Praise for *In Backwater*

"When Maggie's cousin goes missing after prom night, then turns up dead at the marina where she and her ne'er-do-well father live, Maggie knows something about it but not enough to solve the case, or does she? She's really just trying to survive as a smart and non-gender-performing girl whose mother is AWOL while her father drinks himself to death. To make sense of her world, she classifies: animals, plants, humans. And maybe she spins a yarn or two and escapes to her imagination. In this realist/Gothic hybrid coming-of-age novel, Nieman achieves a suspenseful narrative full of compassion, haunting, and desire, and instruction about the power of storytelling."

–Elaine Neil Orr, author of *Swimming Between Worlds*

"*In the Lonely Backwater* is not only a page-turning thriller but also a complex psychological portrait of a young woman dealing with guilt, betrayal, and secrecy. Equally compelling is Nieman's deep sense of the wonderment of the natural world."

–Dawn Raffel, author of *The Strange Case of Dr. Couney*

"Gripping and graceful in equal measure—charting a community in crisis, friendship and family, and the more complex geographies of the human heart. Maggie Warshauer is quite the character, her story one you won't soon forget."

–Art Taylor, Edgar Award-winning author of *The Boy Detective & The Summer of '74*

"This outstanding novel is both artful and thrilling, a rare and wonderful accomplishment! It is also profoundly entertaining."

–Fred Leebron, author of *Six Figures* and director of the MFA program at Queens University of Charlotte

"With gorgeous description and elegant prose, Nieman transforms a North Carolina village and marina into a haunting character in this fine literary novel. Readers who enjoyed *Where the Crawdads Sing* will love this story and its likeable teen protagonist, Maggie Warshauer. Beautifully written and perfectly paced, *In the Lonely Backwater* is a great choice for book clubs."

–Donna Meredith in the *Southern Literary Review*

"Maggie's observations—informed by her fascination with Linnaeus and his classification of species—are carefully revealed.... (her) confidence brims with a mature bravado but often clashes with her negative physical self-descriptions. Themes of sexual awakening are raised; they drip with phrasing that conflates desire, regret, confusion, and fantasy as Maggie wrestles with internalized shame."

–*Kirkus Reviews*

"Maggie Warshauer, the intelligent, conflicted and often inscrutable narrator of Valerie Nieman's *In the Lonely Backwater* has, against all odds, managed to carve out a life living on a rundown houseboat with her alcoholic father who she helps with his duties as marina manager. With an absent mother and few friends, Maggie turns to the natural world for solace and constancy. She's most at home sailing her little sailboat, exploring islands and the wildlife she finds there. The marina is a sort of village where everybody knows everybody, and where a murder, like a stone dropped in a pond, sends out unsettling repercussions. Maggie's heightened awareness of this insular world and its occupants gives the novel a powerful grounding as well as deep emotional resonance. I love this beautiful novel for everything Maggie tells us and for everything we sense she's keeping to herself."

–Tommy Hays, author of *What I Came to Tell You* and *The Pleasure Was Mine*

IN THE LONELY BACKWATER

Valerie Nieman

Fitzroy Books

Published by Fitzroy Books
An imprint of
Regal House Publishing, LLC
Raleigh, NC 27612
All rights reserved

https://fitzroybooks.com

Printed in the United States of America

ISBN -13 (paperback): 9781646031795
ISBN -13 (epub): 9781646031801
Library of Congress Control Number: 2021943782

Interior layout by Lafayette & Greene
Cover images © by C.B. Royal
Author photo © by Al Sirois

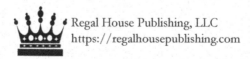

Regal House Publishing, LLC
https://regalhousepublishing.com

For all my teachers, and for absent friends.

PART I

"It would have been wiser, it would have been safer, to classify (if classify we must) upon the basis of what man usually or occasionally did, and was always occasionally doing, rather than upon the basis of what we took it for granted the Deity intended him to do."

Edgar Allen Poe, *The Imp of the Perverse*

1

This is how I remembered it.

2

There wasn't anything wrong between Charisse Swice-good and me except that she was her and I was me, and with the family history and all it was just natural. She won the genetic lottery—tall but not too tall, good boobs, smart but not too much, green eyes and blond hair, and all that. Played volleyball, played flute, sang soprano. And her family owned more land than God and always seemed to know what to do with it. Grow cotton when prices were high, grow tobacco when an allotment was pure gold, grow square footage in second homes when the lake went in and they were suddenly blessed with water views along the acreage they'd left in piney woods. The Swicegoods went back to the Carolina settlement, like the Cobles and the Alfords. My so-called mother was an Alford, so Charisse was related, but we were like the Black Penders and the white Penders, all one big happy family in the phone book but anyone local knew the code of who was white or Black by the address after the name. Of course, Charisse and me looked about as like each other as those two branches of Penders.

So, here I am, Maggie Warshauer (what I call myself even if I'm legally Lenore), with, I guess, not all that much going for me except a real good brain and a strong body. If you turn back the yearbook page from Charisse, you'll find my picture at the end of the junior class, and it's the way I really look—straight, short brown hair and a chin that wouldn't look so big except I have a little pug nose that is maybe all I got from my as-they-say biological mother. Track and Field (discus, javelin), Ecology Club, Scribblers Club. There's no place to list my real work.

Charisse and me were pretty much okay with each other, a few squabbles—it's not like she was one of the idiot flag girls or something—but we had another fight in school the week before she disappeared, a big one, and then I wrote that stupid thing on Facebook. You know how it goes. Finally she messaged, *I hope that we can talk this out sometime.* And now she was missing, and the yokel cops were looking for something because they didn't know anything.

I was outside the principal's office, not a place I'd spent much time, waiting in the lineup on the hard wooden chairs along the wall. The police were using Miss McGehee's office, so she was bouncing off the walls. More than usual. The woman has no tolerance for change—any little thing gets her off track and she spins out of control. At the moment she was haranguing the secretary about whether the student files were sufficiently secure, and how the cops weren't going through her students' lives without a warrant, or a lot of warrants. Miss McGehee has a voice like Vin Diesel going through a sex change and the attitude to match, but she's like five-feet-nothing, and a puff of wind would blow her flat against the wall. She has good hair but keeps it cut butch-short. No nonsense, that's how she would describe herself.

The door to her office opened and Garrett Yancey slid out. He went past me without a word, hands pushed down deep in the pockets of his baggy jeans.

"Next?"

I went in and sat down in the too-small chair provided for students who had crossed Miss McGehee. The deep, padded wooden chairs stayed against the walls for adults, and the cops hadn't changed the setup. In a strange way, I felt less intimidated than if Miss McGehee had been behind the desk. This guy from the sheriff's department had thin hair and the owly glasses and too-big Adam's apple of the classic nerd.

"Good morning." He looked up from the papers in front of him. "Miss Warshauer?" He said it without the Rs, *Washaw*, like they do over East. "I'm Drexel Vann, a detective for the London County Sheriff's Department. I appreciate you giving me some time away from your studies."

I nodded. I didn't expect a detective to look like my dentist.

He waited, watching me like an underfed hound. If I were

going to place him in the marina, I'd say he was a fishing boat. A small one, from Sears, not on a slip but parked on the monthly lot. Plain aluminum johnboat with a little outboard.

"We're asking for your help, everyone's help, in trying to find Miss Swicegood," he said. "She hasn't been seen since Saturday night, after the prom, but I imagine you know most everything already."

"I know what I hear around school."

"That's why we're here. There's more information passed around in the cafeteria at lunch hour than we could get in a week of talking with the adults." He half smiled, in a shy way, not a threatening one.

"So you want me to tell you when I saw her last, and what she was doing, and all that."

"Yeah, all that."

He wasn't going to tell me what he already knew. I pretty much had an idea what the other guys had told him, Hulky and Nat. Especially Nat.

"Well, it was prom, you know that."

"And you went?"

I gave what I expected was a withering look. "As if."

He waited.

Miss McGehee's voice clawed under the thick wooden door.

"It's not like I even wanted to go, that whole pink dress and flowers deal. And a lame DJ from maybe, Hartner, if they were lucky. I mean, for most of the kids around here, it's great."

"Did you stay home?"

Home on the houseboat, watching Dad drink, sure. "Me and these other guys went to the Pizza Annex. It's the only place you can sit down and order, unless you go to Norlington."

"What time was that?"

"About ten. I had to help in the store and then do the pump readings and rotate the cooler stock. And Nat closes up at the Pic 'n' Pay at nine. We met up and got a pizza together." Like he didn't know this already.

"And this was you and Nathanael Johnson and David Priddy?"

David, right. No one ever called Hulky by his real name except for teachers. And cops.

"Yeah."

He waited. I guess that was his best feature.

"So we ate and played some video games. And then we hung out."

"At the gas station. The pizza place is beside the gas station."

"Yeah, playing the games. For a while."

He opened a little red notebook and started to flip the pages. It had a spiral on the top, so the pages went up and over, up and over.

"Some of the students said..." *Flip, flip.* "Some of them said that after the prom they were going to go bowling."

"I heard that."

"Anything else?"

"The ones with the limos were going into Hartner for the moonlight bowling, and then they were going to go to Denny's for breakfast."

"That would be Night-Owl Lanes? Where they have the balls that glow in the dark?"

I nodded.

"Was Charisse one of them?" I noticed he wasn't calling her "Miss Swicegood" now.

"Charisse didn't mess around with bowling and a bunch of kids and a chaperone." I could hear Miss McGehee again, her outbursts punctuated by the slam of metal file drawers.

Mr. Vann—Detective Vann—smiled. He had one dimple, odd. "I'm glad I didn't have her as a principal."

"Yeah."

"So Charisse didn't hang with the main crowd?"

"She was way above that. She had a college guy for a date. Some guy from VCU."

"Did you meet him?"

He was getting around to it, to asking what we did while the rest of the junior and senior students were dancing or bowling or whatever. "No, she ditched him. I guess you know that from Hulky—from David."

"The three of you stayed together after the pizza place closed."

"Yeah. The Three Musketeers." That's what we were called: Aimless, Portly, and Asshole. Portly was Hulky, of course, heavyweight wrestler with a heart of gold. Nat was the eternal outsider artist type, gloomy and sarcastic. I was Aimless, which could have been a lot worse. Girls weren't supposed to hang with guys, so I guess those in charge of making up nasty nicknames didn't know quite how to categorize me. "We hooked a jug of dago red and went over to the OT to finish the evening off in style."

Vann looked at me over the top of his little red notebook. Crime noted.

"Old Trinity. The church graveyard. It's not like anyone was buried there recently, or anything. It's just a place to go where no one messes with us." Sometimes we left the cans or bottles there. I don't think the sexton had ever complained, but maybe he had. Nat's dad was going to have a cow when he found out, being as he was a deacon in a church where speaking in tongues not only happened but was expected.

"I see. Trinity Church is pretty close to Charisse's house. She wasn't with her date when she joined you?"

I shook my head. "She said she had to ditch him. Her words, he was, 'Like, a jerk.'"

"And she never said his name, or where she met him?"

"She met him at King's Dominion, that's all she told anyone. And that he was a college student. And he ripped her dress and she dumped him." She was wasted when she found us, and Moms and Daddy were going to be plenty pissed off at their daughter driving the Jag in that condition, much less being perceived as damaged goods for the upscale marriage market.

He glanced up, like *Go on*, but didn't say it. He flipped back in his book and sucked in his cheeks. The fourth-period bell rang. I didn't mind missing Trig, but literature was different.

"She wandered into the graveyard and sat with us. With Hulky and me, mostly. Nat was walking around talking to the dead. Anyway, we killed the bottle, and I went home."

"What did she say?"

"Not much."

"About the dress?"

I shrugged.

"The two boys and Charisse were still in the churchyard when you walked home."

"Yeah."

"Alone." He let that lie there, like something in the road. "Aren't you afraid to be walking around late at night?"

"Seems safer than painting up and going to the prom with a college guy." I realized how smartass that sounded, but it was too late. "I'm not afraid of anything that lives out in these woods." (Not true. I worry about rabid foxes, rabid skunks, rabid whatever.) "There's a trail over the hill to the marina. So what have you found out about Charisse?"

He didn't seem to like being the one asked the questions. He flipped the notebook closed and stuck it in his jacket pocket. "We know she didn't make it home. We towed in her parents' Jaguar from the road near the churchyard entrance."

I wondered if they had gone over it inch by inch for evidence, like on TV. Hairs and skin flakes and body fluids. Probably just poked around under the seats and took some fingerprints. I sat forward on the chair.

"You live with your parents at the marina? Do you have a house there?"

I sat back. This guy was not going to let me get to English class. "I live with my dad. He's the marina manager. Not exactly a house—we live on a houseboat."

Vann looked at me as though I'd finally told him something he didn't already know. "That sounds—unusual."

"It's different." He must not have heard about my dad.

"Must get pretty lonely there in the off-season."

"It's okay."

"So, the other night—prom night—was the moon out?"

This guy veered around like a water strider.

"At first." The sky had been deep blue, with big puffy clouds moving along on a wind that didn't show on the ground. The stars were washed out by the three-quarters moon. Later, the clouds lowered. Later, the storm.

"Enough to walk by, without any trouble, then."

"Yeah."

He rubbed his eyes. "Well, I think that will be enough. Thank you for your cooperation, Miss Warshauer. Keep an eye out, okay?"

I had my books and was almost out the door when he cleared his throat and I thought, Well, here it comes, he's going to ask about the Facebook stuff.

"What are you planning to do when you get out of school?"

"Wow. Ummm. I'd like to be a marine biologist."

"Sounds good." He opened the door. I squeezed past and kept going before he came up with any other off-the-wall questions. One of Charisse's girls was sitting in the outer office, picking at her fingernail polish, waiting.

3

There hasn't been anyone buried at Old Trinity since 1932, so we never felt any problem with sitting on the graves at night. The bones went to powder a long time ago, the spirits cut free to go over Jordan or just wander the nights. Nothing lived there except for the birds. Never a cold touch or a voice in the mind, nothing. Nights we'd go there to hang out. It was walking distance from all around—the marina, the tobacco farm that Nat's parents owned, the trailer park where Hulky lived.

When it was built in 1748, the road was a path and the graveyard sat properly back, but now three paved lanes shoulder up to the stone wall around God's Acre. The church has a pointed roof but no steeple—just a cross mounted above the door—and is so plain that it might belong to one of the religions that don't hold with wine or music. It was built of round stones picked up out of the river, slate cracked out of the hillside near Troubled Creek, pine and oak timbers. A bell, green with age, is mounted in a kind of cage above a plaque saying it was a gift of the Royal Charter of Queen Anne to Extend the Word of God Among All Peoples. The church is white, inside and out.

The graveyard beside the church has stones that go all the way back—some are smoothed blank, while others hold words where the weather didn't hit or the stone was harder. The white marble ones from around the Civil War are the most interesting, the loopy inscriptions melting away—*most precious daughter of, beloved wife, faithful husband*. They were real specific about life, and death—*died aged 26 years 5 mos and 3 days*. Lichens and black mold grow on the marble.

I was scared the first time there, when Nat got hold of some wine and wanted to go somewhere we could drink it. It's just weird, at first, sitting in a graveyard. Even an old one where there was never any fresh dirt. A hound dog howled, and an owl screeched. "Listen, Maggie, the ghost horse is come to carry off the transgressors," Nat said, but I knew better, since I had read my bird book back to front and knew the common name and Latin name and could even make the sound and did so later on, making him jump off a tomb. *Otus asio.* Common screech owl. Found from the tip of Florida to Maine. All year round. "A mournful whinny" is how Roger Tory Peterson's field guide describes its voice. A small owl that comes in red phase or gray. Strangely enough, the long-eared owl (which I have heard just once, a low moaning sound) is called *Asio otus.* It is supposed to be here only in winter, Peterson says, but I heard it once in summer. The year before Charisse.

The churchyard is shaded by old cedar trees and two immense oaks whose limbs spread wide. The cedar trees are dense and black at night, but in the daytime even really old and impressive ones have a sort of weedy look. Bare twisted limbs, scabby trunks, rusty foliage. Just not a great tree as trees go. I think the settlers were homesick for English yews and this was as good as the Piedmont was going to give them.

The settlers—those Brackenbills and Granstaffs and Pinckneys lined up in the cemetery—were all good Church of England people. They brought everything they needed for religion and education, all the mental furniture, even if they had to make wine out of scuppernongs. Trinity has a church register that records the births and deaths and marriages going all the way back. You can see it, in a locked cabinet with glass fronts showing off the old Books of Common Prayer and lace-trimmed garments turned the color of old photographs.

Not one eerie thing ever happened to me in the graveyard, but the church, that's another story. That's where I got my calling.

The church is kept locked except for Sunday morning service (a pretty sad affair since most everyone is Baptist these days) and Sunday afternoons when historical society ladies hope for the occasional tourist.

It was the summer I turned fourteen. I had wandered the back paths and ended up there, just killing time. I was reading

the gravestones when I heard this creaky sound, like a door
going back and forth on its hinges. I went around to the front
of the church. The left side of the double red door was open
a crack and just barely moving in the thick air. No cars in the
driveway. I walked quietly up the stairs and across the little
porch, and peeked inside.

The church had the not-open-for-business look you'd expect
any day but Sunday. At the front was a board with numbers for
last week's hymns. Shiny wooden banisters on the altar rail, white
walls, hard pews with black books in the racks. Empty niches on
the back wall behind the altar table. Hanging lamps like medieval
lanterns with heavy iron frames. Like a museum.

Except that the small door behind the pulpit was open.

I waited. Nothing. Not even a stir in the dust hanging in the
air. The hinges had squalled when I opened the heavy front
door, but there wasn't any answering sound. So I went in and
walked down the aisle, opened the gate in the altar rail, went up
the step between the two skinny podiums, and looked into the
room behind the altar. Choir robes and felt banners hung from
nails on the wall. One banner was still on the pole they used
for carrying it, and it swung back and forth just a bit. A door to
the outside was ajar, too, so whoever had been there was gone.

A wooden cabinet with crosses carved on it had been broken open, and books had been pulled out and scattered on the
floor. Bibles and hymnals with all shades and conditions of
bindings. Older books, too, leather-bound. I opened up one
after the other, the geography of the Holy Land, history of England, biographies, poetry. Inside the cover of one by Marcus
Aurelius, someone had written with brown ink fading into the
paper: *Let it be Known that, by the Grace of God and the Charity of
the Faithful, through the auspices of Dr. Tho. Bray, S.P.G, this volume
is one of a great Athenaeum of Learning provided that Christian peoples in the Colonies may be instructed in all things necessary to Worldly
Progress and Eternal Salvation, this being the Property of Saint Thomas
Parish in Pamplico.* I flipped open some others and found some
with the same kind of writing—one was inscribed only, *Maj.
Christopher Gale, Kirby Grange.* No telling where Kirby Grange

is, but Pamplico must be Pamlico. How they got up here, in
the scruffy edge where the coastal plain rose to the Piedmont,
was one question. And whether anyone tended to them or even
cared anymore was another.

I sat down and read. The printing was strange: an *S* looked
like an *F*, and the letters were sometimes crooked where they
were pressed into the page. These were the real deal, books
maybe touched by George Washington even. Brown spots on
the pages, brown string holding them together. Boring stuff,
though the medical book was interesting in a horrifying way,
with plasters and purges and illustrations of plague sores.

I placed the remaining books in the cabinet, but one had
come apart in the thief's hands. The pages were scattered and a
lot of them had been stepped on with a fat lug-sole boot, torn
and marked.

*In the road to this spring stands a steep hill called Brevikberget, which
I climbed with great difficulty. In the clefts of the rock lay several wings
of young ravens and crows, with feet of hares, &c. 'See,' said I to my
companion, 'here has been the nest of an Eagle Owl!'*

I pushed back a stack of pages, some with rough drawings
on them no better than I would have made, mountains, a baby
strapped in a cradle.

*On arriving at the next crag, a little higher up, we discovered a pair of
birds of this species* (Strix Bubo) *sitting in a hollow of the rock. Their
eyes sparkled like fire, for the iris in each of them was luminous in itself,
like touchwood, glow-worms, or rotten fish. These birds were as large as
young geese. I durst not venture to attack them with my hands…*and the
page ended with a ragged tear.

This was an adventure, someplace strange and wild, a scientific adventure. I sorted the pages, trying to put them back
in order, when I had a cold chill of someone watching, the
burglar maybe. I folded the pages into a bundle, stuffed them
into the waist of my shorts, and dropped my loose old T-shirt
over them.

I should have felt guilty, but I didn't.

I hustled the pages back to the houseboat and spread them
out on my lumpy bed. The page edges were uneven, and through

the deep-printed text you could see the ghosts of letters from the previous page. I located the title page: *Lachesis Lapponica, or a Tour in Lapland, now first published from the original manuscript journal of the celebrated LINNAEUS*, and on and on, until the date, 1811, so this was not as old as the church but came there later somehow.

The first place I looked up Linnaeus gave the name of Carol, and I wondered how she was able to wander around a wild place like that back when women were wearing corsets and dying at seventeen of the fever. A little more looking and I learned that Carolus and Karl and Carl and Von Linne and Linnaeus were all the same, and a man. It was like the different names of creatures and plants that people used, so that no one agreed on whether that bird was the same one in England and in Africa. Until Carl—that was how I thought of him—organized everything.

I already knew that plants and creatures had Latin names. The biology teacher had gotten that far before spending the rest of the semester dithering over creation versus evolution, scared to death he'd say the wrong thing. He must have because the next year he was gone.

His love of truth and nature were not more ardent than your own, nor was his mental profit more. That line caught my attention first thing. J. E. Smith was the man who had translated the journal into English, and I wondered if the notebook he worked from had been travel-stained and marked with blood and rain and green streaks of plants. *Not the awful preceptor of the learned world in his professorial chair, but a youthful, inexperienced student, full of ardor in curiosity, such as we ourselves have been.*

It was knowing that Carl was young—pretty young, anyway, twenty-five when he went to Lapland—that really made me want to read those pages. He was observing and categorizing, rearranging how people looked at the natural world. That was what I did, sorting the world out so that it made sense, even if I was stuck in the worn-out tobacco land around the marina, and not in faraway Lapland. From that moment on, I had a purpose other than making it through each school day.

4

Usually I'd be in school on Monday afternoon but with Charisse missing and parents jerking their kids out of classes, the school board decided to send everyone home at noon. Some of the seniors were taking part in a grid search, walking out from OT and filling the gaps between police and firefighters.

I spent the day on housekeeping duty. Jesus, Mary, and Joseph (more about them in a minute) were cranking the docks higher after another heavy rainstorm upstream. The lake had stayed high this spring; the metal ramps connecting to the gas dock and boat docks had been steadily creeping up toward the parking lot. Yellow pollen scummed the floating leaves and branches carried into the bay.

I dragged my cart of sprays and brushes back from the ginormous houseboat at the end of D dock. The owners were flying in from Pennsylvania for their annual spring visit, guests coming and going until the blowout party on Memorial Day weekend. The rest of the time, the floating mansion grew algae on its pontoons and sheltered a family of otters. I knocked down the mud-dauber nests and the swallow nests and scrubbed the red clay and gull droppings off the decks. The inside cleaning was minimal, mostly airing out, wiping mildew, clearing spiders. Inside smelled lemony-fresh now, but outside smelled like low tide. When Pastor and Lawyer, two more of our workers, moved the pump-out barge over there, they'd use a pressure washer to clear out the nooks and crannies under the docks where the otters had stashed clams or vomited bones and scales.

I had one other boat to clean up, a Bayliner called *Randy Mandy*. This was a post-party call. I stopped just long enough to let myself in and open the ports—it stank of cigarettes and spilled beer and an overflowing head until I could hardly breathe. No way was I working in there until the stink cleared out. I took a break and headed to the store, where "Klassic Kountry Kountdown" was twanging through the open window. At the counter Dad was dumping cups of Ol' Roy puppy kibble into plastic bags and zipping them. People who visited the marina—not the boaters who actually docked here—liked to buy something to feed the ducks that nested and squabbled across the cove. The kibble also attracted huge catfish that lived under the docks; scary big, they made thick, mucousy swirls as the pellets hit the water. There was more fecal content in that backwater than I wanted to think about.

"Hey, punkinhead."

"Hey." I walked past my dad, trying to get a whiff that would tell me where he was on the drunk-o-meter. Yeasty smell, beer, not the hot stinging scent of hard liquor. I eased on back to the cooler and pulled a Mountain Dew.

"You wanna mark these?"

I grabbed the price gun and hit each bag with an orange 99-cents sticker. Dad had explained how you never used round numbers, like one dollar, because they looked bigger and scared people off. I stacked the duck food in the shoebox beside the cash register. It sold well, like ice and Nabs and sodas. The shelves of boat plugs, shackles, rope, grease, gelcoat repair, all the other accessories and necessities, were mostly for dusting.

Dad shoved the bag of dog food under the counter and sat down on the stool. He'd shaved this morning and the raw scrapes just added to the redness of his face. I was happy he wasn't any worse, after a night with the photo album and a tall bottle of dark rum. It was all about my "dearly departed" mother. He just couldn't live without her, so at least once a week he'd get stone drunk and start writing. Sometimes the letters would be lying around for days, getting covered with coffee cup rings and greasy crumbs before he balled them up and stuffed them in the trash. Sometimes he mailed the letters to the last address we had for her. They always came back. He had this picture of her in a silver frame, taken when we lived at the beach, and he'd talk to her as if she were sitting across from him. When I see that picture, I remember the converted boathouse where we lived, and the ocean always breathing just outside. Dad was sunburned dark then, like a pirate, his black hair long, with a short beard. I remember *her*, too, but she never got that kind of love hook into me, even if I was her child that she stuck with a fancy romantic name. *Lenore Marguerite.* Some mother-child thing didn't take. Maybe she couldn't see anything of herself—blond and big boobs and long legs—in me. Maybe it's a good thing that when Dad looks at me, he doesn't see her.

I watched as he bent over, as though looking for something under the counter, before he stood up and wiped his hand across his mouth. Characteristic behavior, routine as a nuthatch working headfirst down a tree. It wasn't as if he expected I wouldn't see. Just that neither one of us would say anything. He hit the preset on the radio, cutting some yokel off in mid-yodel to switch to "The Best Mix of Today's Hits and Yesterday's Gold." I gave him a smile because he had done that for me.

"How you coming with the boats?"

"Okay. I'm letting that Bayliner air out." They hadn't bothered to put away their porno CDs, which I'd pop in and watch on mute while I emptied the trash and wiped down the galley. I was in and out of a good many boats, cleaning or doing safety checks, and you'd be surprised at what people leave around and not care that I see it.

He laughed, short and hard, not like he did when he was happy.

I finished the Dew and tossed it overhand into the trash bin.

"Nice shot," he said.

"Inside the three-point line."

Some '70s rock anthem came on. He started to follow the drumbeat with his fingers, but just when he was hitting it good, he saw something outside that made him snap off the radio.

A posse was plodding down the long launch ramp toward the water. A literal *posse.* The men were wearing ball caps, T-shirts, and blue windbreakers, but they were on horseback, so it was a posse even without the Stetsons. Sheriff Chesley Richardson had organized the mounted unit three years ago for searches in the big tracts of piney woods that London County was noted for. He sat on a palomino horse like a Texas Ranger.

Dad yelled out the window to them—"Come on in for some coffee"—and when he did, a flock of ducks erupted from the cove, squawking and flailing up off the water. One of the horses reared a bit, and another backed and slipped on the slimy concrete and halfway fell but didn't. I was impressed that the rider hung on and guided it back onto four hooves.

After letting their horses tank up, the riders tied them under the trees and most of the guys headed to the facilities. The backs of their windbreakers were printed with "Deputy Sheriff" in large white letters.

Dad went out, leaving me at the register, but I could hear everything through the window. Sound carries over water. "Hey, Sheriff," he said, "Drinks in the store if your men want."

Nods all around.

"'Preciate it." The sheriff always sounded like he was on a bullhorn.

"Any luck?"

"Not a trace. Don't figure how she got far with a long dress and heels."

"Shoulda found something in the woods, was she on foot." Some other voice, a man with his back turned.

"Maybe she got a ride," Dad said.

"Maybe. Maybe."

"You ever locate who she was with?"

The sheriff didn't answer. He waved his hand toward the store on A dock, toward me, and the deputies were released from where they stood swaying from one foot to the other. They clumped down the gangway to the dock, most of them fat, or at least what you'd called beefy. Some of them weren't genuine full-time officers—they were deputized temporarily for searches like this—but you couldn't really tell one from another. They nodded and "heyed" as they came inside, letting the flimsy excuse for a door slam against the sheet-metal wall so everything vibrated. They grabbed sodas and some of them got chips or candy bars as well. Dad hadn't said anything about snacks, and I wondered if Mr. Malouf would be okay with this generosity, but I didn't ring those up either. They walked around, swigging and chewing, extending their time in the air conditioning, looking at the big map of the lake, talking about whether they were going to have to drag it, given how big and how deep it was. "Hunnert feet!" one exclaimed. Which was wrong, it was seventy-five at the deepest. I don't think all together they had the brains of that detective, Drexel Vann. They made their thanks and dropped their bottles in the recycling bin on the way out.

I hung the Back Soon sign on the door and went out. The day was heating up, more like summer already. The smell of sweat and horse droppings mixed with the smell of slack water and pine trees.

Jesus, Mary, and Joseph had finished C dock and were standing around waiting for the next task. They were talking low among themselves, the sound of their Spanish different from English even when you couldn't hear the words. Jesus, Mario, and Guillermo, those are their real names, but Dad tagged them with the nickname that he never used where they could hear it. Everyone lumps them together as Mexican, but I have learned that Jesus, who is short and wide, his forehead low and eyes heavy lidded, is from Guatemala. He speaks the least and does the heavy work without complaint. Guillermo is the leader, perhaps because of his height. He is maybe five-foot-eleven, and wiry strong, his hands too large for his wrists. He is also lighter-skinned, more of the conquistador in him, and he has the most English. Mario is very young and looks to Guillermo the way a dog does its owner, not just for orders but for love, and Guillermo treats him like a difficult son—few smiles, a few more cuffs on the shoulder, but with a glint of approval in his eyes when Mario accomplishes some task. If Mario is related to Guillermo, we don't know. If he knows any English, he's never let on, so we just say, "Vaya con Guillermo," and that plus a few more words were all that was needed.

The sheriff was asking Dad about them, his big voice reduced, but a whisper for him meant the men could still hear everything. I could see by the way Guillermo tilted his head that he was listening. "Up on the highway," Dad said, or I thought he said. "Good men."

The sheriff motioned them over, asking what they had seen, what they knew. Jesus and Mario didn't say a word, just nodded or shook their heads, but Guillermo went back and forth speaking with the lawmen, standing tall and looking directly at them. The deputies stood in a semicircle like they were going to rush the Mexicans, and Jesus and Mario were very still and their eyes flicked from one side to the other.

Satisfied or not, the sheriff motioned for his posse to mount up. I ducked back into the store as they went clopping back through the parking lot to the road.

"You still cleaning?" Dad asked.

"The Bayliner? Right?" I said. He couldn't remember a thing.

"Oh yeah. Help me with the gas pumps. I didn't get a reading last night."

I got the logbook and he read off the figures. Gas sales were pretty slow until Memorial Day, bass fishermen mostly. The gas-sucking speedboats and cruisers were what added up.

Dad sat on the side of the dock and I joined him. No hurry to get back to that floating sex pit. The sky was clear blue (Dad's stupid joke—how do you know God's a Tarheel? He made the sky Carolina blue). The lake was flat under the high pressure that had moved in, a perfect sunny day after the prom-night storm dumped two inches of rain on top of all we'd had. Seemed like forever since I'd pointed *Bellatrix's* prow up the lake, but there wouldn't be enough breeze today to fill even my baby Lightning's sails. "So they think the guys did something?"

"Not really," he said. "They hauled in her prom date, though, once they found him and got him dried out."

Dad kept looking at me. I watched water striders zooming around in the warm shallows. I watched the geese with their fuzzy young in tow.

"So—all this—how are you doing?"

"Okay."

An escaped boat fender bobbed next to the tree branch that had snared it.

"I know you're not close, but she is your cousin." He stopped. "After all." Stopped again. Dad always embarrassed himself when he tried to do this fatherly small talk.

"We don't run in the same circles."

"Yeah, I understand. Everyone's got a group."

He left that hanging. I figured "his group" in school had been the jocks. It's kind of funny, because I'm a jock too I guess, a jock/geek, but girls don't have the same testosterone thing going. I just show up for practice and heave the javelin as far as I can.

"You enjoying the internet?"

Left field. "Yeah. When it's up."

The owners had finally installed Dish TV at the marina, when the yachtsmen started talking out loud about moving their forty-foot boats somewhere they could watch football. And more importantly, internet service—it wasn't the best, but at least we had made it into the twentieth century.

"You don't run into anything you shouldn't, do you?"

Other than bomb-making directions? S&M porn? White supremacists?

"No, mostly research." Facebook wasn't something he'd understand.

"I just hope you don't turn into one of those kids that's hooked on the internet. There's a lot more to life than computers. Or school and books and research." Pause. Pause. He was working up to something. The breeze brought around that scent of old beer.

"Like prom night. I keep wondering why you didn't have a date or—"

"Dad." My tone of voice should have been enough to freeze him out, but he just kept going.

"You're a pretty girl."

Pretty wasn't a word people would use for me. Sturdy,

maybe. Strong. Active. Healthy. Not pretty. I once heard one of Mother's friends say that I must have hid behind the door when they were passing out good looks. My so-called mother didn't say a word in my favor. It was because of her that we were here, and she was the reason why we would never leave.

"I would have bought you a dress, anything. You never brought it up."

"I don't have any interest." When I look in the mental mirror I see myself in jeans and a T-shirt. In the woods. Out on the water, that's the best. Sails taut and rudder humming in a fresh breeze.

"I mean, you raised me to like boats and the outdoors." He looked the other way. "Me and my friends, we can talk."

I watched the last couple of loons, white checkerboard markings on their backs, riding along low in the water. They had their breeding plumage. They should have been north by now, making loon babies.

"I don't have anything against Nat or David. They're not bad guys. But at your age—I can imagine what your mother would say about you hanging round with them. It's just—"

"Not normal," I finished. "Sure. Like living in a floating trailer is."

He didn't move, but I saw his ear move as his jaw tightened. "It's what we do," he said.

5

Dad didn't have anything against Nat, like he said, but I know he'd rather I found some normal girl to hang around with.

I had friends who were girls when I was little. Not many, though. When they had slumber parties, I wasn't invited. And when they started to get into training bras, their minds changed too. While they were getting giggly and whispering, I drifted along the edges of the guy-crowd, competing with them, being their friends sometimes like with Nat. And so the Three Musketeers, not as tight as people thought, but tight enough.

The last time we'd been together and things were normal was in March, when we ganged up at the Pic 'n' Pay. We were sitting at one of the tables between the cases of beer and the window, eating chips and hot dogs that Nat put on the cooker special for us so they were fresh and not greasy.

We were just being smartasses, watching people being people, commenting on them as they sang along with the radio, argued, or picked their noses when they thought no one was looking.

"Shrunk in the wash," Nat said, lifting his jumbo cup toward a guy whose shirt threatened to pop its buttons.

Hulky chuckled and pointed out that he was buying a twelve-pack of Old Milwaukee. "Don't blame it on his old lady's washer."

"What's up with that?" I asked, lifting my chin toward a guy wearing full camo overalls, though it wasn't any season for hunting.

"No telling with him," Nat said.

"Who him?"

"Alan Ledsome."

"Yeah, really?" Hulky asked. "He had less hair when he was selling deer corn at the Southern States."

"Hey, maybe there's your prom date," Nat said, snickering.
"Up yours." He could be some kind of snarky asshole sometimes.

I guess Ledsome heard, because he gave us a long look and
we focused on our food until he slid out.

I watched an old lady struggle to get her gas cap off. Her
hands were knotted up with arthritis. Another car pulled in and
Genevieve Welborne, still in her dentist office whites, got out
and set her nozzle on automatic, then came around and got
the old lady's cap off and her pump started. I thought that was
pretty nice.

Ellen Andrews came in, all in a rush, headed somewhere important or not but all painted up as usual. She graduated a year
ago and was in cosmetology school. Her clothes were tight,
too, but deliberately, a leopard-print top and a short black skirt,
showing off her breasts and her fat rear end.

"I bet she has a hot date," said Hulky, who usually could be
counted on to see the obvious.

Nat looked at me and raised one eyebrow. His light-brown
eyes looked sort of green in the fluorescent light. He was skinny and edgy, with his black hair flopping around. Hulky was big
and sort of a medium-light black color. Anyone would think
that Nat was the sensitive one, because he was musical and all,
but it's Hulky who is the big marshmallow.

Nat pulls people in. He's a dark star, lots of energy but it
doesn't show unless you are close. Damped down. We had become friends over a science project in seventh grade. I did the
science, and he did the artistic presentation. A-plus. We didn't
really bond up as a group until the day some guys were taunting
Nat and me, which turned into pushing, which was when Hulky
waded in and told them they should try someone their own
size. As Hulky was way bigger than them, they all slunk off. His
soft heart doesn't let him fit in with the jocks like he should. I
don't recall how he started being with us, on and off, but I think
it was Nat doing it just to piss off his oh-so-Christian bigot
parents. I guess the one thing that we have in common is that
we despise bullies.

Ellen leaned into the car to get her purse. Hulky just stared.

"Think she's getting any?" Nat stuffed the rest of his hot dog in his mouth and checked the time on his phone again.

"Fifty-fifty," I said.

"She keeps doing that she will," Nat said. "That how you attracted Fletcher?"

I knew I was red, so I got up and went to the drink machine and topped up my Mountain Dew. By then my face had gone back to normal and I could start the conversation in a new direction.

6

Things tend to float up into Filliyaw Creek. The creeks run down from the mountains to the river, and when the river hits the dam it spreads out, pushing back into the forests and tobacco fields. Where streams used to run into the river, the lake makes coves that are filled with half-drowned trees part of the year, then muck in spring, tinder in summer. When storms hit, trees come down. It's a backwater, as they say. As the Corps of Engineers decrees, the water rises and falls.

I was helping to pull a giant pine tree trunk onto the concrete ramp when Guillermo found the body.

Pastor and Lawyer were helping me, or I was helping them. Those are their actual real names, not nicknames like JM&J. Their parents wanted them to have great futures, and maybe Pastor would have without Lawyer. His older brother is a foot taller but thinks like a five-year-old. Pastor has had to watch out for him, take care of their mother after their dad died, then take care of Lawyer altogether when their mother passed on. Pastor never complains, though sometimes when he's watching his brother bumble around, I imagine he thinks about whether he could have been somewhere else.

We had gotten ropes around the trunk and extracted it from where it was bashing between the dock and a cruiser, worked it out past the finger pier and over to the launch ramp. Pastor was getting the work truck to pull it out when Dad came running up the walkway, his face all red and knotted up. "Watch the store!" he yelled and took off in the truck.

"Makin' tracks," said Lawyer.

I helped Pastor get the dead tree shifted to the side of the lot and was headed for the office when the first police car showed up.

"Where's the storage dock?"

"Next cove. Go back and take the first left."

Lawyer helpfully added a two-handed wave.

The deputy peeled out with his lights going.

I had the marine radio on Channel 16 and could hear chatter about where the stripers were hitting, and Sea-Tow was headed up the lake to the Society Islands to rescue an inboard/outboard with busted controls. But the radio didn't have police frequencies, so I just had to watch out the window as a slew of cops showed up, and an ambulance. Then the coroner, who was just Mr. Young from the funeral home. I sent Pastor up to meet them at the parking lot and turn them around to where they belonged.

Jesus and Mary were huddled on the workboat, paralyzed without Joseph. I could hear some of what they said, "muerta" and "que fue violada," and between high school Spanish and working beside them, I had enough to understand it meant *death* and *she was raped*.

I found out that Guillermo had gone over there to do the usual walk-through, checking on the unused boats tied up on the storage dock or undergoing repairs, making sure the lines were good. He saw that the lock was hanging off the door on the big houseboat that was only ever used in August, annual vacation for people from Ohio. He opened the door and poked his head inside and saw what he saw. Charisse, dead.

Seemed like forever till Dad came back. His jaw was clenched as if he was holding something in his teeth and couldn't let it out. Then a few cops, who shuffled up and down the docks, staring at boats and making the halyards clang with their heavy footfalls. They must have taken her out in the ambulance. I wondered if they carried her body out on a stretcher or in a bag. In the TV shows mostly the body bags are black plastic but on one show I remember the bag was royal blue and had gold trim, some class.

This crappy old brown Ford pulled in, taking the handicapped space nearest the walkway. Then it backed up and nosed into a regular space. I recognized Drexel Vann as soon as he got out, with those huge glasses and his brown hair lifting up in the

light air. He walked with his head down, and as he got closer, I
could see his lips moving.

"It's a sorry business," he told Dad. "Sorry this problem's
come onto your place, Andy."

"Yeah, well." Dad kept his head down.

The detective looked at me, as if he was sorting, and finally
said, "Miss Warshauer. Maggie."

"Right."

"I'd like to talk with your father, and then, with his permission"—and he looked sideways at him—"with you."

"Sure, whatever will help. Maggie, can you go home for a
piece?"

Calling it *home* was a stretch. Small enough to dock near the
store on A, the houseboat had been white once upon a time,
but now was streaked with black, with brown strings of algae
waving along the pontoons and a reek of dead fish all the time.
She used to have a name—the *Annamariner*—from the owner's wife. Anna Marie. When they separated and neither one
would pay the rent, the marina had slapped on a lien and then
tried to sell her. The For Sale sign faded to the color of old
mercurochrome and fell off one night. The accountant said we
should pull the boat and store it on the hard, among the weeds,
but Dad asked if we could live there instead. At the time we
had an apartment over the top of a jewelry store in Smathers,
twenty-five miles away, and the rent and the drive were killing
us. The accountant said the corporation could expense it since
Dad would serve as live-in staff and (unpaid) night watchman.

Moving out of Smathers was going to be the death of me,
I had just known, since I couldn't walk to the grocery anymore
or the DQ, couldn't get internet or even cable. But I learned to
enjoy my personal Lapland, and eventually the Dish network
came. And full web access, which was and wasn't a good thing.

"Maggie? Ahoy there!" Vann was leaning on the rail near
the rusty barbecue grill, but he stayed on the dock and did not
set foot on the boat until I came out and met him. Somewhere
he'd learned that, learned about boats and etiquette. If he knew
boats, then he knew our tub wasn't much.

A couple of lawn chairs were set on the deck, but he didn't seem to want to sit there. "Do you mind if we go inside?"

Great.

I imagined what he was thinking. A kitchen with kid-sized appliances, a rickety table with two chairs, and the "living room"—a bench seat and a pull-out sofa where Dad sleeps. Cheesy nautical lamps. A fifth of rum on the counter and the smell of liquor from the bottles poking out of the trash. I could tell by the way he looked around that he had questions that weren't just about Charisse.

"I have my bedroom, back there." The door was open but it was too dark for him to see anything in there, with the shades pulled down.

He sat on a chair, and I took the couch.

"So…" He waited.

"Well, what happened to her?"

"Charisse is your cousin?"

I nodded.

"I'm sorry to have to tell you, Maggie. She's passed over."

He was picking his words. She was dead, but he wouldn't use that word. Passed over. As if it was a game, choosing sides, and you could start over. I knew he was keeping things back, concealing the details, like on TV. Playing games with my head, like I'm poor old simple Lawyer or something.

"I'm sorry," I said, because I should, but when I did there was a bigger stone in my gut than I'd imagined.

"Tell me again about the night Charisse disappeared."

I tried to remember exactly what I had told him in the principal's office. They like to trip you, detectives.

"Me and Nat and Hulky went and got pizza and hung around in the arcade. Then we went to the church. To the graveyard. It was really hot. We had some wine. We were just talking and stuff when Charisse drove up."

"You could see her car from where you were?"

"Yeah, right on the road, she just pulled off alongside the wall. It was just her."

"And she was drunk?"

I wondered if he had memorized all the stuff in that little red notebook, which was nowhere in sight.

"She was messed up. I don't know if it was drinks or something else. There was that big rip down the front of her dress."

"Did she say anything about that?"

"Not to me. She and Nat went back in the trees and were talking. Then they came back and we all sat around and finished the bottle. I walked home."

"Leaving Charisse and Nat and David all in the graveyard."

"That's right."

"Anything else you remember?"

He didn't need to know all that I remember. I remember better about the real world than all this stuff with Charisse. I remember that Easter had come right when it was supposed to, the woods filling in green, with dogwood and fading redbud coloring the edges. Prom day came two weeks after Easter, even the oaks pushing out their leaves by that time. It had been a cool spring, late frosts, but the Thursday before prom the winds shifted; a breeze filled in from the southwest and put a chop on the lake. It turned really hot really fast, ninety degrees that afternoon. It was enough to raise a sweat during the day. By the time I got done with work and made it up to the gas station, it had cooled, just warm and nice, smell of cut grass and narcissus. The air began shifting around, more from the west, gusts and then dropping to nothing. By the time we headed to OT, clouds were filling in fast.

I remember in the graveyard, the smell of flowers rising up from Wisteria Lodge, a fallen-in plantation house whose owners now lived under the gravestones we sat on. I remember how headlights from cars on the highway moved across the graves in a certain way, depending on if they were headed north or south. But then lights swung all the way across as a car turned onto the pike and stopped, and the lights stayed on, casting giant tree-shadows against the church for a long time. We could hear the motor running. Nat came out of his funk and was looking like *WTF?*, and Hulky stood up and started that way, then the lights and the engine cut off. We heard one door open and close. Next thing we knew, Charisse was standing inside the gate.

"Hey, guys?" Her voice rose way up at the end.

"Hey, Charisse," Nat blurted out. She followed his voice, uncertain as she walked across the graves, maybe because of high heels, but when she got to us we could see she was barefoot and there was a gash down the turquoise shimmer of her dress. Her face didn't look right, but everyone looked ghoulish as the moon went in and out of the clouds.

I could feel the boys sweat, see how they repositioned themselves as they sat. Charisse was *Charisse*. Not Maggie.

"How was the prom?" Hulky asked.

"Oh hell." She sat down on a tombstone, just like us commoners. "Oh fucking hell."

"I bet it was so friggin' hot," said Hulky, unable to bring himself to use the word that fell so easily out of Charisse's mouth. "Me and Nat were riding around earlier, riding around in the truck, you know, an' all these kids were standing in front of their houses and just sweating buckets while moms and dads took pictures."

Nat laughed once, almost a bark. He didn't go to prom because his family didn't hold with dancing. And other reasons.

"It was some kinda time. I hope they enjoyed it." She began pulling apart the smashed flowers in her white and yellow wrist bouquet, shredding the petals into her lap.

"Buncha assholes anyway," said Nat. "I'd rather be here. I bet you're happier here too."

Charisse smiled on one side.

I knew what the guys were feeling, that they wished they could have put on a rented tux and showed up at Charisse's door in a limo and taken her to the prom. I even felt like that, some. Wishing I could put on a show, that I had a dorky regular dad and mom to fuss over me and get me a dress that they secretly thought was too revealing or too expensive. And I had hated myself for this wishing, just like the guys, and we all would have denied ever feeling like that.

"Tell me more about that rip in her dress." Vann hadn't gone anywhere, though it seemed like he had. The little red notebook had materialized from somewhere. "Did she look like she'd been hurt? Any marks?"

I wish I'd asked Nat more about what happened at his interview. Hulky and Nat and me, we had each other's backs.

"It looked like someone had grabbed the neck of it and tried to pull it off her. She'd used a safety pin to close it up." But I didn't tell him that the bra showed through, lace the color of a peach.

"*Someone* being the college guy?"

"I guess."

"We've been talking with him. From Richmond. Whatever happened with Charisse, when she left him he caught a ride into Norlington and spent the night drinking."

"At the Stop-Inn? That must have been a treat."

"Anyways, it appears he was already there when she was still in the cemetery with you all." With a look. "If the timeline holds up, it looks like a pretty solid alibi."

"Maybe not for the dress."

Vann chuckled. "You're right. Maybe not for that."

It sure would have been a relief if the college guy could be the one who killed her, somebody they had their hands on. I felt that rock rise up in my stomach, trying to get into my throat.

He took off his glasses and looked down at them, and I could see from where I sat that they were smeared and dirty. He looked around. I got him a paper towel and he polished away, breathing on them and then polishing, polishing, before he finally set them back on his nose.

"Did you and Charisse have any problems?"

Oh man, what to say about that. "We weren't close."

He nodded, and now I really wondered what the guys had told him, about Charisse crying and wanting us to make up, and that whole weird scene that I did not want to talk about.

"I could see the storm coming in. I left and walked home, over the back way."

"Did you see anything else? See anyone?"

What I could tell him, which wouldn't matter, but which was

real—was that as I had walked home, lightning went from flares on the horizon to streaks. The wind picked up and petals came flying off the dogwoods. I didn't need much light to follow the dirt bike trail that went past Wisteria Lodge and then down the lane lined with huge cedars, and came out on the road that once crossed a valley that was now the lake. I passed the tall house with its four chimneys, the roof and porch caved in from the weight of the wisteria, and when the wind eased, I was almost suffocated with the thick old-fashioned smell.

The storm broke as I came down the hill toward the marina, rain so heavy I could feel the clay melting under my feet. I made it home like a ship coming into a familiar harbor, following the howl of wind in the rigging and the dusk-to-dawn light by the office.

But he didn't care about that. I decided to tell him all I wanted to tell, and all that he had to hear.

7

*D*earest—
   I'm writing you this tonight because I am thinking of you, you know I am always thinking of you, and the marina is really still, seems like there is not another person alive in the world, not a blessed soul, but if you were here this would be heaven.

   I don't know if you are sending these letters back, or maybe it is your new H. or a servant or something. I hear tell that you are rich, and so you probably got butlers and such to get the mail and open it up. If someone else is reading this, I pray to <u>GOD</u> that you will let her see this letter—I know my Angel is lost to me forever and I will not try to mess in your new life, but she should know about her daughter.

   Maggie—she won't answer to Lenore now—is grown up strange, and I worry terrible about her.

   She's smart, way smarter than you and me put together, but she's all to herself. She don't open up to me, I guess a girl needs her mother when she gets of an age. She don't have boyfriends, just guys she hangs around with, like she's one of the guys, she dont tell me nothing. And now we have this mess up here, I suppose you heard, they found Charisse dead right here in the marina. I think it had a bad effect on Maggie, being her cousin and all. The girl was tied up and been abused some way, hid on a houseboat so we didn't find her for a spell. It shook me I'll tell you that. The police have been all over here, and I had to get interrogated, and they talked with Maggie twice. She don't say much. I wish you were here to talk w/her.

   Maybe you cld send a phone # and she can call?

Well, I'm tired and I'll sign off here, and tell you I love you and always will and I hope at least that you are happy.

Yr lover Drew

8

As I said before, this backwater, this flooded valley of worn-out tobacco fields and pine scrub, is my Lapland. When Carl went to Lapland, it wasn't as if no one lived there or had ever named anything or seen any of the plants. But he saw it for the first time as a scientist. So, if I'm seeing this plant or spider for the first time, it's a discovery for me, even if someone from Chapel Hill has the thing dried out and pinned down in a forgotten case somewhere.

I almost quit categorizing, right after I began. We had come back from down at the coast, Dad trying to keep my so-called mother happy. I saw a tree that wasn't a willow begin to sprout willow catkins. I told my teacher, Ms. Nickels, one of those well-meaning but not very bright women they put in charge of fourth graders. She nodded and smiled, smiled and nodded. So I went and climbed the tree and broke off a branch, early the next morning, and took it to school. We had a visiting biologist that day.

This was the biggest thing I'd ever seen, or done. Hybridizing, right there, you could see it.

The guy patted me on the head. Really. I can still feel his damp hand patting my hair. He explained that birches are in the same family as willows and have the same kind of fruiting bodies. That was okay, till I saw him make that shitty little smile at Ms. Nickels, like, aren't kids just the cutest? It was quite a while before I went out exploring in the woods again, but eventually I got bored on the docks, and just went back to what I had been doing, at that point not really categorizing but just—looking. It wasn't until I found the *Journey to Lapland* that I got excited about Carl and his work and decided to make it my own.

Snowy mountains encompassed me on every side, I walked in snow, as if it had been the severest winter. All the rare plants I had previously met with, and which had from time to time afforded me so much pleasure, were here in miniature, and new ones in such profusion, that I was overcome with astonishment... (This was a special page for me, titled *The Lapland Alps* and written on my birthday of July 6.)

Carl isn't remembered for the *Journey*, from what I can tell. That was a work of love. But he wrote *Species Plantarum* years later, and what he saw in Lapland helped him create a whole new way of thinking, like Darwin and the finches. He was ahead of Darwin. That I know: *If we contemplate the characters of our teeth, hands, fingers, and toes, it is impossible not to perceive how very nearly we are related to Baboons and Monkeys, the wild men of the woods.*

He created a system for naming plants, two words, the genus and species, the group and then the type within that group. One thing leads to another, and I don't think you'd have had Darwin until Carl sorted things out. With the organisms lined up properly, when Darwin shipped out on the *Beagle*, it was as if he had the right set of glasses to see what was happening in the Galapagos, old volcanoes from millions of years ago populated by what drifted in or swam or flew there. The visitors either survived and bred or died off. Islands, not like our lake islands, though I guess if the dam holds for thousands of years, the worms and lizards would begin to drift away from their cousins on shore.

We have a fully developed ecosystem right here at the marina, backwater or not, or maybe because it is a backwater, where things have been cut off and left to evolve on their own like in the Galapagos. Just like Darwin said, you have competition for resources. Some do better than others.

Here is my system:

FILLIYAW POINTE MARINA
WORKING
Permanent
Marina concession owner
Mr. Malouf, owner of FPM, LLC. Invisible. He lives at Oriental, where he has a bigger and better marina.

Manager
  Dad, Andrew Warshauer.
Regular Crew
  Guillermo (Joseph)
  Jesus
  Mario (Mary)
  Lawyer
  Pastor
Cleaning Crew
  Deloris Pate

Itinerant
  Sea-Tow
    Big Paul
  Crafts
    Brightwork man
    Sailmaker
    Mechanics
    Carpenter
    Plumber
    Electrician
    Dish TV installer
    Jack-of-all-trades
  Government
    Tax office—gas pumps
    DENR
    Mailman
  Deliveries
    Ice man
    Bread man
    Sundries truck driver
    Pepsi man
    UPS
    FedEx
    Gas delivery

The Wheeler-Dealer
> Mr. Canty, who owns the only sailboat dealership within a two-hour drive.

The PIs
> I place them under "permanent" although it's a rotating cast. There's always at least one here, snooping. I call them City Slicker, Bounty Hunter, and Highway Patrol. It's always about divorce.

BOATERS
Customers
Gas buyers
Bait buyers
Soda and snacks buyers
Jet skiers
Boat launchers
Platypus
> That's what I call the guy who has an experimental aircraft on pontoons. He launches it from the ramp and takes off with a long run out from the cove.

Tourists (non-paying)
Dockwalkers
Toilet users
Boat lookers

Tenants
Powerboaters
> Bass anglers
> Cruisers

Speedsters
Houseboaters
> Weekenders
> Occasionals

Liveaboards
> Loners and old cranks

Pontooners

> Partyhutters
> Fishermen
> "The Simpsons"

Sailors

> *Boat bums*
>> Guys working on their boats, silent
>> and competent.
>
> *Hopefuls*
>> They've bought an old boat and hope
>> they can get it working.
>
> *Daysailers*
>> Mostly couples.
>
> *Yachtsmen*
>> Thirty feet or better. Usually with flags
>> on the rigging.
>
> *AWOLs*
>> Boats where no one ever shows.

Me, I'm a creature like a bear or raccoon, I can live lots of ways. Daughter of Andrew, cleaner of boats, sailor of *Bellatrix* that I built from a derelict, roamer of woods, scientist, stalker of plants and animals, teller of tales.

9

What did you tell him?" Nat's voice, never much of an instrument anyway, nearly disappeared in the slap of backwash against the dock. Out here at the end of B dock, I thought it would be quieter, but it's never altogether quiet around water. I pressed the phone up tight against my ear.

"The same stuff." I watched a heron lift one foot slowly and set it down slowly. "We were at OT, she showed up drunk. I said something about her dress being ripped."

"He already knew about that. Hulky told him."

Huh. "Well, Hulky couldn't hardly keep inside his skin, looking at her." I heard my own voice say that, like some of Dad's old hillbilly talk.

The heron had its head pulled back as though it was going to stab something, then eased down and shook its neck-feathers. Nat didn't say anything. I watched the bird and waited on him. *First one to speak loses*, so says Dad.

I waited some more, but I must have had more questions than Nat. "So what did *you* tell him?"

"Yeah, well, all that," he said. "She was crying and messed up."

"Did you tell him about what she did?"

"No."

"Well, he must have known something, 'cause he was asking me about if we were close."

"I told him Charisse followed you." Nat was almost whining. "That's all."

"Oh, great." I could see Vann putting *that* down in his little book.

"I just told him the truth. You took off and after a while she went the same direction, toward the lake. I never said anything before."

"Why'd you now?"

"He was saying we looked good for it, Hulky and me. We were the last ones with her, the last ones to see her." He was talking so fast I could hardly understand him. "We didn't do anything to her. You know that. We shouldn't look good for it. Anyway, Hulky probably told him too."

I remember Vann asking, had I seen anyone when I was walking home.

Clouds underlit by lightning. Wisteria smell. Below the old plantation house, down by the fallen-in cabins, something white had come out of the woods and flashed past me. Big. I heard the leaves scatter, the drumbeat of hooves. It was one of the albino deer that show up around the lake—I realized that, even though my heart was hammering and I stopped on the path and listened before moving as quickly as I could down the hill to the lake, the wind banshee-howling in the shrouds of the sailboats.

"Anyway, they found her in your backyard."

The great blue had stalked deeper into the water off the point. Now he was cocked like a gun—one foot up—then fast-fast he struck and brought up a good-sized fish.

"Some friend you are," I said.

The heron tried to swallow the fish, throwing it up on the air to take it head first, but it was too big. He waded to the shore and began to bash it, wiggling, against the rocks.

Nat didn't say anything, so I did. "How was the funeral?"

"People noticed you weren't there," he said.

"Dad tried to make me go. He said people would talk. I said I didn't care and he couldn't make me."

"Your choice, I guess. People were talking about your fight. Kids, anyway, not the old folks."

"I imagine they turned her into a saint."

"Gobs of flowers, a table full of pictures, sappy music, yeah. But you still gotta feel sorry for her parents."

I didn't have an answer to that.

The fish was coming apart. The heron ate it a piece at a time.

"So did you tell Vann about what happened?"

"What part?"

"You know."

Charisse showing up at Old Trinity was about the last thing any of us had expected. She'd come wheeling up in the Jag, staggering in to find someone to talk to, where she knew we'd be. "Hey, guys," she said, weaving over the fresh-cut grass to where we were. Hulky let her have the big Robards stone he always sat on, then hovered. Nat and I sat opposite her, on each end of the Brackenbill tomb. She sang a couple of slurred lines from "Beauty and the Beast" (you can guess what role she had in our production) and kicked her feet, her painted toenails glittering when the moonlight showed through, her ankles white and the bottoms of her feet black.

"Where's your shoes?" Hulky asked.

"One here, one there." She lifted her legs in a gymnast's pose, until her beaded dress slipped to the tops of her thighs and Nat got up and walked away into the dark under the cedar trees.

"Here." Hulky pulled off his shoes and socks, set them down beside her. His favorite Chuck Taylors.

"Maggie has all the boys," Charisse said.

"Yeah," I muttered.

"No, it's true. You have booooooys," she dragged out, "and you have friends. You have boy-friends."

"Charisse, just go home."

"I could drive you." Hulky, of course.

Charisse shook her head, slowly and emphatically, one side to the other and back, like something mechanical.

"Why'd you come here, Charisse?" I asked. She kept staring into the trees. "You don't want anything to do with us in the daylight."

She didn't answer me, just talked into the dark. "I thought maybe we should bury the hatchet."

That didn't make me feel any more comfortable. We'd been cutting eyes at each other for weeks, got into arguing loud and heavy by her locker one day, until she said one thing too many and I slapped her. Then she made those comments on my Facebook page, calling me a sad, pathetic liar, and me commenting back. Harder.

She stood up, teetering for a moment from the uneven ground or her uneven equilibrium. "Actually," she said. "I'd rather kiss and make up." She put her hands on my shoulders. She leaned forward. I could see the peach lace through the gash in the front of her dress. She leaned in, and I tried to lean back but her hands were stronger than you'd think. She had opened her mouth and pressed it to mine, deep and soft, the smell of liquor and sweat and vomit.

"I didn't tell Vann anything about *that*." Nat's voice came from outside my memory, washing it away. "I said we finished the bottle and you left and then she left, walking toward the lake. And Hulky and me went home, and our parents knew when we got home. We have alibis."

Great. Everyone's got alibis. The dock boards were cutting into my legs. I pushed myself up and when I did the heron took off from the point, making that pterodactyl noise.

"Can we just not tell Vann anything more about all this? It's embarrassing, you know?"

"At least I didn't tell him about Fletcher."

10

Observation: Chipmunks

Kingdom: Animalia
Phylum: Chordata
Class: Mammalia
Order: Rodentia
Suborder: Sciuromorpha
Family: Sciuridae
Tribe: Marmotini
Subtribe: Tamiina
Genus: Tamias
Species: Striatus

Species rise out of species, like out of like—that's the rule, that's how it works—but sometimes creatures that are in no way related come to look alike or live the same way, as though the universe was interested in trying out that same idea from another angle. Sometimes the same question is answered different ways, with bats and chimney swifts both swooping around the night sky. Nature comes up with the design for eyes over and over, or wings, or a streamlined shape, turning little dog creatures into horses that run and live like antelope.

It's not really the same, but it seems to me that chipmunks and wrens have sort of the same thing going on. They couldn't be more different, birds and mammals, but they're also a lot alike. I see them both near the bathhouse, the chipmunks with their dive-holes under tree roots or the edge of the building, the wrens nesting overhead. They have the same coloring, that fall-leaf blend of rusty browns and white and black. They have the same movement, quick and erratic, moving from vantage point to vantage point, always watching with bright black eyes.

When movement on the ground catches my eye, a jerky shift from here to there, I'm never sure which one it will be.

Mostly it's attitude. Alert. Interested. Cocky. The British call it cheeky and I think that's the best term. Cheeky.

11

I read that DNA is causing scientists to shuffle the taxonomy in birds and a lot of other creatures. Which birds are the most primitive, that kind of thing. Ones that look similar may really be pretty far apart genetically. All Carl had to work with was feathers and bones, but it turns out that evolution had worked the same problem over and over. Like penguins and seals and otters.

I was thinking this as we lined up in the marina office and waited for the crime-lab geek to get his tubes and swabs arranged. Drexel Vann had come with him, but then went out on the docks. I guess he didn't have to mess with that kind of work.

Dad got the call and closed up shop—not a big problem, with the sudden chill around the marina, and not just from the recent cold front that had dropped out of Canada. We weren't getting people in the store. Boat owners were walking past with cans of gasoline bought elsewhere, and the fishermen weren't gawking over the shiny new lures and reels that I'd arranged with some care around the old stuff to make it look like we'd brought in a lot of new stock for spring.

"Okay." The lab guy held up a swab. "Just open your mouth. It only hurts if you bite down."

Mario jittered one leg and looked like he was going to run away. Guillermo put a hand on his shoulder and they moved forward together.

Jesus, Mary, and Joseph, and Pastor and Lawyer. Lumpy old Deloris Pate, who came in twice a week to push the dirt around in the bathhouses. Dad.

"I need her too," and the lab guy pointed at me.

"Why?" Dad bulked up the way he does when he's mad, his shoulders going up and his chin down, ready to scrap. I see myself in him, or him in me, I guess, more than I want to admit.

"I just go by the list." The lab guy pointed at the clipboard. "Everyone who has access to the keys."

"That don't seem right."

Just like in the movies, the door opened dramatically, and Vann walked in, trying not to lose a bunch of papers to the wind.

"Vann, what's going on here?" Dad asked.

The detective squinched his nose to resettle his glasses higher. "The tests?"

"Yeah, the tests. Why's Maggie dragged into this?"

Vann looked at him, as if what was evident *was* evident, but Dad just balled up his fists.

"Mr. Warshauer," he began. "It's like with fingerprints. We use tests like this to eliminate possible suspects."

"Why Maggie? She's a victim here. Wasn't it her cousin? She's traumatized by the whole mess. Why you think she ain't in school like she oughta be?" He always went hillbilly when he got angry. And he got red in the face. "What about all them people, the boaters and all?"

"How many people had access to that boat, Mr. Warshauer? More to the point, how many had access to the key to open that padlock?" Vann's voice was calm and seemed dangerous because it was.

"Any of 'em mighta stole the key."

"Was it missing?"

Of course not.

The tech held up a swab. It seemed to give him pleasure. I didn't want him putting that in my mouth. Dad looked at me and I wish he'd looked more horrified, or had some kind of expression other than the doubt I saw edging in. I opened up and the tech rolled the swab around my cheek. I tasted latex from his gloves where his fat hand pressed against my lips.

"Thanks for your cooperation, folks." The tech wrote my name on a label and pressed it into place.

"This everyone?" Vann asked.

"Everyone that gets into the key box."

"Craftsmen?"

"I sent you the list. We keep the same contractors."

The lab guy got himself out the door, moving pretty well despite his size and all the boxes and pouches. But Vann hung back.

"Mr. Warshauer, I believe I need to speak with your daughter again."

That ran a cold chill up my spine. I waited for Dad to swagger up again, tell Vann no way, demand an attorney. I looked steady at him, but he didn't have any more fight. His shoulders sagged and seemed to kind of collapse as he tipped his head.

Thanks, Dad.

This time Dad left and we stayed in the office. Vann was shuffling his pile of papers and printouts, some of them highlighted with fluorescent yellow.

"What can you tell me about this, Maggie?"

He laid the pages out, one after the other, like a deck of cards. The Facebook stuff looked strange, pulled off the screen and printed out in big type.

Maggie Warshauer

Work

> Scientist in Training

Education

> London County Prison Camp. Sentence ends in May!

Living

> Hometown: Somewhere Else.

Basic Info

> Sex—Female.
>
> Birthday—July 6.
>
> Languages—English, sailing.
>
> Political Views—I am strongly in favor of living things.
>
> About—My passions are sailing and taxonomy. My heroes are Carl von Linne (you can look it up!) and Thor Heyerdahl and Anne Bonny "The Lady Pirate."
>
> Favorite Quotations—"In wildness is the preservation

of the world." Thoreau

Relationship—Hmmmmm.

Status Update

Soon as the wind comes up I'm outta here. Headed for the Society Islands *Five likes.*

Status Update

Found an interesting plant today. Time to get out the ol' botany book.

Status Update

Bellatrix lived up to her name today. The lake was choppy and the wind W-NW. Tough beat all the way up the lake but a great ride home! *Three likes.*

There was a lot more of that kind of stuff, just reports on the marina and things I saw. Those all seemed so long ago. I read the lines almost the way Carl would have read a scientific treatise from a library. In Latin.

"What are the Society Islands?"

Anyone around the lake knew that. "The islands halfway up the lake. They used to be hills. Just old hilltops with oak trees and stuff on them."

"And *Bellatrix*?"

"That's my sailboat."

"Nice." He looked like he had just caught the punch line of a joke. "A warrior woman."

Now it was my turn to be surprised. "Most people think it's from Harry Potter. As if. Actually, it's the name of a star in Orion."

"The Amazon star."

"Huh?"

"I know a little astronomy," he said. "Bellatrix means female warrior. It's the 27th brightest star in the night sky."

I sure would have rather talked about the sky, but he turned back to the printouts.

Status Update

New photos posted: Society Islands.

Bora Bora sure is pretty now! *Six likes.*

52   VALERIE NIEMAN

COMMENTS

Swangurl Charisse—I call it Bora-Boring!

Goober Greene—I'll tell ya, these are some empty snaps. Where's the people?

Maggie Warshauer—It's not so empty. What U don't see U don't know

Swangurl Charisse—Don't tell me you had company?

Taylor Hayworth—Must be the invisible man then, cuz all I see is trees. *Three likes.*

Maggie Warshauer—I was not the only one on society islands!!!! Followed footprints & saw him sleeping with no shirt on OMG.

Goober Greene—Unh-hunh.

Swangurl Charisse—Sure, like I believe that. Maggie all alone like always.

Vann said, "You and Charisse weren't exactly pals." He wasn't asking a question.

"No."

"Seems like she had most everything going her way—popular, pretty, well off."

What he didn't have to say was that I didn't have any of those things. But I have more smarts when I'm asleep than she has wide awake.

"Yeah, I guess. As long as you didn't have to work with her on anything for school."

"Did that happen to you?"

"We got teamed up for a project in English. Not my idea."

"What did you get for a grade?" Sometimes I wondered how his mind worked, if he was doing what he should be doing as a detective or if he was just nosy on his own.

"B."

"And you're a straight-A student. Am I right?"

I nodded.

"Charisse?"

"She wouldn't do her part at all. We had to present in class and she flubbed around and giggled. We got a C." I wished my face didn't show how hot I felt inside, remembering that disaster.

"Make you mad?"

His eyes were magnified by the glasses, innocent as a puppy's, but Vann wasn't a puppy. I didn't know what he knew and what he was guessing at. And what the others had said, or believed, or thought they knew.

"I told her how I felt."

"Charisse gave you a hard time about boys?"

I could hear her, the remark flung over her shoulder after the fight about the English project. "At least I can get a date."

Status Update
> He looks like a pirate—tanned, black hair, barefoot. *Two likes.*

COMMENTS

Swangurl Charisse—Arrrgggggghhhh Capt. Morgan

Elizabeth Smith—Hahaha. Right off the bottle.

Maggie Warshauer—Jealous?

Status Update
> Fletcher sails from VA. 22ft Catalina he keeps bristol. Happy me! Only thing keeping us apart is dead calm. *One like.*

COMMENTS

Taylor Hayworth—Whats a bristol?

Maggie Warshauer—It means perfect condition, a boat kept in perfect shape.

Status Update
> When Fletcher kisses me I feel it right to my toes. *Three likes.*

COMMENTS

JJJones—AWWWWWWWW! So schweeet.

Goober Greene—Soooo romantic. >;)

Elizabeth Smith—SOOOOOO FAKE!!!!!

Status Update

> Fletcher brought a sleeping bag. We got in together and
> he zipped it up. He is so hot.

COMMENTS

Swangurl Charisse—Yeah, I'll bet it was hot.

Maggie Warshauer—He's the hot one.

Swangurl Charisse—OK guess u don't like girls after all.

Maggie Warshauer—Not the right equip.

Elizabeth Smith—You lose your phone? How bout a look
at this guy?

Status Update

> New photos—Fletcher. Inspiration for when we are
> apart. *Six likes.*

COMMENTS

Elizabeth Smith—Look like U got him @Dollar Store. *Five
likes.*

Goober Greene—lmao!!!!

Swangurl Charisse—He is 2 hot 2 be real 4 sure.

Maggie Warshauer—U couldn't handle how real.

Elizabeth Smith—O tell us Yr not cherry anymore. Yeah
right

Maggie Warshauer—Fletcher makes me scream.

Vann looked at me over the pile of pages he was still holding.
"So who's Goober, these others?"
　　"Swangurl is Charisse. Of course."
　　He nodded. "Odette."

"Yeah?" I didn't get the connection.

"*Swan Lake.* The swan queen is Odette. Charisse's middle name is Odette."

This cop knew the strangest things, for a cop. But she did take ballet classes. Of course.

"Goober?"

"Someone she knows."

He just waited, looking at me.

"Elizabeth is one of her girls. The plain girl she keeps around for contrast. Taylor Hayworth is a jock. Loudmouth." I pushed the pages across the counter. "It's just Facebook stuff. Just crazy stuff."

"And Fletcher?"

God, I could feel the red in my face, feel myself breaking out into blotches and sweat. I didn't want to open my mouth. Didn't want to look at him. I knew this was coming, but still. "Fletcher." I didn't want to say any more.

"Fletcher," he repeated.

"Fletcher—isn't real."

"Really?"

That made me smile at least.

"I made him up. That we met on the island and that we sailed there to meet and have sex and all of that."

"What about the pictures? He's some good-looking guy."

If my face was red before, now it was on fire. I knew what he was thinking, like Charisse and the rest. Too handsome for me. "I found them on the web." But the pictures *looked* like Fletcher, *was* Fletcher, the man I could see in my mind's eye right down to his freckles.

"Still, your friends believe he's real."

"My friends are idiots." I wanted to take that back; they weren't idiots. They were friends and so they believed me. And that made the others believe, even Charisse after a while, even if she just couldn't stand it that I had a boyfriend. I remember the first time I told her, and she kept asking questions and I answered them, the answers coming easily, just making it up as

I went along, but the doubt was still there so that I had to keep telling people, keep the thing going.

He turned to the next page. I didn't have to see the yellow marks to know what the detective found interesting.

Maggie Warshauer
Work
Voyager.
Education
The best education is self-education.
Living
Hometown: Atlantis.
Basic Info
Sex—Female.

Birthday—July 6.

Languages—English, sailing.

Political Views—I am strongly in favor of living things.

About—My passions are sailing and taxonomy. My heroes are Carl von Linne (you can look it up!) and Thor Heyerdahl and Anne Bonny "The Lady Pirate."

Favorite Quotations—"Forget not that the earth delights to feel your bare feet and the winds long to play with your hair." Kahlil Gibran

Relationship—In deep.

Status Update

Great day. So warm like July. We had sex in the boat tied up at the beach. *One like.*

COMMENTS

Swangurl Charisse—Here we go again.

Maggie Warshauer—Then a squall line hit while we were sailing, so Fletcher hove to and we cuddled up.

Taylor Hayworth—Did you say ho?

Maggie Warshauer—Those quarter berths are so narrow.

Sore.

Swangurl Charisse—Sore from doing yourself, you mean.

Goober Greene—[: lmao.

Taylor Hayworth—hahahahaha. U know which is which?

Elizabeth Smith—Do it matter?

Swangurl Charisse—She wishes.

Maggie Warshauer—Jealous?

Swangurl Charisse—What's to be jealous of? You are just a sad pathetic liar.

Maggie Warshauer—I hope U choke on your rotten words. Choke to death. Just because someone w/out everything gets to have a boy friend, a man friend not boy w his tongue hanging out, U cant stand it can you. I hate your guts forever.

"I understand there was an…altercation…in school," Drexel Vann said.

"She said I was a liar. I said she was a stupid whore. It was a cuss fight—no blood, no foul."

"I heard it was more than that. That you backed her into her locker. That she pushed you and you slapped her hard."

"People blew the whole thing up."

Vann shuffled the pages back together.

"So you made this whole thing up, this Fletcher, and kept it going for—what, weeks? Months?—because Charisse gave you a rough time about boys." I could hear the doubt in his voice. I'd gotten good at spotting doubt.

"It's not the easiest thing, being a girl that looks like me."

"Why is that?"

"I'm not petite. I'm not blond. I don't have the—parts. And I won't giggle and prance around and pretend I'm stupid to make some stupid guy feel better about himself."

I think he wanted to smile but wouldn't allow himself. "So… do you have a boyfriend?"

"I don't think that's any of your business." Now I could feel my dad in me, almost feel my shoulders coming up and making me big and threatening.

"That might be none of my business."

If he was waiting for me to cave and admit I was a virgin, it wasn't happening; anyway, I knew plenty about sex, way before any lame-ass health class.

We sat for a little while, with me looking out the window and wishing someone would come buzzing for gas or knocking to get in for a drink and chips, but all I could see was one of the Hunters putting out past the no-wake buoys, a woman at the tiller and a man pulling the sail cover off the main. Daysailers.

"You watch a lot of TV?"

Dang. Where did that come from? "Some."

"You got cable out here a while ago, right?"

"Yeah, finally. Not cable, Dish."

"That really opened things up, didn't it? Just the Raleigh stations before, right?"

I nodded.

"What do you watch?"

"I like Discovery, PBS, nature programs. National Geographic."

"You have HBO here, Showtime?"

"Yeah."

"And the internet."

"Yeah."

"Some pretty graphic things you're writing about in this Facebook here, Maggie. You know there's more."

Now I understood what the questions meant. He thought either I had a lot of sexual experience, which meant Fletcher was real, or else I had to get it off TV or some porn site on the computer.

"Fletcher is imaginary. I told you that. I made him up. I *read*. I write *stories*. I have an *imagination*."

"Well, Charisse's was not an imaginary death." His eyes went from barn owl to horned owl, soft to sharp. "She died from breathing her own vomit. Choking on her own words, exactly as you say."

That ran a shock through me. I kept my eyes on the water, watching the sail rise and fill on the Hunter, watching it heel a bit.

"Charisse followed you that night. I've seen her feet, Maggie, and they were cut and bruised terribly. She was barefoot—how could she have walked into the woods like that?"

I flashed on her dirty feet, Charisse sitting on the tombstone, kicking her feet up in the air, the bottoms of them black already. And Hulky trying to get her to take his Chucks.

"I've seen people do some strange things, but all the time I keep wondering, why? Why did she follow you into the woods, barefooted, with a storm coming?"

I could feel that Vann had leaned closer. I would not look at him. His eyes would pry it all out of me if I did. *I'd rather kiss and make up*, she had said. Her dress was torn and the wrist corsage was shredded, just the button centers left where the petals had been pulled off, and the wrinkled and dirty ribbon. Then her hands were on my shoulders, and her mouth pressed into mine. Deep and soft, the smell of liquor and sweat and vomit.

Heat bloomed low in my belly. I knew the feeling, sort of, but this was more than some rubbing and a quick release. Was this the feeling that was supposed to come from being with a man? Was this it? That kind of melting need?

"You're awfully quiet, Maggie. I wonder what you are remembering. Or who." Vann stood up and gathered his printouts. I turned toward him but kept my eyes on his hands, not his soft, intense, demanding eyes.

"I find it hard to believe this Fletcher is imaginary, Maggie. Maybe his name, maybe some details to protect him. Maybe you make some things up, but not everything."

12

Observation: The Nest

I almost kicked the thing over, running down the shortcut between the bathhouse and the campground.

A dome made out of sticks and grass, it was like a giant bird's nest turned upside down.

I walked around it, seeing how it was put together. It was loosely woven out of twigs and grass and weed stems, just like a bird nest, but nests were usually, well, nest-shaped and small and up in a tree. I looked up. No branches over the path that looked like they could support this. And birds that built something this big, like crows and eagles, used big honking sticks and not little stems.

There was an opening at one end. When I looked inside, there was nothing but the bare path, and sunlight arrowing between the branches to burn white spots on the dirt. I picked it up and turned it over, light as I expected, and a little wobbly, the weaving not close and regular like a human basket maker would do. Birds wove nests—like house sparrows that are really weaver finches, and that make tall grass nests with scraps of plastic or cloth woven in. But this was way bigger than any sparrow.

I started to carry it home, like other things I find in the woods, but then I had a kind of creepy feeling about it. Superstitious, maybe. I stashed it in the machine shed, on a top rack behind the oil cans, where I could look at it again.

I searched the internet, but it wasn't much help (though the Cornell Lab of Ornithology site is *great*!). Bird nests come in cups and plates, burrows, mounds, and scrapes, and some odd things like the bags that orioles hang from branches. The closest thing I found was the ovenbird, which makes a domed nest on the ground.

But the ovenbird would have to be as big as a cat. At least.

13

S ome memories are frozen, like faces caught in photographs, and there's no way to make them better or worse. We were living in a converted boat shed at the time. My dad was leaning against the pea-green bead board nailed between raw wood planks, and even if I didn't remember my mother taking the picture, I would know she had because I see it in his eyes. This is who my dad was: a pirate, a fisherman, a survivor of the Spanish Armada. A really excellent boat mechanic. He was leaning on one hand—the other one, out of sight, probably holds a cigarette or a glass of rum and Coke. He had on a fresh white shirt from the Neuse Boat Works. He was dark and ruddy, black hair and thick black curling hair on his arms and a weekend growth of beard, his nose and cheeks and lips red from the wind and the sun. He could be a Moor, or partly one. He was looking straight into the camera, or into the face of the person holding the camera, and his eyes gleam *sex sex sex*. That's all he was thinking, sex. And in the foreground, my face washed out by the flash, I was looking at her too. My eyes are her eyes, clear blue, and my lips are my father's, full and red. I have his ears—you can see that so clearly—and his eyebrows. My hair is light brown, stuck between the black and the blond, either one more desirable. I have a fat, likable face and I got my hair cut at the barbershop with my dad. Most people think I'm a boy when they see me in pictures from that time.

Right before the picture was snapped, she had announced that she had landed a job at Sharkey's. I guess we were happy, because money was tight. She'd get good tips from the yachting crowd.

Guess what I did today? she'd said, sashaying a little with her shorts pulled out at the corners like a skirt.

You added a layer to your tan? Dad had said back.

She'd closed her eyes and lifted her chin, turning away as though she'd been mortally insulted. It was one of those gestures she'd copied out of the movies, probably *Gone with the Wind*. If she could've gotten away with it, she would've said, "Fiddle-dee-dee." But even she wouldn't push things that far.

No, smartass, I got a job.

Yeah? Dad sat halfway up on the rotten old couch set on bricks instead of legs. *Where at?*

Sharkey's. They need a waitress for the weekends.

He didn't say anything, just nodded. Sharkey's sounded like a dive but it was the primo place on the waterfront, with expensive wines and thick-cut steaks, not just the usual Calabash seafood. That was where the men who owned hundred-foot yachts and expensive racing boats hung out, bragging and boozing.

She dipped and danced toward us, the camera in one hand and the other making loops in the air. *We can afford a few things now. Lenore, what would you like most in all the world?*

I said the first thing, the thing I wanted most in the world. *A Hobie Cat. The one over by the machine shed.*

The smile tipped down a little. *Oh, honey, I don't think we'll have that much. Daddy needs tires for the car and Mommy needs some new dresses—for work. How about a new outfit for you?*

I nodded. She'd get what she wanted to get. I didn't care about any outfit, which meant jeans and a shirt from Maxway that smelled stiff and had the colors of a cereal box. The boat wouldn't have cost as much, maybe. It was an old one the owners kept for back payment, or storage, or maybe it was just abandoned—it had sat there with the grass growing up between the hulls, which were beat up and patched but okay. Sails were in a bag inside the shed. I had plans. But I wouldn't plead. I had learned not to ask her for things she didn't want to give.

Then she'd lifted the camera and said for us to smile because it was a celebration—I am too close to the camera and have the half-smile I seemed to have in every picture, but not until I found this one did I see how my father had looked. Leaning back and looking at her, all his need was in his eyes. There was a direct current from him to her—I was just caught in the glare.

14

I took the package all the way down A dock to *Free Bird*. Mr. Yardley was working on her, as usual. He was one of the most diligent of boat bums, making his Catalina as gorgeous as you could make a production boat like that. He was redoing the teak, though it was pretty much perfect before.

"Your stuff's here," I called.

He looked up with a scowl, then smiled. He was a real loner. Privately, I call him the Gray Man. Whatever color his cap and shirt and pants had been once, they were always gray, all gray like his close-clipped hair and beard.

"Thanks." He reached his left hand for the package, never letting go of the narrow brush he was using to apply brightener to the wood.

"That looks great," I told him. "Just like new."

He stepped back and squinted along the surface. I could tell he was pleased.

"It's so nice when someone pays attention." He reached his brush into a corner with a kind of flourish, but his hand began shaking a little and he hit the fiberglass. Zap, he had a rag out and the mark was gone.

"I always mean to tell you, I like how you keep your little boat," he said. "She's just as clean and nice."

"Thank you." I trotted back down the docks, feeling bubbly with his recognition. I'm as proud of *Bellatrix* as he is of *Free Bird*.

She's a Blue Jay, which is a great little boat—fast despite a short rig, and with a nice cockpit. She was designed by Sparkman, a name that means a lot in sailing. He created the Lightning too. They call the Blue Jay a baby Lightning.

Just like that Hobie Cat, I had found her in the boneyard, a terrible fate for a boat. Derelicts that people had stopped caring about, when they quit paying slip fees, were pulled into the weeds above the old road. My little boat was weather-worn like the rest, her aluminum mast and boom bare, the numbers faded off her bow. Dad checked the marina records (which the previous manager had left in a mess) but found no hint of who had left her there. The hull number went back to a long-dead owner. As he had the say-so, with my biological mother not around to squash the idea, Dad let me fix her up.

Some Blue Jays are made of wood, but this one was fiber-glass; a wooden one would have been a pile of sawdust by now, what with carpenter ants and beetles and hole-boring bees (*xylocopa*, from wood-cutter). I compounded the hull (what a pretty V-bottom, she *looked* like a she!) and then waxed it until it shone. I'm always on the lookout for serviceable line tossed out by boaters, and was able to fit her up. You'd be amazed what goes into the dumpster every weekend—Lawyer and I work them every Monday, me pulling out usable boat parts, and Lawyer bagging aluminum cans to sell at the recycler. I got the rudder and tiller back in shape, with a new gudgeon to replace the one that was a bit bent.

Dad sprang for registration, used sails, and new deck hard-ware. And I found the name after weeks of pondering and writing different ideas in my notebook. I painted it myself on the stern.

15

When he left West Virginia, Dad says, he *shook the dust of that place offen his feet forever.* Weird sayings he comes up with, from back there. His own daddy was a coal miner (dead, roof fall) and his mother a store clerk (dead, lung cancer) and his brothers worked the strip mines. When they weren't on an excavator they were in jail for drinking and fighting. Sometimes with knives. Drew must have been the pick of the litter. He finished community college and went to work at a marina up there at Stonewall Jackson Lake, until he broke out and headed for blue water.

The first job he found in Carolina was doing repair work at Filliyaw Pointe. Fate intervened, as they say. Angela's family had a Sea Ray on B dock. She and Dad got together, despite what all the Alfords and their kin had to say, and they got me started and got married that summer just before I arrived. A real comedown for her, marrying a grease monkey from West Virginia, which in North Carolina is like saying the ghetto. We knocked around the state, Dad working at marinas here and there until we landed at Oriental. That's about where his telling ends and my memory kicks in. I started school there and learned to swim and learned to sail and was just beginning to understand two-stroke engines when my biological mother decided that this daddy's-girl stuff had gone too far. She wanted to get back to her momma and the red dirt and a "proper environment for Lenore."

Mr. Malouf already knew Dad's work at the boatyard, and with my so-called mother's family working the other end, Dad got the managership at Filliyaw Pointe. We lived with the Grands, in a wing of the plantation house, so that I could "get to know my heritage." And get properly broken into being a female like my mother. That didn't work out any better than the marriage. When she took off, we moved out of the big house but Dad stayed running the marina. He was sure she would come home eventually, and he wanted to be right here waiting. He has the true-believer thing going, but if she wasn't coming home for her momma then she sure wasn't coming back for him.

I miss the ocean. I even miss the shack we lived in, with shower curtains for room dividers. We go to the coast now and then, to pick up a boat or some parts or something. It's never for long except at the Christmas break. Dad fishes and mopes, and I catalog what washes up on the beaches. Summers are too busy for vacation, and I guess I'm okay with the winter because I'd rather look at birds and shells than people anyway. I plan to major in marine biology down at UNCW. If I get a good enough grade on my SATs.

So I don't have any family. I do, in a physical, genetic sense, but not in the way of having people that you go see at holidays. Cousins that you roll around with and play Wiffle ball with and torment.

As I've said, the Alfords don't like to claim us, my daddy being one of the wild mistakes that my so-called mother made on her way to Florida and a "good marriage." Husband Number Two is twenty years older than her, some kind of financier, and Dad says his ex-wife is just a hood ornament on a hundred-foot yacht. And he's Cuban, which is barely up the road from Black for people like the Alfords, but money works wonders on the complexion. So, I don't mingle with the Alford clan, and the Warshauers are all in West Virginia and would be as mythical as unicorns except for one trip we took a couple of years back.

I had looked forward to that trip after hearing all my classmates talk about family reunions and Christmases, never having a thing to say back when they asked how I spent Christmas, other than *on a smelly houseboat sloshing around in a deserted marina.* Just me and Dad and Rudolph on the VCR. Or in some ratty apartment that his buddy let him use at Atlantic Beach. When he said we were going to West Virginia for Thanksgiving, I thought that was Disneyland.

West Virginia wasn't something he talked about a lot, but I had a pretty good idea—Hatfields and McCoys, miners, lots of wildlife such as bears. I read somewhere that there is only one real lake in the whole state, the rest of them all being rivers that had been stopped up by dams.

He said we were going to Fairmont, look on the map. I looked it up. "Pretty mountain." I was eager for mountains.

It was a long drive. I-77, I-79. The hills and curves wear you out, leaning. I'd see a church steeple, maybe, or a little town wedged down between the mountains, but mostly just trees and the names of places on the interstate signs. We made each other silly with them, Flat Top, Lost Creek, Nutter Fort. The trees were mostly bare except for oaks, so everything was smoky looking, with bands of pine trees dark as scars against the purple-gray hills.

We saw some coal mines. One had a conveyor belt coming all the way down the mountain. The buildings at the top seemed flimsy and old, just sheet metal. A railroad track curved around the bottom of the mountain. It was an awesome thing to see, the coal pouring down, the cars ahead out of sight around the curve, all full, and more waiting to be filled. They did that every day.

"Not that kind of mine," Dad said when I asked about where our family worked. "Strip mines. Surface mines."

We finally drove past one. It didn't look like much.

"That's the reclamation side," he explained. "All finished up. You cut the trees and peel off the ground down to where the coal is, and shovel that off, and then put back the spoil. Carve it into benches so the rain don't just pull the whole thing down the side hill. Plant some grass, and there you go."

And there you go. I wondered how people could live where the land around them was being torn up and reshaped all the time. I wondered how the mountains even stayed standing, with the insides being pulled out.

Turned out we weren't heading to Fairmont. That was just the name on the exit. We were headed out to some little town with a single stoplight on the main street. That might not have been much different from the boonies where I live, but everything else was. The houses were made of round stones or wood, but small, and pressed up close to the road, right against it—a slice of grass and then the house, right there, and behind it a river or a hillside. Everything looked gray, maybe from the diesel smoke of the trucks running by so close. None of the businesses looked like they were open, except for a convenience store at the edge of town and the post office and the Word of God Church.

We drove right through that place, Grant Town, and kept going. The roads got smaller and smaller, like rivers going backwards to streams and brooks and then springs that rise out of the ground. We turned across a rickety one-lane bridge, then took a narrow road that went along the edge of the hill, riding above the creek until it was level with the tops of the sycamore trees, and hardly a shoulder to the road and just a section of guard rail here and there where it looked as if you would just slide right to death. Another turn, and now the road was so narrow that there were pull-offs so cars could pass each other on one thin strip of blacktop. When he turned at Rock Hill Run, I thought they had to be joking—the road was just dirt and went straight like a driveway, but there were mobile homes and little houses along it, until we were nearly to the top. We gunned up a dirt path with grass growing down the middle. The hill leveled off and there were open fields around an old two-story farmhouse with barns and other buildings, beat-down ground where a garden had been, and then more woods, like a watch cap pulled down over the top of the hill.

"There's your uncle Philip," Dad said.

Coming around the porch was a skinny version of Dad, with the shadow of a black beard and going bald. I knew he was younger than Dad but he didn't look like it.

Dad had tried to fill me in before we came, but the family tree was a mess, the lines broken and tangled, like trying to sort fossil strata after an earthquake. His older brother Simon was in jail. James was out west somewhere for reasons no one was talking about, his wife here at home with the babies. Sisters Johnna and Barthie had moved in together after Barthie lost her baby and she and her husband split up. Philip worked the coal mines—this was his house, his wife and his sons and one grown daughter living there with a baby while her husband was in the army. Just regular old family dysfunction.

"Hey, bro, good to see you!" Philip came up and grabbed Dad's hand and slapped him on the back. "This your girl?"

"All mine, right, Maggie?"

"Yep."

"Well, she favors you, no doubt of it." He bent closer, as if he was looking for my mother somewhere in my face. His breath smelled of Tic-Tacs and coffee. "You're in luck, Maggie, they's a couple girls here for you—the Warshauers most all make boys. C'mon in, c'mon in." Philip motioned like a carnival barker, like we might reconsider, run away, bounce down the road and back to Carolina. Maybe he could read minds.

The house was overheated and packed with people, along with a hyper Chihuahua. From the tiled fireplaces to the heavy dark woodwork with carved circles at the top corners of the doors, you could see someone had put a lot of care in building it. Lots of cigarette smoke, and a familiar sweet harsh smell of liquor, but mostly noise. Noise thick as smoke. Dad and Philip, Uncle Philip, took me around the room to meet "the family," aunts and uncles and cousins, a screaming baby, a hand-wave at some boys out back.

"Glenanna—meet your Rebel cousin." Philip turned the dark-haired girl around from where she was watching a video with another girl. "She's Simon's daughter. And this is Faith." Faith had hair the color of a squirrel. I don't know whose she was.

"Hi." Faith kept looking back at the video. It was Britney Spears, dancing with every corner of her body.

Glenanna tossed her hair and moved her shoulders up and down in time to the music. "Who do you like?"

"Me? Like as in…?"

"Music, you know, videos and stuff."

"I mostly read."

Faith turned to look at me like I was a strange specimen formaldehyded inside a jar. "What grade you in?"

"Ninth." That was two years ago, almost three. Seems like longer ago, but I remember, ninth.

"Gawd, I bet you don't even wear makeup, do you?"

I was saved from having to answer when the little rat-dog bit one of the men on the ankle. He cussed and kicked and the dog flew into the corner, where it backed up and showed its pointy teeth, yipping and quivering.

The TV blared and the dog yapped and that started the baby crying. Then the adults, so-called, started arguing.

I slid out the back door to where the boys were.

"What's going on in there?" said a boy with black hair, thick and wild. He stood by the back porch, apart from the three bigger ones who were clustered around a stack of hay bales back by the woods.

"The dog bit someone."

"Goddamn thing." He swaggered his cussword. "That ain't no kind of dog. We got coonhounds, beagles, a whole pile of dogs. You got dogs?"

"No."

"You're from down South."

"Yeah. Maggie."

"Gary. Me 'n' the others are shooting. Bow and arrow."

"Yeah?"

He started walking toward the others. As we got closer, I saw that one of the boys looked like him, kind of fat, but that same coarse hair. One was taller, older, and the last one could only be Faith's brother. They were trying to stand a plastic dummy of a buck deer against the hay bales, but it kept falling over. The dummy already had holes in it, places the arrows had been pulled out. Finally they leaned it far enough back that it stayed upright, though it looked sort of like it was lounging.

The boys were around my age, I guessed. They were all shy and wild, cutting their eyes at me, but none of them said anything to me. They had compound bows, all wheels and pulleys, not elegant like a long bow. It must have been familiar for men who were used to car engines and mining equipment to hunt with those things.

We walked back toward the house.

"You see Keith's deer?"

"Yeah, I seen it. Eight points."

"Can't eat horns."

"Can't eat horns. Now a young doe, that's good eating, Dad says."

"Wouldn't mind a set of eight-point antlers on my wall."

They nocked arrows and got ready to shoot. Faith's squirrel-haired brother stood first, pulled the bow back to where the pulleys took over, sighted, and let fly. The arrow went over the deer's shoulder and into the haystack.

"Aiiiiiir-ball! Aiiiiiirrrr-ball!"

"I was going for a backbone shot—you know, the really tough one?"

"Yeah, right."

"Stupid anyway," said Squirrel-Hair. "I'm gettin' a thirty-aught-six next fall for sure."

"Ain't happening. It'll be more 'just remember what happened to Eli' and that's all she wrote." Big Bear-Hair had spoken.

The tall kid hit the deer right in the middle of the body. Lots of talk about gut-shots and stinky innards and waste of meat. Then Big Bear-Hair shot wide. Finally Gary had his turn, the arrow taking off with a *whuuusssht* and hitting the dummy right where the back leg met the belly.

"Shoot it off, why don't ya?"

"Right in the privates." Squirrel-Hair glanced at me and snickered.

"Right in the dick."

"HEY!" Apparently, Big Bear-Hair was in charge, even if he wasn't the tallest. They snorted and poked each other for a while, while I did what Dad always said, *consider the source,* and ignored them.

Gary held out his camo-painted bow. "You wanna try?"

I'd never shot anything, even a BB gun, even at a plastic deer. The bow looked like some medieval torture instrument, an evil twang in its cables.

"Go on, it don't take no strength, the compound does it all for you," Gary urged, setting an arrow to the string and showing how it worked.

"She looks strong enough," said Squirrel-Hair.

The fourth boy, the tall one who didn't look like much of anything, or have anything to say, was smirking at me as he ran his forefinger back and forth through the V of fingers on his other hand.

I grabbed the bow and leveled it at an old car, rusted and sun-faded, and I pulled back the string and let fly. The arrow thudded into the door and stood there quivering. It was done before I could understand why I was doing it, and the boys just stood open-mouthed. I threw down the bow in front of the tall boy, went up the steps into the house, and didn't look back.

The Bear-Hairs came boiling in after me and told. "She shot Uncle Jimmy's car! Put a' arrow right through the door!" It was easy enough to say my finger slipped. The adults believed that, of a girl, though the boys knew better and gave me the stink-eye for having pulled it off without getting a whipping.

I spent the rest of the afternoon hanging with the adults in "the den." It had wood paneling and a scabby deer head (six points), and one of those talking plastic bass on a plaque that would go off when people walked past it. I saw bows and arrows hung up, but strangely enough, not a single gun. So much for mountain feuds. The TV cycled through soap operas and judge shows and talk shows. Like they were part of the TV, the adults went around and around the same topics: who was sick, got the cancer, probably from smoking, no it was black lung, well he's just a-wasting away, who's out of work, who's got work, who's knocked up, what happened to Tony, his momma would roll over in her grave, bail bond, Eye-talians'll take care of their own, put up the place, when's the trial?

Sometimes when you are categorizing you have to sit still, like in a blind. Just blend in with the flowered furniture. There are country people and rednecks, that's what I learned. Country people know how to do things—make jelly and slaughter hogs. Rednecks get their moves from beer commercials and the country music station. The older folks had skills, but I don't think the Bear-Hairs or the Britney watchers would ever know how to do anything worthwhile.

After they had dissected the lives of everyone up the holler and down the run, the women drifted off toward the kitchen. The men were mostly drinking beer, but some had pints in their pockets too, and Dad was right there with them. I could see him getting red-faced, and Philip looked just like him, except he was too skinny to swell up and look intimidating, mostly just thin-lipped nasty like a rattlesnake.

The death-and-misery talk slid over toward politics. I don't know who got onto that topic, except it was a bad idea, with some of the room shouting they were "yella dog Democrats" and others mad about the "damn rich bastard Republicans" and glaring at each other. I'd never known Dad was a Democrat, never remembered him voting, but he was howling mad now at his brother over something with the mines, like he should care, being in North Carolina.

"Can't see any farther than the end of your nose," he said.

"Man's gotta eat, Andy."

"What you gonna eat—or drink—when the mine acid poisons all the rivers?"

Then they were all shouting, and Dad hit his fist on the arm of the chair and said we were leaving, but everyone got quiet and Philip said it was growed dark, and no sense to running off into the night. "We ain't but started to get to know each other again," he said, almost pleading. Next thing I knew they were all settled down to watch *Sports Center* and talk football.

The next morning, the men held their coffee mugs with both hands while Mrs. Philip (I don't remember her name) made eggs and greasy fried potatoes and bacon cut thick. I stuck to Cocoa Puffs.

We left as the sun was climbing over the ridge top. There was still fog in the creek bottom. We threaded down the narrow roads, meeting a coal truck on one turn and hitting the gravel shoulder as the truck was over on our side of the road. We were near Grant Town when I saw ghosts.

"Look."

Thin gray threads emerged from the ground. A person who was superstitious would take them for ghosts.

"What is that?" I asked.

Dad slowed down and stopped. "Mine fire," he said. "The coal is on fire underground."

I looked carefully and saw a couple of dim red places at the foot of the smoke columns, and I saw how the smoke didn't come evenly but in gaps and belches, one puff rising and then another. He rolled down the windows and I could smell sulfur, like a box of matches all going off. "That's the sulfur in the coal here, what mixes with water and makes acid mine drainage. Kills ever'thing it touches."

I imagined the rivers bubbling with acid, burning things to the bone. I *tried* to imagine it, anyway.

We kept driving through the ragged fields and places with beat-in and rusty mailboxes, in some ways like home, the poorer parts of home, but more angry. The houses hunkered under the mountains and seemed to glare at you, dare you to step foot, and the people were the same way, mean as chained dogs. We may be country in Carolina, but we have blue sky above and ground underfoot that is not just a thin crust over hell.

16

The Rumor Mill

Sheriff's deputies maybe aren't supposed to talk about cases, but the clerks read the reports as they file them, and they talk. And the deputies will talk to their wives and buddies, and to each other at lunch, where people can overhear them—the clerk, the customers, the fat counter girl they ignore as she fills the sugar dispensers. Word gets around.

This wan't no normal rape, not Henry gettin' horny and jumping the neighbor girl.

That's why they ain't solved it. They got nothing. Nothing.

Not like *CSI*. They find DNA everywhere, semen, all those little flashlights, the evidence glowing.

Law and Order too. You can always tell, the first suspects ain't the ones. Gotta go a half-hour before the real suspect starts to show. You look at this case—they was keen after that girl, I heard, what's her name? Washington? Warshauer. Crazy, right? But with no evidence then it could be anyone.

My friend works in the sheriff's department and he says the boat they found her on was some kinda sex den. Red velvet, mirrors, peacock feathers.

Feathers?

They got their uses.

Hah!

No, you're wrong, 'cause I seed the pictures. No feathers.
What about her? Was she naked like they say?

Her prom dress, the poor girl. It was peeled off her like a banana.

More like a san'wich, ya know? In foil, and you peel it back. She was lying on her dress but it was cut apart and folded back.

Anyways, still under her.

Naked.

She was gagged with her own undies. Victoria's Secret. Jesse delivered the package a week before prom.

Bet they was something.

Wrong-oh, buddy. I heard she was gagged with an old sock.

Nope. It was the panties, but he used duct tape to hold the gag in there. The funeral director said her hair was all pulled away by the tape. Acourse that was around the back of her head, didn't show.

So what do you know about funeral parlors?

My girlfriend does the makeup and hair. I know plenty, let me tell you. Other than her wrists, she was clear of damage as a peach just been picked.

She wasn't bloated up?

Nah, just starting. Even if she was, you'd be surprised, be surprised what they can do with bodies. They got this stuff they inject, even drowned people. It can be done.

She looked just like herself, once they got done with the embalming.

They did a' autopsy, didn't they?

Of course.

They do it so's the incisions can be covered up.

You'd a thought she'd been bruised an' all, but he never touched her face.

Here you go with he again.

He, he, he. Yep. Wasn't a woman did that.

So who knows? She wasn't raped.

Yes, she was.

No semen, remember?

I know what they say, she was raped with something. They ain't saying what, or don't know what. So she was raped, not by a man proper, but I'll never believe anyone other than a man.

CSI would find out.

Enough with the *CSI*. That's TV.

But realistic. Based on real-life cases.

So why'd he kill her?

She died on her own. She threw up and choked on it. Drunk.

There you're wrong, for all you got friends down at the sheriff's office. She was full of Ecstasy. That's what killed her.

Whatever.

Admit you're wrong.

Both right. She was drunk and high and she threw up and died.

She was tied up with that cheap yellow floaty-line they use for waterskiing. Said it took all the skin off her wrists.

Thought your girlfriend said she wa'n't marked.

I said, her wrists were.

I heard there was some kind of kinky stuff. Handcuffs.

Whatever. The undertaker used makeup and put a bouquet of white lilies in her hands.

I admit they do wonderful things, those funeral homes. Wouldn't believe the people who get open caskets after wrecks and all.

They can just do wonders.

The undertaker said he never prepared a more beautiful body.

17

Observation: The Kill

I saw a young hawk on its kill today.
I think it was a young one. I didn't have my book to check for plumage, but it seemed to be having trouble finishing the job. It hopped on the prey and dragged it along the ground, and then pecked at it. I could see the gray body moving on its own. The hawk waited, then pecked some more.

Finally the hawk lifted the creature up onto a log, and sat there a while as though it was getting its breath. It took off and began to fly, low and heavy, carrying its kill across the road and into the trees on the other side. The squirrel dangled by its neck, the body limp and swinging like a kite tail.

18

My Angel:

 Things has got bad to worse here. I don't know if you ever see any news from NC where you are at but it's all over the papers. I suppose you hear from your folks. It is a real mess and Maggie is smack in the middle of it. She had got herself a boyfriend. They say she wrote about him on the computer, about having sex and all. She says not, and I believe her. You know how she always made up stories from when she was way little.

 The police are all around. I cant hardly run the marina for them. And people just looking, curious. Oh I wish youd call Maggie, please. She is your own flesh and blood. I remember what you said that you were never meant to have children. Why would a woman not want a baby? She was so beautiful. I remember tho I remember it all. I told you this baby coming was fate and all. We could buy her pretty dresses and walk on the boardwalk by the ocean. Everywhere people'd say she was a beautiful child.

 But you never took to her, after she was born, you couldn't stand the poop and all. I didn't mind, I helped raise my brothers, a dirty didy was no big deal to me. You being an only child, I guess it was.

 I wonder now about what happened. Living like we did. Only when she went to school could we think about having a real bout like you know BETTER than ANYONE how, and sometimes we just wanted each other so bad, it didn't matter.

 The Raleigh paper says that Charisse was tied up. Horrible stuff. You know how wild she was. I hate to say it but she is like you, just too full of life for living around here. But the paper says there was "inconclusive physical evidence." So the police are plain baffled and looking any old place, sure that this boyfriend of Maggie's wha' did it. They even hint that Maggie's involved. Good God are they nuts? Our little girl.

I am right scared, Angela. So much I don't know about her. You always hated her being with me, working on the boats, but she was happy then. Now shes growd up and its different. You always said you were on the outside looking in, now I feel that way. Secrets. All these secrets, and these weird boys she hangs with.

She tells me she made this whole thing up about Fletcher, that's the boy, but i don't know as I buy it.

This has been a real long letter but I cant say to you the things I need to say and what Maggie needs.

Come on home baby any time I will come and get you wher you are. Please please

Forever and ever your Drew

19

The Johnsons lived on Tabernacle Faith Chapel Road, which was also the name of the congregation they attended and where Nat's dad was the deacon. I don't know if the chapel came first or the road or the farm, but they were linked together from way back. I marched up the path from the lake toward Nat's place, across a corner of a tobacco field and back into woods. I expected to see people working somewhere, but the fields were empty and the tobacco leaves limp under the sun. What I didn't expect was to see Nat anywhere outside in the daylight. He did his work in the shadows.

A new stick hut, like the one I'd found before, had been built in the middle of the fork where one path went down to a branch of the lake and the other headed upcountry to Nat's house. The first one I found might have been made by a beaver, wasps, or termites, or some creature, but there was no question that this one was human made. It was better organized, as if the builder was learning how to put these things together. The twigs were woven more tightly. The space around it had been cleared, with grass pulled out and then the dirt smoothed down. And a single flat stone, a smooth oval of pure black (basalt?), had been placed in front of the doorway.

Black. Well, that made me think of Nat. A black stone, plus the fact that it was pointed right at his house. He was spooking me again, or trying to.

The Johnson house was big and old, white with heavy black shutters. Around the front, a few flowers drooped among the sad-looking azaleas. The porch went around two sides, but it was bleak, with one straight-backed porch swing and two wooden rocking chairs. The smell of bread baking came out of the open windows.

I knocked at the screen door, feeling like I was being watched from inside.

Nat's mother came to the door, wiping her hands on a towel.

"Hello? Why—Maggie. How are you?" She unhooked the latch. "Come on in."

I followed her into the living room. It hadn't changed any. A huge Bible on the coffee table. No television. Mrs. Johnson wore her hair in a thick braid coiled up into a bun. I wondered how long it was when she let it free.

"Nathanael. Your friend is here." She said it strangely, probably Biblically, not "Na-than-Yel," but "Na-than-A-el." She looked up the stairs and called again.

He was probably curled up, listening to forbidden rock music on headphones.

I heard a washing machine cycle into spin. Mrs. Johnson stood and waited with me.

"How's your daddy?"

"Oh, fine." I always wondered what people heard about my dad.

"You tell him I asked after him." She turned and gave me a long look and a kind smile. We seemed to be in something together.

I heard a door slam upstairs and Nat came down two at a time. He was wearing a plain white T-shirt and had combed his hair. His neck and his skinny pale arms were red—sunburned.

"Hey, Maggie."

"Hey, yourself." I wasn't real happy with him, and I guess it showed. He knotted up his forehead.

"Isn't it nice you have a—friend come to see you," his mother said to Nat, with that hopeful-but-doubtful tone of voice. He shot her a look and she glanced back and forth between us, confused. Now I was turning red too. His mother was so wrong, *so* wrong.

"I'll leave you young people to talk." She wiped her hands again, though they were dry, and disappeared back in the direction of the bread smell.

"Look," I said. "I guess you think it's all funny, but I don't appreciate you messing with my head."

"Are you demented?"

"Those stick things you're building over near the marina? Some kind of shrine or something? Trying to creep me out when I have all this mess!"

"You *are* demented."

"Well, if anyone would know demented, it would be you." That was a cheap shot and I was sorry.

"Gee, thanks. Join the chorus around here." He started to have that whiny edge to his voice that appeared when he was stressed out. "But I really, *really* don't know what you are talking about."

I sighed. "You—or someone—is building these little stick huts around the marina. This one had a black rock in front of it, like some kind of symbol, and it was right on the path over here."

"Cool," he said.

"Not cool."

"As much as I'd like to say I have the leisure to design totems and build them out in the woods, it's not me. Dad's had me working, and when I'm not out there, I'm under guard." He jerked his head toward where his mother was lurking. "As though I'd be doing something like that anyway. Guess you don't know me very well."

We both knew what we were remembering. If he brought it up, I was going to smack him.

"It's not me." He made an elaborate sign like a scout's honor crossed with a Roman salute.

"Okay. It's not you."

Then who?

20

The swallows were dive-bombing a newbie boat owner who was repairing an old Irwin. They swooped and cheeped, but he kept his head down and hat on and kept scraping. Every year the birds build their nests in the ends of the booms on boats that never leave the slip, ones that are gray with mildew and neglect—like the Irwin this guy must have thought was a bargain. He'd evicted the birds and started working on the derelict, but soon enough he'll find out that the hatch leaks can't be fixed, and the diesel needs a rebuild. Eventually the boat will be abandoned again under its tarp, to saw back and forth on stiffening dock lines. And the swallows will go back to raising their chicks in peace.

I shouldn't be so negative—occasionally one of these Hopefuls, cooked under the summer sun, will metamorphose into a full-fledged boat bum, and an old hulk will be shined up and become worthy of the phrase "ship-shape and Bristol fashion."

I quit watching out the window and went back to work, shoving the broom under the fishing tackle display and scooting out the rest of the duck food. A tourist had dropped a bag and it exploded, sending the kibble all over. The display racks were all bolted down so they wouldn't shift if we had heavy weather, so all I could do was poke around under them with the broom. It needed doing anyway, from the crud that was coming out along with the kibble.

I was taking care of the place while Dad made a run down to West Marine. No one was coming in anyway. It was too hot. This whole year had been extreme, sizzling or freezing. A morning breeze died before lunch to occasional cat's-paws, but clouds were building in with the promise of a front out of the northwest. The A/C cycled and cycled, trying to keep the tin hut cool and almost doing it.

Even Channel 16, which we monitored in the store and at home, was becalmed. A burst of talk now and again—Sea-Tow was headed into Filliyaw Pointe after delivering fuel, good news for a slack day. Big Paul would have the latest gossip. Then another call came in. Sea-Tow was turning around to free a boat stuck on Neptune's Nose. A Beneteau, too, and that was a shame. It's my favorite boat, the insignia high up on the mainsail so curving and elegant, a horse's head rising out of the waves. No reason for that kind of boat to go aground—full electronics, but no one paying much attention what with passing the wine and cheese.

The lake level had been falling steadily since Easter, with hardly any rain in the mountain headwaters or locally. People forgot that this lake was allowed to rise and fall, that it breathed like the ocean tides but more slowly, over weeks instead of days. Some of it was natural and some was the Army Corps of Engineers keeping water levels stable for the next lake downstream, where the shorelines were developed. We could tell where things stood—trees knee-deep in water when it was high, points extending farther out when the lake was down. The Nose, a former hilltop that rose out of the deep just outside the Paradise Channel, was usually eleven or twelve feet below the surface, but when the water started dropping, it headed toward the surface, eight feet, six feet, high enough to catch the keel on one of the oversized brag-boats that people kept here—as though they had a special outlet to the ocean none of us could access.

This lake's rise and fall keeps it wild. Houses have to be built above the pool elevation maximum—back in the woods, where they may have a view of the water but are not right on it. All you see on the water are the campground, the boat ramps, and the marina. We post the daily pool elevation on the message board, and Dad painted a bright orange band on a pine by the parking lot to mark the historic flood. The lowest level came when I was a kid. The lake had dried down and down, red clay showing all around like the ring on a bathtub. That year dead trees had come back up out of the water like bones out of graves.

Jesus, Mary, and Joseph finished leveling the gas dock. It's a regular routine, keeping the docks right. They have to unlock giant gears and crank the docks up or down and adjust the length of the metal ramps. One year in the spring there was so much rain in the mountains that the lake kept going up and up and up. The access ramps were shortened as much as they could be, until you actually had to walk *uphill* from the middle of the walkway to the gas dock.

Big Paul was getting a fix on exactly how the Beneteau had got itself hung. The worst way—sailing downwind in the channel between Bora Bora and Tahiti, running its wing keel smack into the Nose, and the breeze just pushing it deeper aground. The skipper was trying to sound calm, but you could hear the tightness in his voice right through the radio. Yes, he'd tried backing off with the engine. No, it didn't come free, stirred up a lot of mud, engine getting hot.

A blade keel would have come free.

Big Paul said to hold tight. I'd say they didn't have a lot of other options.

I can't believe Drexel Vann didn't know about the Society Islands. I think he was just playing me. Everyone around the lake knew that name. Of course it's a different culture, people on the water compared to people not on the water. I guess this might as well be the South Pacific for all they know of it.

I saw the islands when we first got here, the Grands taking us around the lake on the Sea-Ray and showing off the sights. "Folks call them the Society Islands," Granddad said.

"High society?" Dad said.

"I hear sometimes." And they all laughed.

When I had my sweet *Bellatrix* ready to go, the Societies were the first real place I sailed, soon as I got a good wind to take me up and back.

The morning we launched her, Dad "liberated" some wheels from a stored trailer and stuck them on the Blue Jay's trailer, which needed greasing and new wiring and all, but it wasn't going on the road anyway. It worked enough to back it down the ramp and release *Bellatrix* into her natural element.

"There she is, darlin'," he said, as he tied off the painter to the dock cleat.

"Thanks, Dad."

"You earned it. I should pay you a real salary for all you do around here."

I could agree with that, but right at that moment I was just crazy happy. My little boat bobbed beside the dock, pulling at her lines, eager even with bare poles to be off. She's the only one on the lake. To categorize her properly:

Blue Jay
Sloop rigged, one design sailboat, designed 1947 by Drake H. Sparkman of Sparkman and Stephens Inc. The International Blue Jay Class Association was formed in 1954.

Specifications

Length	13'6"
Beam	5'2"
Weight	275 pounds
Total Sail Area	90 square feet
Main	62 sf
Jib	28 sf
Spinnaker	56 sf
Draft (board down)	4' x 0"
Draft (board up)	6"
Mast	19' x 6 3/4"

Of course, as soon as I launched her, we came under a massive Bermuda high, and the lake was flat as a puddle for days. I'd waited for so long for a boat that a few days seemed like months, before a front scooted through at last.

I stayed pretty close to home on those first sails, making sure everything was proper, getting used to how she handled. Sweet! Then came the Thursday morning with a nice steady southwesterly forecast all day, a broad reach to carry me there, the wind a little forward of the beam for a cooler ride home. Without an auxiliary engine, I have to be sure that I have a promise of good wind both ways.

I'd stared at a chart of the islands so long that I had them about memorized. Tahiti is the largest of them, with a pretty tall hill right in the center, pointed, almost like a volcano if you don't look too closely. Bora Bora has a couple of little low hills and a nice sandy beach. Then there are all the Societies—picnic islands with a few trees, then even smaller islands, bare rocks, shoals with swampy vegetation that erupts during summer low water. The best direct passage is the Inner, which cuts west of Tahiti.

The Paradise channel is good most seasons—but not today, when keelboats had best thread the Inner or avoid the islands altogether, keeping to the main marked channel that loops to the east.

Anyway, that first run up the lake was special. *Bellatrix* handled the occasional wake and the quartering chop, the tiller humming under my hand as the rudder sliced through the water. I watched a fisherman boat a big striper, and saw a pair of eagles circling their stick nest on a tree at the end of a rocky point. A snapping turtle raised its beaky head from the water and disappeared as the bow slid past.

I raised the centerboard and ran *Bellatrix* up onto the tiny beach of Tahiti. I made the boat fast to a handy tree and then walked all around the island, to see what was there. I found what I expected, and some things I didn't. My list from that day on Tahiti:

Plastic water bottles
A Clorox jug
Some partly burned wood
A deflated shiny balloon
Chunks of Styrofoam
Broken cattails
A good Taylormade fender that I kept
Two drink koozies (one from Filliyaw Pointe)

A bright orange-and-yellow plastic leg from some kind
of toy animal
A long feather from an eagle or osprey
A sneaker turned green from mold
A piece of twisted metal
A snarl of fishing line with a bobber
Dog poop (and dog footprints)

And human footprints. Those were made by a boat shoe,
from the zigzaggy lines they left in the mud, and big, a man's
foot. They came out of the woods to the beach and then went
back. I followed them through the underbrush, along the hillside, over to the west side of Tahiti, where they were confused
with a lot of other footprints around the remains of a fire. Other fire pits dotted the little strip of sand, along with a pile of
beer cans. A grassy slope led up from that edge, a perfect place
to lie back and watch for boats coming up from the marina.

I could imagine being a sailor marooned on an island, like
mutineers who hide on uncharted atolls or shipwrecked men
cast upon rocky shores, living with what the land provided, like
the Laplanders that Carl saw sleeping on carpets of moss. I
could spend my days facing the one direction I could expect
help to appear from, and my nights tending a fire so that a ship
wouldn't pass by a dark and empty shore. Hunting the slow,
trusting land turtles for food like on the Galapagos.

There had been people on the Galapagos before Darwin
visited, sailors and whalers and I suppose maybe settlers. None
of them paid attention to the tortoises except to eat them.
None of them paid attention to the little birds at all. But he did.
Like Carl, he looked at things closely and saw how they were
connected. He went home to England and pondered and wrote
the book that changed the world. I wonder if he had read the
Linnaeus book that I found. I'm sure he must have:

Close to the road hung the under jaw of a Horse, having six fore
teeth, much worn and blunted, two canine teeth, and at a distance from the
latter twelve grinders, six on each side. If I knew how many teeth and of
what peculiar form, as well as how many udders, and where situated, each

animal has, I should perhaps be able to contrive a most natural methodical arrangement of quadrupeds.

And, of course, he did.

The finches that Darwin saw must have been blown onto the islands or brought there by people, and with just a few birds, they began to try new ways to make a living. Some of them went on eating seeds, some started to hunt insects, some drank nectar. The craziest of all, the vampire finch, learned to peck at the necks of the big seabirds and then drink the blood. If there was a finch family reunion, I could imagine all the rest of them moving away, horrified at what had become of that branch of the family, the little seed-eating mousy ones afraid of the vampires, all in black, like goth-girls, familiar but creepy. I wondered if that vampire capability was in them all along, so that it wasn't difficult for them to go that way as they bent to the environment, or if the pressure to survive just created an entirely new capability, maybe like dinosaurs learning to fly.

The Society Islands aren't far enough away from land for that kind of evolution. The plants and trees were there when the lake was flooded, or the seeds were carried there, but they could also be pollinated by the wind. I don't know about the squirrels and rabbits—I guess they might swim over. Maybe worms or ants, things that couldn't get off the island, they might evolve. I wonder how long it would take for them to change, to make themselves over in order to survive, to morph into something else?

PART II

"...and the heat in my blood and in the sunshine are one, and
the winds and the tempests and my passions are one..."

- W. H. Hudson

21

A white box sat exactly at the center of the table in the galley. I looked through the plastic window on the top—a cake, white frosting with loopy second-grade handwriting and pink roses. I opened the cover and pushed my finger into the space between "Happy" and "Birthday." It went right to the bottom, through tepid ice cream melt. They had cakes like this all made up in the freezer at the DQ—it didn't have my name on it or anything, and besides, I despised pink. No telling how long it had sat there. I was almost afraid to move it, but it hung together when I lifted the box to set it in the freezer. The tiny freezer was half-full of lumpy, frozen crystals from the humidity, so I slid the cake out on its cardboard and into the space with only a few roses scraped off.

Dad would say that was shutting the barn door after the horse got out. If he was sober enough to say it. But now he was snoring—whether the booze came first, so that he forgot to freeze the cake, or later because I didn't come home, didn't really matter.

I was supposed to be back hours earlier, but the wind NOAA had predicted for three to five knots with some gusts had died, and I sat in the middle of the lake with not a capful of wind to fill the sail. It was midweek, so it was a while until a bass boat came by and answered my hail, giving me a way faster tow than *Bellatrix* liked.

I was at fault for not taking my cell. I could have. But the signal was sometimes there and sometimes not. And lately I didn't much like having it on, with the text messages that still came in. So I left it off most of the time, and then it didn't seem like it was so glued to me as it used to be. I felt best when I was just *away*. I could glide out of the dock, feel the boat lift to the pressure of the wind. It was pure. Not like people. The warm wind and the lake water just as warm, showing darker toward the north and east as though I could sail past the islands and right out to sea.

Dad snorted and rolled over on the couch, his tummy showing slack and hairy where his T-shirt was rolled up. I used to sit on his stomach when I was a kid. He'd put his feet on one chair and his shoulders on another. My so-called mother said I was a "chunky monkey" and would break him in two, but he just laughed, said it would take more than the flesh of his flesh to break him down. He was strong from hauling engines and shoving boats around. It seemed as if he had done such work single-handed, but probably not; it's just how I remembered. The people here in the backwater don't know him. They call him Andy instead of Drew, and they treat him like one of the abandoned boats, dirtied by the weather, stuck in the slip though the dock lines were fraying. Yeah, my so-called mother. She could wait tables and bring home big tips. She could flirt and she could shop, but she couldn't stick around.

His hand rolled off the edge and hit the floor hard, and I jumped. It woke him a bit and he looked at me, woozy. "Hey, sweetie." He squeezed his eyes shut. "What time is it?"

"Five," I tell him.

"Okay." His mouth stayed open and he drifted back off, snoring.

I got my Linnaeus and a bottle of Mountain Dew and prepared to clear out for a few hours. It didn't pay to wake him, even if I had found him on the floor. Not that he was violent or anything—some nasty drunks will take a swing at just about anyone—but he forgets where he is. Last November he got really bad. He'd sent off a letter to my dearly departed using a new address that he got from a friend who was substituting on the mail route to the Plantation. Big hopes. But the letter flew back like all the others: Return to Sender. I came home from school and found him flat on the deck of our houseboat, passed out, the rest of a half-gallon of dark rum spilled and dried under him. I could have left him there, let him come to by himself, but it was chilly and about to rain. Dad's hands were pressed together under his face, like a child gone to sleep on his prayers. I couldn't leave him like that. So I turned on the lights, propped open the door, and started pushing him and rocking him until he woke up.

"Whooouuuuuuu."

And then he was asleep again.

"C'mon, Dad."

I felt a few raindrops and I thought about getting a tarp.

"Whyyyyyuuuuuuu. Uuuu."

I rocked him until he got on his knees, and maybe he could have crawled inside to bed, but he began to really wake up.

"Sorry, baby. Sorrybaby sorrybaby."

"It's okay. Let's get inside."

He made it to his feet and lurched to the railing, grabbed hold and slumped back to his knees: "Woooah." I hoped he wasn't going to puke, or that if he did, it would be on the deck and the rain would wash it away.

"One more time." I helped him get on his feet, and he shuffled to the door, letting me lead him by the arm. He scrunched his face against the light inside and stood there, wavering.

"Sorry."

"Yeah, sorry, I know, me too." He put a hand on my shoulder and we got inside, his toes catching on the lip of the door so that he stumbled forward, grabbing me around the waist and propelling us into the "living room." We were dancing. Sort of. Around and around the little space between the door and the kitchenette table. His head was down on my shoulder and his weight against me, so that if I tried to ease him toward the couch then he staggered sideways, pulling me with him, and around we went again.

"Love you," he said into my neck. "Love you love you SO sorry."

He started to stand up better, and we slowed down. Good news. I steered him backward.

"Time for bed," I told him.

His eyes were closed and his mouth was slack open—almost asleep, I thought. But as he sat down hard on the fold-out couch, he grabbed at me and pulled me down with him, falling sideways, me on top, and then his hands were all over me. My breasts. I felt his erection against my belly. I pushed away from him, standing up by shoving him flat.

"Angela, oh, Angel baby, oh oh, I'm—" He caught me around the knees and burrowed his head into my thighs. "Uuuuuuu. Uuuu—I love you don't go away, don't go."

"I'm not Angela," I shouted, and smacked his hands away. I got out of reach. Sick. *Sick.*

He opened his eyes really wide and seemed to focus, and his face changed. It had been all loose and red, but now his face stiffened, his mouth turned way down and big tears started to leak out of his eyes.

I went into my room and closed the plastic door and put my plastic chair against it, not that it would hold. I could hear him sobbing, big whooping sobs, and I wanted to sob myself but I wouldn't.

The next day, he didn't wake up till noon, and then he didn't seem to remember anything. And I have never told him, or anyone, especially the shrink that the school has required me to see so that I could "process my grief" about Charisse. Better that I spend my time with Linnaeus, who wasn't free of "spirituous" drinks but had the advantage of being long, long dead.

So I left Dad to sleep. Maybe I'd make hot dogs with chili and chopped onions for dinner. He usually liked those after a bender. But that was hours away, so I got my *Lapponica,* which I store in a Trapper-Keeper so the pages won't get wet or rumpled, and walked up the dock.

Painted ladies and cabbage butterflies were everywhere on the fluffy white flowers of buttonbush. It was a tough plant that would last through floods or dry times, the flower balls becoming reddish fruit clusters in the fall, and birds would be the visitors then. Dad complains there aren't as many butterflies anymore, not like when he was a kid. Not as many kinds and not as many, period. I don't know. I think we have quite a lot. Maybe it just seems like that to him, the way he remembers. Things were all better in the past, even butterflies.

I was going to go sit in the picnic pavilion, but people were lounging at the tables and the pig cooker still sat just outside, smelling of grease. They'd had a hootenanny, that's what Dad calls them. Big parties, mostly the houseboat people, and their friends who roll in on golf carts and ATVs from the camps and trailers close by. The yachters tend to hold parties on their boats anchored up in the islands, and if they were loud and obnoxious, nobody heard them. The hootenannies were just drinking and cookouts and crappy music, usually from a boom box, but this time they shook out some cash and hired a band. The lead singer was a sort of Kid Rock clone, hair but no voice. The big attraction was the drummer, a woman barely keeping her big tits inside the wife-beater as she flailed away. It went on all night, something you couldn't avoid if you were in the marina—the noise just pounded through the boat hulls and it didn't matter how many pillows I put over my head, it still came through. Happy birthday to me.

I slid on past the leftover 'nanniers with their beers, and went around the road to the campground bathhouses. It was quiet up there. The raised bed of an old railroad runs past, straight for the water, where there used to be a high bridge over the river, back in the day. There's a story about an engine catching it on fire, and the bridge burning down. All this area was logged over, more than once, and so a lot of the plants you'd expect to find in a virgin forest are missing, but there are still quite a few wildflowers in that area, along with some great mushrooms after it rains.

I had asked Dad to set up a picnic table in the clearing between the bathhouses and the woods. He didn't say anything, but after a while he did, and that's where I hung out a lot. Deer would walk past me if I stayed quiet and the wind was right. The dusk-to-dawn on the corner of the building attracted moths—already there were green wings on the ground, the remains of a luna moth. It seemed early, but with the spring so hot everything was running too fast. Nothing was right this year. Charisse unloading all her needy shit on me—if she'd been half-straight she'd never have gone into the woods at all, much

less in a prom dress and no shoes—but that night everything
was upside down. The moon, the way she showed up and made
us all feel weird, the thunderstorm like one from late summer,
the funeral-home smell of the flowers, the feelings that went
crashing back and forth inside me like the white deer spooked
and running hard.

Enough of that.

I sat at my table and spread out the pages. July 6. My seven-
teenth birthday.

July 6

*In the afternoon I took leave of Hyattan, and, at a distance of a mile
from thence, arrive at the mountain of Wallavari (or Hwallawari), a
quarter of a mile in height. When I reached this mountain, I seemed
entering on a new world; and when I had ascended it, I scarcely knew
whether I was in Asia or Africa, the soil, situation, and every one of
the plants being equally strange to me.*

Sometimes it takes only a small shift and everything becomes
different. Seems like this past year has been like climbing that
mountain, and now all the familiar things are different. The important days just fall on you like a downpour that's been holding
up in the clouds. Or maybe a huge limb, stuck in the treetops,
and one day it just lets go and you're under it. Like that.

I never minded about the girl-thing, much. My so-called
mother had been trying to fit me into the mold ever since I was
born. She'd buy me pink dresses and put ribbons in my hair
and make me wear shiny shoes. I hated those the worst, hard
patent-leather shoes with buckles, shoved on over frilly socks.
And then we'd go walking down through the town, my so-
called mother swinging her skirts or holding a big-brimmed hat
against the sea winds, or if we were at the Plantation then we'd
go to church. Not that they cared about church, at least not for
the right reasons. She had to show off, and Dad went wherever
Angela wanted. I'd kick my shoes against the pew until they
were scuffed, and get down and crawl under the tables at the
social hour, not out of meanness like she said but just because
I was bored and itchy. She gave up for a while, when we were

living at Oriental, and that's always been the favorite time of my life. The ocean right there, always the sound of the water and the birds and the boats, the ocean permeating our shed with its smells and dampness and sounds—almost like living on a boat. Sometimes I'd hug my pillow on my little daybed and feel like I was lifting and falling on the waves. But when we came back to London County, it was double jeopardy. Not just dresses now, but bras and hair salons, making up for the grubby days in our beach shack, for the grease and sand grit and salt on the tongue. She tried so hard to get me to fit in. I guess it was important to her, something she could picture but not make reality. It was funny, really. She'd "help me get ready" in the morning with a little mascara and blush, and I'd scrub it off at school while the other girls were layering on the makeup that their rock-ribbed Pentecostal mommies wouldn't let them wear.

None of it mattered. I mean, who doesn't have problems with their parents? I suffered in silence, until my so-called mother began to be gone for nights, then weekends, too, so she didn't have time to fuss over me. And then she was gone off to Florida with one of the men she'd met way back at Sharkey's, a guy with a big boat and the money to keep her in high heels. Me and Dad, we were on our own.

But then everything started at school with Charisse and the others. *Maggie can't get a boyfriend. Maybe she's a lezzie.* It didn't used to matter, then it began to seem like it did. I thought maybe I could pair up with Nat, that we could sorta slide from being friends to being perceived as a couple.

One time I had actually tried the girl thing on him—I excavated the stuff Mother had bought for me and showed up at the OT with lip gloss on and mascara and a nice green silky shirt. He just looked at me. "Hey, Nat," I said, sitting down on the other end of the same tomb. He glanced sideways and got up, drifted into the cedars, and the next thing I knew, he had disappeared for home without a word. Hulky realized something had happened but didn't know what, and he headed out right after. I walked home alone in the dark, feeling like a fool. I threw away the mascara. Nat and me went on being regular friends, but sometimes I'd get the feeling that I'd ventured past the edge and it could never be the same. *Entering on a new world.* After that, I spent more time alone, which was the only way I felt whole and real. I sailed to the islands, walking around the biggest ones and finding all sorts of stuff. It was a few weeks after finding the footprints on Tahiti that I was over on Bora Bora and saw more footprints and found the hidden place sheltered between the two hills where someone had pitched a tent. The moss and grass were smashed flat and the holes where the pegs had been pulled out spilled little hills of sand. And it was like Carl on that mountain, everything looked different. I could almost see the man who camped here. He had a little gray mountain tent, and as the morning came up he would have been sleeping with his mouth open but not in that nasty way of Dad when he was drunk, just gentle and innocent. I imagined that I might sit down and wait for him to wake up. The first thing he would see, looking out of the triangle of his tent, was me, Maggie, a new creature. Not the Maggie everyone else knew.

I guess people would say Fletcher was a lie. That's the easy way to look at it. But the worse things got at school and on Facebook, the more real he became. I wasn't making things up—I was *finding out* who he was, discovering him like some new species of flower or bee, *true* things. Fletcher (and his name wasn't there at first, it just showed up one day as I was writing in my journal, Fletcher) has glossy blue-black hair and a short beard sometimes, sometimes not. His hair is a little long, because he spends most of his time on the water and in the woods, but not raggedy. He trims it himself with a pair of old silver scissors that look like a water-bird. The scissors were from his grandmother. And he trims his beard with them, too, using a little round mirror that is fastened to the teak in his gorgeous boat. His face is as clear to me as my own round face. His hands with the calluses laid down by lines and anchor chains are as familiar as my own. I like him best in a red T-shirt faded from the sun, his arms and legs bronzed from the same sun, his feet bare and the grass showing between his toes. Fletcher.

I remember him as clearly as I remember prom night and

the smell of wisteria, the clouds massing, the rain opening up as I reached the marina. He is more real than Charisse now, even though I had smelled her sweat and perfume and tasted her lips.

And now Drexel Vann won't leave me alone about him. He's asking everyone who knows me, who is this Fletcher guy? Have you met him? Is she actually seeing someone from school? He's been around to talk with Nat, and Hulky, who won't say one word to the police because his family, being Black, fears the law from forever. And the stupid girls in my homeroom. Even the Grands. God, that was awful, hearing from Dad that the police had asked Grandmom and Granddad about whether I had a boyfriend. I don't like how they look at life at the Plantation, but still, they're old, and they still think I play with dolls or something, like they tried to get me to do for years. My last birthday they bought me a "girl's spa weekend" at some place with a glossy brochure about pedicures and hot-stone massages and facials. This year I guess they seriously didn't know what to do, or think, because they sent me a card (pink) with a fat gift certificate good anywhere at the mall in Durham. That was my birthday, along with drunk Daddy and a sick cake.

The day was getting along, the sun slanting through the trees. Soon it would be dark, and then the day would be over, and so much for another "milestone" as people called them.

A black-winged swallowtail of some kind—pipevine? spice-bush?—came fluttering through the open woods. It spiraled down to check the shriveled orange tubes of trumpet vine, fallen at the base of an oak tree. The flowers were hidden high up in the trees, the original stem and the climbing vine small compared with the spread of its pinnate leaves up in the crown. The fallen flowers were a clue, evidence, but you have to look very closely to see where they have come from. Just because you can't see where the flowers come from doesn't mean there's not a real living plant there.

Fletcher. When I found his photograph on the internet, it was verification. Maybe I had shaped him from my thoughts, called him out of his real life, and now he had broken through to my world and was trying to communicate with me, making those bowers in the woods. Maybe we were out of phase in some way, so that he couldn't speak to me. Was he a ghost? Someone from another time stream? I thought of him sailing on a ship that touched at New Guinea, going ashore and seeing those incredible birds and their bowers for himself, watching the birds strut and preen in front of their homes.

He really exists, out there somewhere, someone that I am connected with on another plane and who visits my dreams. So my stories aren't fiction at all.

22

From Lachesis Lapponicus

Chamoedaphne of Buxbaum (*Andromeda polifolia*) was at this time in its highest beauty, decorating the marshy grounds in a most agreeable manner. The flowers are quite blood-red before they expand, but when full-grown the corolla is of a flesh-colour. Scarcely any painter's art can so happily imitate the beauty of a fine female complexion; still less could any artificial colour upon the face itself bear a comparison with this lovely blossom. As I contemplated it I could not help thinking of Andromeda as described by the poets; and the more I meditated upon their descriptions, the more applicable they seemed to the little plant before me, so that if these writers had had it more in view, they could scarcely have contrived a more apposite fable. Andromeda is represented by them as a virgin of most exquisite and unrivalled charms; but these charms remain in perfection only so long as she retains her virgin purity, which is also applicable to the plant, now preparing to celebrate its nuptials. This plant is always fixed on some little turfy hillock in the midst of the swamps, as Andromeda herself was chained to a rock in the sea, which bathed her feet as the fresh water does the roots of the plant. Dragons and venomous serpents surrounded her, as toads and other reptiles frequent the abode of her vegetable prototype, and when they pair in the spring, throw mud and water over its leaves and branches. As the distressed virgin cast down her flushing face through excessive affliction, so does the rosy-coloured flower hang its head, growing paler and paler till it withers away. Hence, as this plant forms a new genus, I have chosen for it the name of Andromeda.

Andromeda polifolia

Kingdom: Plantae—Plants
Subkingdom: Tracheobionta—Vascular plants
Superdivision: Spermatophyta—Seed plants
Division: Magnoliophyta—Flowering plants
Class: Magnoliopsida—Dicotyledons
Subclass: Dilleniidae
Order: Ericales
Family: Ericaceae—Heath family
Genu: ndromeda L.—bog rosemary
Species: Andromeda polifolia L.—bog rosemary

23

The Rumor Mill

What's new?

Not a diddly damn thing. Work work and more work.

You know it.

They hiring at your place?

Nope.

See there's a house going up at Queenstowne Crossing. Mebbe ole Hector'll make a go of that yet.

He spent enough on that big sign, I reckon he best get a house or two in there.

You hear the Ledsome boy's back around?

Living offn his folks.

Not for long if I know Patty.

What'd he wash out of this time?

Building portable log cabins.

What?

Little ones, for camps and such. Put 'em on a trailer and haul them where they're going. Up in the mountains. They're right nice, I wouldn't mind having one.

Not one he built.

Oh, he's good with his hands.

Just lazy in the head.

This makes what, six, eight of these kinda projects?

Don't know. Prob'ly.

His old man still over at the Southern States?

Saw him there Thursday, went to get some tick dope for the dogs.

Bad this year, ain't they.

Terrible. Terrible.

Heard there's some new disease in the ticks.

I heard it was mosquitoes. Fever.

One or t' ther.

Speaking of dogs—my Sassy Lass has come into heat and I got Gordon's Lucky for sire. You always said you wanted to start with beagles so I'm giving you second pick, if you're wanting.

Mebbe. Let me see what the old lady has to say.

24

The kitchen at the Plantation wasn't anything like the rest of the house. No displays of artificial flowers or gold-painted Valentine cupids holding up lamps, no bright-colored couches or polished furniture. It was a working place, my grandmother's office.

We had moved back from that shack at the beach a few months before. The house had plenty of room for us all. I had enjoyed it at first—good cooking, and new places to explore. But that morning was a visit to hell.

I sat in one of the spindle-backed chairs, next to the enamel table where Grandma made pies.

"Now this will give your hair body, Lenore."

Maggie, I said to myself. *Call me Maggie.*

Mother put her hands under my limp damp hair and lifted it. I heard her nails click together like tiny rodent teeth. She raised it up a couple of times and let it fall back.

"It's just hopeless without some help," she said.

A permanent wave box sat on the table, with a smiling woman pictured on the front. Her hair rolled like amber waves of grain all around the sides of the box and onto the back, as if she had three times the hair of a real person. I sat wrapped in a towel with a thin plastic cape over that. Mom was laying out her implements: comb, plastic roller-things, rubber gloves, squares of tissue paper, and a jar of Vaseline.

"This won't make me look like an old lady, will it?"

"No, honey, this is a body perm. We use these bigger ones." She showed me gray and white rods. I tried to take an interest, as though this were an experiment in Mr. Palko's class.

My so-called mother was dressed in her oldest sweat suit, but even in that she looked beautiful. It didn't matter, she could have worn a garbage bag. Her blond hair swayed in its ponytail as she worked around me, rubbing a layer of Vaseline along the top of my face and around my ears. She had on lipstick (bright pink), even to do this. I loved to read the names on the bottom of her lipstick tubes, all passion and roses and love and fire.

She took her comb and began marking off my head like a map, sectioning my hair, and then she began to wrap pieces of hair around the rollers.

She put on the rubber gloves and began to squirt stuff onto my head. It smelled horrible, and ran over the Vaseline wall and toward my eyes. I pulled my arm out of the plastic and rubbed it away with my sleeve.

"Well, that's another shirt ruined," she said with a sigh.

I didn't know this was dangerous. I put my arm back under the plastic and sat very still. I could feel my head itching, like the stuff was peeling the skin off me. She set the cooking timer and I watched the time crawl and crawl. This didn't seem like a good idea now. I wondered why she hadn't taken me to the hair salon that she went to and always came back looking like a soap opera star.

After ten minutes, she unrolled one piece, but rolled it right back up.

Finally she was satisfied and began to rinse the stuff out with water that was too hot. She patted my hair with a towel, and I thought, *done*. But there was more goo, and this felt really cold. Finally we got to rinse that out, and she began taking the rods off and tossing them on the table.

I put my hand up to feel the first parts coming free. My hair was curled up so tight.

"It will relax, honey."

My butt ached and I really wanted for it to be over. I don't think I had ever sat so long, not even in school. Hours and hours. But I was eager, too, to see if this would make my hair look like hers, bouncy and shiny.

She was about halfway done when Dad came in.

"How's my girls?" He put his arms around her and danced her across the room.

"Oh, Drew, I'm a mess!"

"You are *never* a mess." He squeezed her tight, and she tipped back her face and he gave her a kiss. "You are one sexy dame." I saw her hands go down around his bottom. I watched the kiss get serious. I sat there, helpless under my silly cape, my head itching and half rolled up and half down. I saw how he rubbed himself against her.

"Fine, I'll do it myself!" I ripped off the plastic sheet and flung it, not really at them but sort of in that direction, and I reached up and tried to figure out how those rod things came apart.

"Oh, Lenore, you will just ruin all my work!" She pulled away from Dad, and came back and really started to fly, pulling the rods out and not caring if it hurt me or took half the hair off my head. She was in a hurry to get away and go upstairs with him.

I hated her. I hated the way she smelled of strong perfume. I hated how she was always checking herself in any mirror or window she walked by. I hated how her hair was perfect and stiff, how she couldn't do anything with her hands in case she might break off a nail. I hated that she had named me stupid romantic names. I hated that she could lure my dad away from anything, any time, by touching him, or even just looking at him.

When she was finished I went to the bathroom and looked in the mirror.

That was when I understood that beauty couldn't be added on, like frosting on a plain cake. It had to be there, in the bones.

25

Nat always was a creature of the night. Even in the full afternoon he had that moon-shadow look.

I heard the clang of footsteps on the metal ramp and looked out the small window of the marina store. He was staggering down the incline under a heavy backpack. I ran out and helped lift it off him before he toppled into the water. It was packed all wrong, the weight on the top and to one side; no wonder it had nearly flipped him. His pale face was blotched red, and sweat had pasted his hair down over his forehead and was dripping into his eyes.

"Shit, man, what's going on?" I asked.

He slid into one of the chairs and let his bony hands flop.

"You got anyone might be headed to Raleigh?"

"Like Dad? No, he's—well, you know."

"They don't have to be coming back." He said that just as flat as could be, but the words vibrated.

"Huh? Are you, like, running away from home?"

"Like that." He made a little mouth at how I used "like." I didn't mean to but had picked it up around school. He pushed his hair out of his eyes. Nat usually tried too hard to be haunted and deep, but this wasn't just an act anymore.

I thought quickly. "The brightwork man is over on Dock B, restoring a deck. He doesn't have much left to do. He lives down near Raleigh somewhere." I waited, but he didn't say a word. Just looked at the floor, as though he was reading something in the worn-out carpet. I guess he'd talk about it when he was good and ready. I went back to watching the Discovery channel.

Dad came in, red-eyed and glary, as he was way too often these days. Nat being there wasn't going to help.

"We're outta here," I breathed, and Nat shouldered up his bag and followed.

"Don't get too far. Don't be patrolling around in those woods. God knows who's out there," Dad said.

"Yeah, yeah, Charisse and all that. Just going to talk. At the picnic shelter. Okay?"

Dad made a big deal about clicking off the TV. *Fine.*

It was the usual massively humid summer day on the lake. The picnic shelter was on the other side of the parking lot and out of Dad's sight. Out of sight and out of mind. It had a view of another arm of the backwater, now down to a thin snaking channel that used to be a stream, surrounded by greenish mud that stank as it dried. Heat and stink and annoying noises, the cicadas rasping away, kids screaming as they were towed on inner tubes, boat engines winding up and the pounding of the hulls, the pulsating dentist-drill sound of whatever tool the brightwork man was using. I wished I could drive so that we could go to Raleigh, but the state of North Carolina, in its infinite wisdom, has this graduated license thing. Always rules and restrictions. Such as—if I were a boy, like Nat, then I would be allowed to shuck off that icky wet T-shirt he had on (Lamb of God, bones and fire) but even though he could, he just sat there with it stuck to him.

"Okay, I'm tired of waiting for you to say something." I hopped up onto the tabletop and sat there looking down at his bowed head. "Give it up."

"I got busted. My stupid. Now it's time to..." He made a swooping gesture with his hand.

"What for?" I figured it was pot.

"I had this—item. And I tried to pawn it over in Smathers. Next thing I know the cops are coming in from all over and they got their guns drawn. I about pissed myself."

"This *item*?"

"A bracelet. A gold bracelet."

"Where'd you steal that from?"

"Charisse."

"Charisse!"

"I didn't steal it, by the way. Thanks for the vote of confidence. She gave it to me."

That didn't sound right. I didn't remember Charisse ever giving anybody anything unless she expected to get more in return.

"Really. She did. To help me."

"Well, pawning it was stupid. Anything with Charisse is gonna get you nailed. I guess that blew your big old alibi."

He shrugged. And went silent.

This was weird. I thought about her talking with him under the trees. Maybe that was when she gave it to him. She wasn't in any way right; no telling what she did that night or why.

"Prom night?"

He shook his head. "Earlier. A couple of weeks ago."

"So were you…"

"Jesus, no." He worked hard at using the name of the Lord in vain sometimes and you could tell he had issues about it. He turned away and looked over the dead stream. The sun in his eyes made them look more gold than hazel. Nat was kinda weedy-looking but he had great eyes, whether he knew it or not.

"So, why?"

"She liked me and I liked her." I kept my face really still. "But not in a boyfriend-girlfriend way, more like brother and sister. We had a special kind of relationship."

"Special relationship." I could taste the bitter on my words.

"Yeah. I could tell her things."

And here I'd always thought it was me and Nat. Like he was my shadow-self.

"She knew I couldn't stick around here much longer, couldn't take the parents, and she thought that might help me get out. The bracelet."

"That you tried to pawn." I would have thought Nat had more sense. Something like that you keep secret. Some things you hide and never show.

"The cops didn't believe me either. You wouldn't think there would be that many people we know, just standing around in Smathers, but while they were handcuffing me and reading my rights, I saw the Blakeleys from church and Mrs. Quisenberry from school and Roger Early and his girlfriend. People driving by and slowing down to watch them put me in the car."

"Shit."

"They put me in a room at the jail, asked a lot of questions. A lot of the same questions—about that night."

"Of course."

"They were back onto me, you know? Because I was there that night, even though I told them she left, told them the truth. Truth was the best thing, right?"

Maybe for him. I was getting a crawly feeling, like a deputy car was going to come wheeling in and I'd be the one in handcuffs.

"Was Drexel Vann there?"

"Not at first. He showed up and kicked out the uniforms."

"He's dangerous. He's a thinker." I don't know why that came out, it was something I'd just realized, that even though he was a nice guy and seemed to care, he was someone who didn't mind waiting to get what he was after.

Nat looked at me funny. "Yeah. Yeah. Like Auguste Dupin." I leaned my head over and looked at him. He sighed. "*Murders in the Rue Morgue?*"

Poe. Of course.

So Vann interrogated him then, he said, and it felt like an interrogation. He couldn't answer him straight, all the words tangling up. So he got scared and asked for his parents, and Vann quit, just like that. "Maybe they were supposed to have my parents there all along."

I wondered if that was true, and why Dad had let the detective talk to me every time without listening in.

"So the deacon comes," he said.

"I'd rather take my chances with Vann."

"Yeah, maybe. I knew what he was going to say. *Don't lie, son. Tell the truth and shame the devil.* But the more I told them that she gave it to me, the more they didn't believe it."

"Been there."

"I guess so. Bet you wish they'd catch the guy and get this over with."

"If he's even around anymore. Dad's watching me all the time. He sees murderers under every rock." The only time I could get a breath was when I went out in my boat, and even then I had warnings and deadlines. Rules.

I picked up a pine cone that had fallen on the table and winged it into the brush. A bird came squawking out. Robin, the squirrel of the bird world. (Starlings being the rats.) "Still, you gotta admit, the bracelet thing does seem pretty weird."

"You and the damn cops! She *did* give it to me!" Nat slammed his hand flat on the picnic table, which scared me more than anything else. He never acted out—was always remote. "Why wouldn't she? She had lots of things, it wasn't anything to her. Didn't she ever give something to you?"

I felt crawly again.

"Then they started in on the Fletcher thing. They asked if I knew who this Fletcher was, if I ever met him, or maybe even if *I* was Fletcher."

I could feel my face getting hot, so I jumped off the table and went and stood under the half-dead pine trees, watching the water. Yeah, Nat, you coulda been Fletcher. That one time I'd tried to interest him, he had just faded into the woods. Who knew that he was tight with Charisse? And there was something, like right now sitting with him, I felt that vibration even though we weren't touching or even looking at each other.

"So she gave you this bracelet."

"She said it was worth plenty, it was solid gold from someplace in New York."

Dang! I remembered the week after her sixteenth birthday, she wore it to school to swank around for one day before it went back into the safe. It was from Tiffany's, she said.

"Why did you try to sell it?"

"So I could get money. So I could leave forever."

"I don't get it. If anyone ought to be running off, it would be me. They're after me all the time about Fletcher, and they don't believe me either. You don't have any problems like that."

"Oh no, not me." He laughed, a hard exclamation, and I remembered him laughing like that the night Charisse showed up. "Just having my parents weighing whether to stand behind my story or not. Just being the designated class wacko. Choosing between being Asshole and Freak. The pit and the pendulum. Like I told Vann—and right in front of the deacon, I had to—I told him that I'm not into girls."

"You're gay?"

"No, I'm not *gay*." He said it in a mincing, high voice. "They think I'm gay, sometimes I let people think I'm gay. But I don't feel anything. For anyone. Any attraction. Nothing. Nada. I'm just a fucking freak of nature. Or not a fucking freak. A non-fucking freak. I just wanted to get a bus ticket and go somewhere I could figure it out, where I didn't have any crazy family, or church six days a week, or school, or friends, or any of it."

Now I felt like the freak. I stayed facing the water, like I was really interested in the osprey that was fishing. It hovered and dove and came away with a fish. Not like I hadn't seen it a hundred times. But it was all just too much, that I'd tried to act the girl thing with Nat, of all people, now that I knew this. Maybe that's why I tried him instead of Hulky, because somehow deep inside I knew he wouldn't respond. Maybe I was *way* over-analyzing what had happened.

"I always thought maybe you knew something about—this."

Why did everyone think I had the answers?

"About being in-between. Because you hung with us and didn't try to play games to get a guy." Maybe he didn't even remember. "Except for that one time."

So I guess he did.

"And then, all this shit about Fletcher. Please! Where did you get that from, some romance novel?"

"Not exactly." I knew what it was like when people really enjoyed sex, when they couldn't get enough of it, when it made them cry out with joy. I didn't have to go to cheesy novels or porno videos or the internet to learn about that.

"So are you really—secure?" he asked. "Like you know what you are?"

I thought I did. Used to think I did.

"Maybe it's like being right-handed or left-handed," I said, just to say something. "Most people are right-handed and they're not even conscious of it, it's just the right thing and nearly everyone is, so it's easy. And some people are left-handed, and they have to adapt all the time, because things aren't set up for left-handed people. They even used to make people who were left-handed use their right hands, because the left hand…"

"Was wrong."

"More difficult."

"Gauche. Clumsy. Wrong. That's me, Mister Lefty. Remember our French class? *À gauche* and *à droit?* Worse than that—sinister." He wagged his left hand in the air. "The filthy hand of Satan."

Bam! It came together, sinister, sinistrorse, how some plants turn left when they climb—bindweeds and morning-glory. *Convolvulaceae.*

"Like I was saying, some people are mostly right-handed but do some things left-handed. I do some of that. I sweep left-handed, my grandmother says."

"So what does that mean?"

"I don't know."

"You and Charisse?"

"That was Charisse, not me." But I remembered the electric shock of her mouth on mine; even with the taste of liquor and puke, her lips and her tongue had connected with mine and I felt it all the way down. I felt the jolt.

"Maybe you're sweeping left-handed." He made that nasty laugh again.

"I don't think so." Time to change the subject. "So I guess you went home. And how was that?"

"It was *The Exorcist*, except I wasn't the one with my head spinning around."

I went back and sat on the bench across from him.

When he told me, it did sound like something out of the movies. They came in through the kitchen, his father as silent as he'd been the whole drive, and when they walked into the parlor (that's what they called the living room at his house) he found Rev. Lipscomb and three of the other elders sitting in a semicircle, Bibles on their laps. There was a hard chair in front of them, and he had to sit in it and face the minister, while his dad hovered around behind him like a guard. The reverend told him they were there to save his life. "For by Leviticus 18 we are told that if a man lies with a man as one lies with a woman, they have done what is detestable."

"So I told them that I hadn't slept with anyone, and they said it was the intent as much as the act, and that if I'd just let Jesus into my heart then I wouldn't have these urges. Funny, huh, since I don't have urges *at all*."

Dad wasn't into church, but I'd been hauled to enough Sunday services and Vacation Bible School at the Baptists that I pretty much knew the line.

"'Just accept the Lord's guidance, Nathanael,' they kept saying, 'These desires are the work of the Devil.' I mean, I expected them to come over and start whaling on me with the Bibles, beat the sin out of me. It was scary."

"So did they give up?"

"I got mad, finally, when they said that with God anything is possible, and I asked if God could make all my problems go poof, then why didn't we just get Jesus to fix me up?"

I nodded. He was spilling now, letting it all out, and I figured that was as healing as any laying-on of hands by the deacon and his cronies.

"They don't know anything about me but they think that they could make me right. Right as they see it. Finally, they wore out, or just didn't have any more arguments. I got up to go and Dad stood up. 'As for me and my house, we will serve the Lord,' he said, like Moses or something. 'If you will not reject evil, then you are no longer of this house.'"

Nat turned away from me, and I knew why. I'd seen him ugly cry before.

"So. Well. I packed up and walked over here."

"They just let you walk away?"

"Dad was still in the parlor when I came down. He didn't say a word. He looked real hard at this," and he plucked the front of his shirt, one of the dangerous rock-music ones he'd traded for at school but always kept hidden, "but Mom was in the kitchen. She gave me a hundred bucks. She keeps back a little out of household expense money for things Dad don't agree with."

Good for Mom. I always thought she had more life to her than most of the fundamentalist women.

"I don't have the bracelet—that's evidence, they took it— but I have a bank account for college. I can get it out in Raleigh, if Dad hasn't already grabbed it. Don't want the prodigal son to have too much ready cash when he goes into the haunts of iniquity."

"I wish I could help."

"It's enough. I can get somewhere, and I can work."

We sat there for a while longer. In some ways I envied him, taking off, making a new path by himself. I imagined doing the same, but I couldn't see myself in a city somewhere. I'd have to head to the coast and work on a fishing boat or something. I couldn't tolerate that many people. I wondered if Nat could either.

Finally the sun got low enough that it was hitting us right in the eyes. I hadn't heard the brightwork man's grinder for a while, so maybe he was finishing up. His truck hadn't come up to the parking lot though.

"Maybe we should see about your ride."

"Okay."

We cut down toward the docks through a grove of pines. I should have known better—loblollies—prickly bastards. One of the cones wedged between my toe and the flip-flop.

"Shit! Damn!" I hopped on one foot while I pulled the thick spine out of my big toe.

Nat dropped his pack and grabbed my foot.

"What?"

He squeezed my toe until blood ran out.

"Hey, that hurts!"

"You have to get the poison out," he said. "Poison gets into the blood. Blood poisoning. The dark wine of the blood is soured."

I don't know which was creepier, the grim sound of his voice, or the death grip he had on my foot.

"Like I'm poison," I joked, and tried to pull away.

He squeezed my toe one more time, hard. "No, but the dirt is, and everything that came in on the thorn." He ran his thumb across the wound and stared at the streak of blood. "That's why stop signs are red. Blood makes us pay attention."

26

Way past time.

It had been way past time to be heading for home. The heat lightning that had flared as we sat at Old Trinity was becoming streaks on the horizon; the wind was gusting from the east, smelling of salt and sea storms. Sometimes the air was full of petals from the dogwoods and scales cast off by newly opened leaves. The trees groaned overhead, and I listened for the ominous crack of a limb breaking. The trail was an uneven path gouged by dirt bikes, but after I reached Wisteria Lodge I'd have an easier walk.

The house appeared before you realized it, the worn-out white of it thinning the darkness a little at a time until you were right there. Four brick chimneys still stood, but the front porch and part of the roof were caved in by the wisteria that crawled everywhere, thick ropes and masses of purple blossoms from the peak down to massive azalea bushes just as old. Flowers were everywhere—on the ground, in the air—and when the wind let up for a minute, the wisteria smell wound itself around you like cheap, strong perfume.

And when the wind eased, I could hear Charisse.

"Maggie! Maggie, wait!"

I turned around and saw her weaving down the path. Limping, and I realized she was still barefoot. It made my feet curl to think about the rocks and sticks I'd walked over in solid running shoes, and she was barefoot.

"Maggie! Oh, damn!" She staggered to a stop.

"What are you doing?"

"Trying to catch up with you."

It almost made me laugh, the princess with her black mascara smeared all around her eyes so that she looked like a raccoon, but there was something regal about her too, not just pitiful, in her gorgeous, destroyed dress. Lace was coming out of the rip like stuffing out of a doll, and a safety pin held the two halves together. She stood up straight, as if willing herself to be elegant even though she was a mess. I stayed apart from her, but she wasn't trying to get close now. She settled onto the stone steps of the fallen-in porch, her back to a pillar. I went and sat on the opposite side. Thunder grumbled and the lightning showed the color of the flowers for a moment, red azalea blossoms and the wisteria dripping over everything.

"I'm sorry, for earlier. I shouldn't have done that."

"Yeah, well." I couldn't help staring at her, as if she were some new species that had just popped up, fascinating and repulsive like that kiss. More than the taste and smell, the looseness, the way her mouth opened all the way and her lips were soft.

"Really, really, really sorry." She rocked back and forth. "Really, really sorry."

I hate that word. Useless word. The word people use when they refuse to be responsible for themselves. When they want someone else to do the hard work of being an adult. I got up, but then she stood too, though she was breathing hard and looked worn out. I didn't know if she would start chasing me again, so I sat back down.

"I wanted to make it up to you. I don't want you to be mad at me. You don't understand how it is with boys."

"Thanks, yeah, I know all about what you think I know."

"No, it's not that. Not the Fletcher thing. Really, I don't care—about me—but you. *You.* Be careful. I know. They are always *after you* with their hands and tongues, just like you're a piece of meat."

"Boo-hoo. I feel for you."

Charisse leaned forward and nearly fell on her face. She grabbed the step and leaned against the pillar again. Her head was tipped back and her eyes were closed. "My date tried to rape me," she said, and it sounded like she was in a séance or something, her voice strange, or maybe just because she was speaking up into the vines.

"Damn."

"I'm a virgin."

"Pu-*lease.*"

"I know you think that's crazy, because I date a lot. But I never let anyone—my parents would just die. I was raised to keep myself pure until I got married." She held up her left hand, where she always wore a ring. It was silver, or maybe platinum, set with diamonds. "My dad took me to a purity ball when I was eleven. I had a white dress and a crown. *A crown.* Flowers in my hair, a crown of flowers. We heard a speech about how God has an intense desire for us and that we need to stay true to the Lord and our future mates."

That sounded truly bizarre. God and desire.

"And then we signed a pledge and Dad put a ring on my finger. For God."

"For real?"

"Not just once. Eeeeeevery year. Every birthday Dad asks for the ring and I take it off and give it to him and we recite Matthew 5:8. It's inscribed in the ring. Every every *every* every. He gives me a new ring and something else. Last year it was a gold bracelet. This year it was St. Simon's Island."

"So you've never?" I thought of all the guys she'd dated, the older ones that she went out with—the VCU guy wasn't the first college man.

"Never. Never had sex. I. Am. A. Virgin. I mean, I've done some other things, but that doesn't count." She let her head fall forward and then sat up straight and folded her hands in her lap and crossed her feet at the ankles. All proper, except that her feet were filthy and I could see, when the lightning came, the cuts and the blood.

"I let them see my breasts. It's okay. And they want me to touch them, their dicks, and so I would stroke them off or suck them off. I kinda don't mind if I've been doing Ecstasy because then they are soooo so happy and that makes me happy." Her voice was very bright now, as though she were introducing herself at a pageant. "If I've been doing X then I feel so good."

She seemed to lose her train of thought. Maybe she was going to pass out. I thought maybe I could drag her into a sheltered place.

"But then I wake up. It's just a sticky, nasty mess, and I remember. I'm so ashamed all the time, because I made a vow and I'm keeping the vow, but then I want to feel good and make them feel good, but when I do it's just—wroooong." The last word just dragged and disappeared into the thunder.

The storm was getting closer. Counting between the lightning and the thunder, it was within a couple of miles, and the wind was cool with rain. I wished she'd pass out, so I could leave her under the wisteria to sleep it off.

"It's so nasty," she said, rousing up. "You're lucky, if you don't know, or maybe it's not like that for you. I know I'm going to have to do that someday, do whatever I'm told to do, get married and have sex whenever he wants and have kids and it all just makes me cringe. Doesn't it scare you?"

"Never had the problem." But what I'd heard of sex, and seen some too, wasn't like that. I remember my so-called mother and my dad laughing, just whooping it up. Their legs and arms and parts all tangled.

"Well, now, this *guy*," she confided, leaning a little way forward but very carefully, keeping her balance. Her green eyes glittered and darkened with the lightning. "He wanted to have sex. *Real* sex. He said he had condoms so I didn't have to worry. And I showed him my little ring and told him about the pledge and said I could get him off but I had to stay a virgin for when he married me. *Aaaannnnnddddd.* And then he got REALLY mad and said he was going to take me up the ass first and did I think Jesus would be down with that? And I was trying to get away and he grabbed my dress and tore it, can you believe that, he *tore* it? But when he did he fell down and I got to the car and locked it and got away."

She was looking at me, very serious, and then she began

to smile, and then started to giggle. "Pretty slick, right? And I drove straight to OT because I knew you'd be there, the Three Musketeers."

Great to be so predictable. I was getting jittery but there was something hypnotic about her, the shifts in mood, up and down, and I really wondered what other secrets she had to tell.

"I swallowed the X, all I had with me—I was ready to get through the night, you know? And I just wanted you all to hold me, just be with me, hold me tight because you all really like each other, not because you have sex, but because you like each other. And you'd help me, help me know what to do, what was the right thing to do. S-E-X, XXX, you understand."

"Which one of us is supposed to know about sex?"

"Why, you! You and Fletcher, sitting in a tree."

"Yeah, me, the 'sad little liar.'"

Charisse tucked her chin down and looked at me with big wide eyes like a little girl who's trying to con Grandpa into more candy. "I thought maybe you—really knew—even if this Fletcher is just bullshit, you knew how it's *supposed* to be. You made it sound exciting and not nasty. You must have had sex *sometime* and liked it."

"Not really."

"Not liked it?"

"No." BOOM! The lightning cracked really close, and thunder shook the ground. "NO SEX," I yelled. "Time to get out of here."

She began twisting her hands and then she had the ring off and was holding it out. "I don't want this anymore. I can't. Take it and keep it for me, please?"

The ring glinted and suddenly I really wanted it. Maybe it was just fear, or relief, but I took the ring and put it in the watch pocket of my jeans.

"So that's it? I've got the ring. Now we gotta get out of here."

"Oooh, is there a boogerman?" She was back to little-girl stupid.

"Stay here and get hit by lightning, then, dimwit." I'd had enough of her, of her crazy druggy talk. I took off.

The lightning cracked again, and the thunder, and I heard her yelling, "Maggie, don't leave me," but I wasn't stopping. It was all too weird. I could taste her mouth again, I could feel her pressing against me, and I thought about sex and no sex and what it was like.

The first spatter of rain hit, but it didn't last.

I was in the long lane that ran from Wisteria Lodge out to the road, huge cedars on each side, like a tunnel. I heard something, turned, and saw something pale and thought that Charisse had somehow caught up with me. I was deciding if I could cut out through the cedars and get away from her, but then I saw it was one of the white deer that lived around the lake, and then it was past me and up the lane, bounding like a ghost chased out of hell. My heart thudded.

I was on the paved road now, headed to the marina. It was a road that had been there from before the lake, one that disappeared straight into the water. I ran down the white line in the middle, as the wind blasted into me, and now it was raining in sheets. I passed the sign for the marina and veered across the parking lot. The ground seemed to be melting under my feet.

I couldn't see much but I could hear the smack of waves and clanging of halyards and shriek of the wind in the sailboat rigging. The water was rolling hard and the docks were heaving. Finally I saw the two pole lights, the dimmer one over by the storage dock and the one by the office.

I skidded across the deck of the houseboat and banged the door open. The lights were on and Dad was dead drunk and passed out in his underwear. He snorted when I turned off the light and slid past him and into my room.

I peeled my wet clothes off in a heap and got into bed. I hugged myself under the covers, feeling the sheet get wet and then cold and then warm against my skin.

Charisse. Now that I was safe in my own bed, I felt some guilt about leaving her helpless as a wet kitten. I shook off and on with a chill, first from the cold, and then with a feeling that I had not done anything, but what I hadn't done was something very wrong.

27

Aggression (My Screenplay)

EXTERIOR: AN INLAND MARINA
ENTER FROM THE LAKE: a wakeboat with heavy metal blaring from the speakers, engine only partly throttled back.

MR. YARDLEY, boat bum, on his docked sailboat, waves his hands up and down, slow down.

BOAT DRIVER gives him the finger.

>   MR. YARDLEY
>   It's a no-wake zone!

>   BOAT DRIVER
>   Up yours. I'm going as slow as I can.

>   MR. YARDLEY
>   Bullshit. You're rocking everyone on this dock.

>   BOAT DRIVER
>   Live with it, you old fart.

>   MR. YARDLEY
> I'm going to talk with Andy. And Maggie's my witness—she
>   saw it all.

>   BOAT DRIVER
>   Call the law if you want. I don't give a shit.

MR. YARDLEY pulls out cell phone and begins to press buttons.

BOAT DRIVER turns his boat sharply and tosses a wake, guns the engines and makes another turn and throws another wake. Boats are banging back and forth at the docks. Clanging noises.

MR. YARDLEY staggers and falls onto the cockpit seat. Cell phone flies into the water.

BOAT DRIVER laughs.

MR. YARDLEY (red in the face)
You'd better be on your boat twenty-four-seven. You'll get yours someday. I'll see to that.

BOAT DRIVER
Hah! Like you think I'd dock at this dump?

28

Investigation: Bowerbirds

Bowerbirds. *Ptilonorhynchidae.* Twenty species in New Guinea and Australia. I saw an old documentary on them, "The Art of Seduction." Some of them are ordinary bird-brown. The satin bowerbird is shiny, sleek, blue-black with weird blue eyes. Others have bands of yellow across their necks and backs.

Carl would have loved them, if he'd known about them. Did he even know about New Guinea? That was something I'd have to look up. But if he did, if he'd been able to take a ship there, he would have made his little drawings, taken close observations of their beaks and feet, and commented on their unusual courtship behaviors.

One branch of the bowerbird family makes things like haystacks, piling sticks around a little tree, sometimes with a roof. Other kinds make roads with sticks in a palisade on each side. All of them decorate with bright shiny objects, anything they can find, flowers and stones and bones, stolen things, plastic and metal trash from people. They even color-coordinate, using all green or blue or red.

This is the cool thing: it's like overcompensation. The pretty bowerbirds, where the males have brighter plumage, don't do this building, or at least not as much. The dull species, where the males look more like the females, that's when they make the special elaborate bowers. It's all about getting attention.

29

My dearest _dearest_ Angel,

I am writing to tell you that we really need you here. Poor Maggie, our poor little girl. She don't know which way to turn these days. The police have been on her steady, asking questions, tho no one thinks she did it any more thank god they still think she knows something.

You remember Lawyer, the retarded guy? He's the latest suspect, crazy, he don't even know which end is up. Saw him yesterday playing with something. You know how he used to pick up little snakes and birds, I thought he had something like that. He was hunkered down on the ramp and dipping it in the water. I asked, what's that, and he held it up to me—dead flowers, dripping mud, but with the ribbons and all, I knew it was a corsage.

Well, I called the cops, of course, and a whole gang of 'em came out and poor Lawyer! Where did he get it, where did he get it, and Lawyer gets excited and just waving his hands like he does. They got him to crying.

Then a' course Pastor gets involved. He don't like them making his brother cry, gets right up in the deputy's face and tells him back off. I thot he was going to jail sure. Then I'd lose my dock hands, so, you guessed it, sweetheart, I jumped in between them and said maybes we could kinda lead Lawyer thru his steps.

So we got him over by the storage dock where he started and asked him to just go where he went, and he went down on the dry ground that's most times underwater, and he mushed around but they found some of his footprints and followed them out to where he dug the thing out of the mud. The cops put out their yellow tape all around, and they looked and looked, but they had their footprints all over, and what could there be now anyway? When that was throwed there, it was high water, six foot deep. Just a miracle it ever showed. Or bad news, one or other.

Dear Angel please please come see us, come put yr arms around your daughter and help her. She's your flesh and blood, you birthed her out into the world, come home.

Ever loving Drew

30

Today was the day to finish the tiller. I'd sanded it smooth and given it a first coat of spar varnish, and last night I had light-sanded that to prepare it for a final coat. It was supposed to be dead calm today; once the dew was off, it was time to complete the job. I tack-ragged it one more time to be sure there wouldn't be any dust or bugs in the finish.

The varnish looked like dark honey in the can. Good enough to eat. I dipped the brush in and leveled it off on the side.

"Maggie!"

I knew the voice before I looked up. Drexel Vann, heading down from the parking lot. I put the brush into a plastic bag and set the lid loosely on the can. I wasn't giving up on my work, but he tended to hang around when he showed up, being a detective, and it was no use letting the brush get dry.

"So this is your baby?" he said, stopping at the end of the dock finger.

"Yep."

"She's a pretty sailboat."

"A dinghy, actually." I held my hand to shade my eyes, as he was standing with the sun over his shoulder.

"Dinghy?"

"You call boats by their length. Dinghy, sailboat, yacht."

"She's not a yacht, I knew that much." Vann hunkered down. "I'm not a sailor, I guess you knew that. My people were into fishing boats."

I remembered imagining him as a johnboat, from Sears. I'd been upgrading him over these weeks and I'd say he was a Ranger now, a great bass boat but not a flashy one, not metal-flake or anything. Black with a gray stripe, maybe.

"It's okay if you call it a sailboat. They all work the same."

"That's what always got me. How do you get anywhere when the wind is against you?"

"It's complicated, but it's not. It's all balance. The wind, yeah, wherever it's coming from you have to set your sails for that. That's what moves you."

"But only away from the wind."

"You can't sail right into the wind, no. An area about like this, you can't sail." I held my arms up to show ninety degrees.

"So you zig-zag," he said.

"Tack."

"Tack." He shook his head. "Never was too good at physics when I was in school."

"Physics, exactly! You also have sideways force, and heeling, when the boat rolls from the pressure of the wind in the sails." I rocked backward to show how easily *Bellatrix* would heel. "Dinghies like this have a centerboard that sticks down, this thing, and that keeps the boat from capsizing—bigger boats have keels. Either one holds the boat in the water. It's like vectors and stuff, different forces. Even where I sit in the boat matters—you sit on the side the wind is coming from—and how much I pull the sails in or out."

"Well, it's mighty complicated."

"Like riding a bike. You can't really explain it, you have to do it. Explaining it doesn't even make sense."

"It's good to have a hobby."

"So what's your hobby?" I wonder how he liked having the questions turned around on him.

He had a way of putting his tongue between his teeth when he was thinking, like now.

"I think you might already know."

"Reading mysteries?"

He shook his head slowly. "No, that's too much like work. And the detectives are always so much smarter than me, it hurts."

I laughed at that. I almost didn't mind him hanging out, almost felt comfortable with him, but then I remembered what he was coming around for and that even if they'd gone after Lawyer now, the cloud of suspicion over me just wouldn't blow away. It hurt that no one entirely believed me, not Vann, not Dad, not even Nat maybe.

"I like astronomy," he said.

"Oh yeah. You knew about Bellatrix in Orion."

"I had a little telescope when I was a kid. I got hooked."

"Do you still have it?"

"Sure do. Dad got it for me."

My ears went up, the way he said Dad. "When you were a kid?"

"I might have been seven, eight. I looked at the moon a lot. Everything else was pretty shaky."

"Is your dad still here?"

The detective looked out over the water. "No, Maggie, he's not. He had the same problem your dad has, and it took him off early. We put his ashes into the Neuse, where he used to like to fish."

There wasn't anything I could think of to say. Finally, I came out with, "But you still use your telescope."

"Not that one. I keep it, of course, but I have an excellent instrument called a Celestron. We have good dark skies out here in the boonies."

He was right about that. I'd seen some incredible things, meteor showers, the Perseids and Geminids. Fireballs the color of green neon. The space station moving incredibly fast and silent across the sky. The full moon rising white or orange, sending a river of light down the lake.

"Have you ever discovered anything?"

"No, not anything new. I like to think I see unusual things on the moon, or in the rings of Saturn, but I know better."

I wanted to tell him about my work then. Categorizing, how I was making the world line up better by connecting one creature with another. And Linnaeus, how much those salvaged pages meant to me, Carl talking to me across time. But that would sound stupid.

Vann always seemed so interested in my life, and I thought it was not just because he was doing his job. I'd told Nat to watch out for him, but it was because of what he did for a living, not who he was. I thought Drexel Vann was essentially a good person. But Detective Vann was not here on a social call, and he spilled all that stuff to maybe get me to spill too. I didn't like it that I was still under some kind of suspicion just because she came looking for us that night.

He reached over and touched one of the soft goose feathers that I had tied to the shrouds, one on each side. His jacket fell open and I could see the gun in a holster under his arm. It seemed small, but I guess it was all you needed.

"These feathers—good luck charms?"

"Tell-tales. Sometimes there's hardly any wind at all, but even a little bit will fill the sails if you catch it right."

"What's good wind for you?"

"Ten knots is great. Just depends. If it's puffy then it makes it harder to sail."

He stood up again; must be his knees couldn't take it. He was probably forty or something. I tried not to smile. I picked up my brush and unwrapped it, looked at it, hoped he'd get the hint.

"So your dad taught you to sail?"

"Some. He can sail but he really likes stinkpots better."

Vann lifted an eyebrow.

"Motorboats."

He nodded, and I realized that he liked motorboats better too, so that wasn't the most diplomatic of things to say. I needed to learn to keep my mouth shut. Dad says if you don't have anything to hide, you don't need to worry, but who doesn't have something to hide?

Vann looked toward the office. His owly glasses caught the water and the sunlight, throwing out shards of reflection. "Are you afraid to be out here, living at the marina? After Charisse? It must be pretty empty at night."

"We have quite a few people who stay on their boats. And summer's busy." I didn't mention how slack it got with the fall storms, and then winter, when we turned the water off on the docks and all but a couple of hopeless live-aboards found winter quarters elsewhere. December, January, people came out only on the nicest days. I didn't tell him how Dad refused to listen to me about getting a gun to protect ourselves.

"I think you're being brave."

"Maybe."

"I wish I could reassure you that we're close to having this solved. We are checking out every possibility, let me tell you— reports of strange men lurking, reports of things being stolen out of locked sheds. Someone had a grocery bag taken out of the trunk of the car while they were carrying the others inside. But does that have anything to do with Charisse?" He shrugged. "Every week, the newspaper wants an update, and it's not easy to say that everything is pretty much the same."

It was strange to have him confiding in me. A few weeks ago, the suspicion was all on the college guy, then me and Fletcher, then Lawyer; I suppose a few others were mixed in there. I guess the pressure must be getting pretty bad.

"I hate how Dad keeps me on a short leash. He doesn't want me up in the woods and stuff. So I'm stuck here all the time unless I go sailing."

"He's trying to keep you safe."

I looked at him. "Yeah. Sure. Do you have kids?"

"Two boys. In elementary school."

"Do you worry about them?"

"Every day. Every single day." He sighed.

"Do you ever wonder if they'll be okay?"

"That they'll be victims? Because I'm a cop?" I could tell he was trying to keep his emotions hidden, but I could see anyway. I was world class at reading little signals, from watching Dad all these years.

"Well, that too, but that they'll turn out okay, like normal, or if they'll be criminals."

That really caught him off guard, and he seemed to measure out what he said back. "I guess it could happen, but I think my wife and I are raising them right. But back to you, Maggie. Nothing to report here, then?"

"Not a thing."

There had been the corsage, coming up out of the mud like a body rising out of a grave. I'll bet he was thinking about it too. I could see it, the way it had looked on Charisse's wrist that night, already shredded, just the centers of the flowers where the petals had been pulled off, and the straggling ribbons. I had her ring in the watch pocket of my jeans. I could feel it when I moved, and I wondered if it even might show. Sometimes when I'm out on the water, I put it on my little finger, because it's too small for my ring finger. Like everything else, I'm just too big for beautiful.

I checked on the brush, peeling the plastic to see if it was getting dried out. Vann wasn't going to get the drift. I wrapped it back up.

He picked up the dock line that went to the bow cleat. It was new, white with blue and red fibers braided into it, not dumpster stuff but the end of a reel that Dad had tossed my way. He turned the loop end of it over and back.

"This knot—what do you call this?"

"It's a bowline."

"For tying up?"

"All sorts of things. It lets you make a loop that will hold fast, but you can also get the knot loose if you have to. It won't slip."

"How do you make one? Seems like a good thing to know."

I picked up the end of the mainsheet.

"You make a loop, first. Then the rabbit comes up out of the rabbit hole, runs around the tree, and back down the hole again. The hole closes up when you pull it tight. That's the way to remember."

Vann made a loop but didn't leave himself enough line. He glanced at me and nodded, like, I know. He tried again and again, finally making a solid knot.

"When you can do it in the dark behind your back, then they say you are a sailor."

Vann turned it over and back. "This was the kind of knot that was used to restrain Charisse. Just like this."

A chill ran through me.

"So maybe whoever did it was a sailor?" he said.

"Everyone in the marina uses this knot but so do truckers. It's just standard, like a clove hitch."

"Another clue that goes nowhere." Vann sighed and tossed the line back to me. "Well, back to work. Maybe we have some new reports of missing flowerpots or mailboxes vandalized."

"See ya."

I didn't tell him that this knot was the left-handed version. I don't tie it the standard way, I tie it backwards. What some people call a Dutch bowline. Sailors argue about it like crazy, if a regular bowline is the only secure knot, or if the left-handed one works as well or even better.

I wondered if Vann meant the knot really was *just* like that. Left-handed.

31

I used to walk all over, all alone, free as Rima the Bird Girl. That was some weird old book that I found in the library discard bin, but the writer knew what he was talking about, at least so far as the forest and the creatures in it. As I read, I imagined myself a girl alone under those incredibly tall trees, talking to the birds and understanding the animals. Free and wild. Free and unafraid, at least until the end of the book.

There isn't any place, no matter how remote in the jungle or deep in my woods or far away in the cold latitudes, without someone stalking the edges.

These punky grown-over woods were my Lapland, my place to be myself and be unafraid. I used to be able to make sense of everything, and now it's all turned over. I try not to be afraid like a girl but I jump at sounds now.

It's not something to compare, not against a life, but I had a free spirit and now I don't. It's not the same. I don't feel the same.

Old people call it peace of mind. I don't have any peace of mind or peace of heart.

It's not just about Charisse. I don't walk around the same because of Dad and his drinking. I don't feel safe at home, and I don't feel safe in the woods. The place that was my refuge.

It's not fair to take what it isn't yours to take.

32

Observation: Cicada Killer

At first I thought it was a sphinx moth, hovering around and around. Big. Thick body. But when it lighted on the ground next to the concrete I saw the hole and the mound of dirt. I toed the dirt with my sneaker and the hole filled. The wasp started digging as if it was the end of the universe, shoving back the pellets of clay with its feet, something down there. It was black with yellow spots on the abdomen, a wicked stinger, and clear amber wings.

So I went to the bug book, written by Mr. Borror, great name, rhymes with horror. But there were not enough pictures. All the wasps it showed were smaller. Delicate. Everything was categorized by wing venation and number of abdominal segments. This is how Carl started, by enumerating the fin rays on fish and the spots on the wings of gnats that pestered him. I wasn't interested in flies or gnats. What I was looking for was this great honking wasp. Or I thought it was a wasp.

The next day I saw a dead cicada next to the hole. The wasp came up out of the hole and dragged the cicada down. Like watching an ant try to move something, straddling and pulling and shoving.

I went back to the book. Right above "cicadas," where I was going to look for natural enemies, was "CICADA KILLER." Just like that, in capitals.

Mr. Borror-Horror writes, "The largest species in this tribe is the Cicada Killer, *Sphecius speciocus* (Drury), which is about 30 mm; it nests in the ground and provisions its nests with cicadas." Kinda dry, but it gave me the name, and I found a lot more about it on the internet. Horror is right. The wasp stings the cicada, but doesn't kill it—just paralyzes it. Then it flies it or drags it back to the cave. The diggings may have ten or twenty chambers, each one stuffed with a living-dead cicada and a wasp egg. The eggs hatch and the larvae eat the cicadas alive.

I always liked the sound of the cicadas, like heat or summer lightning, something that came around in July and filled the afternoon and evening, the buzz hanging in the trees like humidity. But now the sounds seemed more like panic. The tiny, tiny scream of the human head on the fly body, "Help me, help me!!!!!!!!!"

(I turned this piece in for the literary annual and they used it!)

33

Another Bermuda high.

The blue sky was hard as a rock, flat and blue and bright.

I could cook my eyeballs, staring up, the sun starting its downward slide but the sky simmering with the day's heat. Not a cloud, not a breath, the lake flat as a mirror.

I rolled like a porpoise, wetting my face and front, then came back to float again.

A nothing day in a nothing month, nothing to do and no one to do it with. Nat gone, gone, gone, no word to anyone as far as I knew. The deacon and his Mrs. were stone faced whenever anyone saw them out. Hulky's folks had reeled him in, afraid of the Black kid getting the blame, and the only time I ever saw him was in the field cropping tobacco. Yesterday, actually. Hulky and his family were out there under straw hats, might as well have been 1850 or something. Lately he's found him a laughing, fat girlfriend and goes roaring around with her in the family truck. No time for hanging at the Annex or Old Trinity. When he saw me in Norlington a couple of weeks ago, he smiled with a tight face and grabbed his girlfriend's hand. Keeping his distance. So, shit, I had no friends at all, and God knows what school was going to bring.

Maybe not worth going back. Stay ignorant. Pump gas. Seriously learn to drink.

I lifted a handful of water and trickled it down on my face and neck, dry already. Too bad water couldn't just wash everything away, like the Christians said. Dipped under the water and your soul was bleached bright. It didn't take for Nat, I guess. His church did their baptizing in the creek, serious stuff, down three times in the muddy water. I'd been sprinkled when I was a baby and had no say in the matter, but I couldn't tell that it made any difference for me either. Maybe some people were just damaged souls, some of us not meant to be cleaned up with a white robe and some water.

A snapping turtle periscoped up a few feet away, wrinkly neck and flat reptilian eyes and that beak. I could see its clawed feet treading water. I wasn't creeped out by them. They knew what was dinner and what was best avoided, unless they had been hooked and were fighting for their lives. The turtle seemed to check out the sun, and then dove. *Don't blame you*, I thought. Even 50 SPF wasn't going to turn back this blast furnace.

I'd have to go in soon. Before I cooked. I had to walk home and even though nothing had happened in forever, Dad still got antsy when the sun started down. He knew where I was at the end of the old road and he'd be driving over here to check on me. I'd hear the tires hitting potholes and branches snapping, faster or slower depending on what he was consuming.

Yesterday had started out bad. Back-to-school shopping brought out the worst in both of us. We closed the store on Mondays anyway, but Dad was up early and whistling as he got ready. I guess he was looking forward to getting off the lake and away from boats altogether. I dragged myself out of bed and downed some cereal and coffee before I went to the bathhouse. The shower on the boat was just too nasty for words. Like an upright coffin with black mold and a trickle of water that went cold real quick. The bathhouse was utilitarian, but at least I could shave my legs (yes, Mother, I do that occasionally) and have a good hot spray.

We drove to the North Point Mall in Durham, and he was nice enough not to hover. He gave me money and said we'd meet up for a late lunch. Neither one of us liked walking around looking at sweaters and shoes together. There was this empty space we kept between us. Mother always used to make an *expedition* out of school shopping, wanting to go to the best mall in driving distance. She always ended up carrying out more bags than I did.

Anyway, I mushed around at Macy's and Aeropostale and

some of the little stores, and hated on the mannequins with their hip bones jutting out. I got the "necessaries," as Dad called them, because he got embarrassed at talking about them. Bras and socks and undies, plain comfortable cotton, not those lacy things. Docksiders and a pair of cheap kicks. Two pairs of khakis, after trying on a million pairs of pants that were too tight in the butt or the waist or the thighs, too short, the material too clingy. I hated looking at myself in the mirror and seeing the muffin-top once I buttoned the waist. But I found something and got that over with, at least. Shirts wouldn't be a problem.

I headed to the food court. You didn't need directions—the smell of Cinnabon was enough. More crowd than you'd expect for a Monday, I guess because of the school sales. I wove through the mommies with strollers and the kids running wild and the old people moving slowly. I was scanning the tables, figuring that Dad would have beat me there, when I saw him.

Not Dad.

HIM.

Fletcher was at a table near the edge of the seating area, wearing the kind of red T-shirt I had always imagined him in. My heart just stopped. His black hair was long enough to curl on his neck. He had a little growth of beard. In profile, his nose was stronger than I'd imagined, really kind of a Roman nose, and his cheekbones flew away from it. I stopped by a pillar and just watched him. I was ready to duck if he turned my way. Surely if I recognized him then he would know me as well, reach right through the internet vapor that I'd plucked him from, out of whatever alternate time-stream thing had placed him at a plastic table in the food court at the mall.

He got up and went to the Japanese hibachi place and came back with a plate, heaped up. I watched him unwrap a plastic fork and spoon, economical movements. Like a sailor. No wasted motion. He took the lid off the cup and lifted it to drink, ignoring the straw on his tray. I felt like a stalker. No, like Carl watching some wonderful creature there in the mountains of Lapland. He scanned the food court as he ate. Once he looked toward me, and I slid behind the pillar, my hands on the curved rough concrete surface. I waited like a squirrel behind a tree trunk, until I thought I was safe, and then came back out. He was focused on his food again. He lifted his hand and rubbed his lips, and I felt that deep body charge like I had when Charisse leaned into me and planted that kiss. Quaking. Like the earth turned into water, rolling and rocking, a sensation I wasn't unfamiliar with, but it didn't usually come without some steady work on my part.

He took another long drink from his cup, tipping it back, his throat moving. I couldn't have moved now if I'd had to. I just stood there, watching. He finished his meal and stood up, threw away the trash, and stowed his tray. He was taller than I'd expected, leaner, even a bit older. And then he turned around and I saw, face on, how much he looked like Dad. Like Dad used to look. Handsome in that pirate kind of way, smiling and tanned and with a swagger to his walk. I felt my stomach turn over. Was Fletcher just a reflection of Dad? And I remembered it all, the noises in the bedroom that had scared me until they stopped, and then I ran in yelling, "Mommy, Mommy," and Dad was standing naked and Mother was kneeling and he had his hands on her head and her face had been moving below his belly.

I don't know how I looked. Stunned, I guess. Fletcher walked past me, not ten feet away, and never glanced my way, thank God or Buddha or whoever. I just leaned against the pillar as if I'd been blown there by a storm.

"Hey, punkin."

I must have jumped a mile.

"What's the matter?" Dad set his two little bags down and came over and put a hand on my shoulder. "You feeling okay, honey?"

"Yeah." I was afraid to look at him, with that man's face and his face going in and out. I wished he would take his hand off my shoulder.

"Maybe we should head home. You're awful pale."

I breathed deep. "No, I'm okay. Just hungry."

"I'll bet you're starved after all that shopping. What do you want to eat?"

When we were with my so-called mother, we always went to Tripp's and topped off lunch with that great cheesecake they flew in from New York every day.

"You see something you'd like?"

It looked like we were staying here. I scanned the offerings and it was bleak. Fake Mexican, fake Chinese, fake Italian, hamburgers, fake Japanese, subs, cookies.

"How about Japanese?"

I didn't want that. Not now. I couldn't have choked down a bite. "I think a burrito."

"Mountain Dew?"

"Yeah."

He left and came back balancing two trays. "Bet you didn't know I was a waiter once."

"I did not know that."

"It made me decide to spend my time underneath a boat."

I could smile now, my insides settling back to normal.

He had a meatball sub with everything, extra cheese, french fries, a giant Coke. He ate like a starving man, as if he hadn't eaten in forever. I felt a little guilty, because I hadn't been cooking very much. It was tough on the old barge with that little stove, and I didn't like to cook anyway, so we had a lot of spaghetti and eggs and Hamburger Helper.

"Did you get all you needed?"

"Most of it."

"Good." But he didn't ask to see what I bought. Mother was always hypercritical but at least she cared that I looked mostly human when I went to school.

He sucked down the last of his drink and I took our trays to the trash. I hadn't eaten much of the burrito—the chicken was tough, and the whole thing was greasy.

"You ready to head home?"

"Sure."

But we had to stop at Lowe's for roofing nails and caulk and some boards. Then Advance Auto for something. And then

Walmart. I still had some cash, so while he was getting whatever, I grabbed some notebooks and binders, so I didn't have to
use the ones with "Fletcher" engraved on them, and two polo
shirts and a tunic thing. I was used to cheap; it didn't bother me.

It was getting dark by the time we turned down the marina road. The pole lights were flickery as they came on, and it
looked like the parking lot was moving. When I walked around
to the back of the truck to open the gate, I realized that the
parking lot was full of tiny gray toads. Frogs. Toads. Hopping
all over the place. It was some kind of apparition, the concrete
looking like it was coming alive. I picked up a rock and threw it
farther up and saw the same movement.

"What the hell?" Dad said.

"I guess they're eating, or breeding, or something."

He pulled out the sacks without another word. I stayed for a
minute, watching, and tried to catch one, but then I saw he was
waiting at the edge of the dock. Watching me. I let the toads be
and followed.

I'd never seen it in all the years I'd lived there. How could
I have missed it? Or maybe it only happened at long intervals,
like the seventeen-year locusts. Something in Linnaeus—something I read about frogs. I pulled out my pages before I even
emptied the bags.

> *Here was a woman supposed to labor under the misfortune of a brood
> of frogs in her stomach, owing to her having, in the course of the
> preceding spring, drunk water which contained the spawn of these
> animals.*

Linnaeus reported this very soberly in his journal, along with
all sorts of other folklore and superstitions. He wasn't making
fun of them, though he could be real judgmental about the
parsons and schoolteachers who lived in the villages.

> *She thought she could feel three of them, and that herself, as well as
> persons who sat near her, could hear them croak. Her uneasiness was
> in some degree alleviated by drinking brandy.*

It anesthetized her, or the frogs. Whatever works.

I started to put away my new clothes in the tiny drawers. The top of the dresser, if you could call it that, had my trophies and some rock samples and books held up with horse bookends. I clipped the tags off with nail clippers, saving the extra buttons for the pants. I usually lost one or two, and when I sewed them back I used monofilament line so it wouldn't happen again. I emptied my sock drawer and tossed a few thin pairs to the side for work rags, laid in the new ones, flat and clean. Same with the underwear. I had these old raggedy bras that I kept just in case—time for them to go, but not into the rag bin. I was making everything tidy when I heard the ice crunch as it was twisted in the cube tray, then the cubes hitting the glass and then the liquor. I should have figured that, after the mall. The mall was too much tangled up with my mother, and she wasn't here, and so he tried to chase her away with alcohol, but it never worked. Like the woman with the frogs in her stomach. He'd drink until he finished it all, or passed out.

Dad remembers too well. Sometimes it's best to remember differently.

I finished putting stuff away and lay down in my clothes on top of the bed, letting the cool night air blow in through the window. I went to sleep right away, and if I had any dreams of Fletcher, I didn't remember them.

Here and now, in the lake where I lay like a floating log. My skin was hot in the sun and cool under the water, as if there was a line dividing my top from my bottom. I rolled over in the water again and blinked to clear my vision. The shore was farther away, the current pulling me toward the far end of the lake and the dam. The sun was almost down behind the trees. I started to swim back, slowly, feeling the heat in my face that would be sunburn in the morning.

Maybe that's what happened with people. Divorce was like the woman and the frogs. Everything was going fine, normal, and then one day you took a drink or a bite of something you didn't look at real careful. Something started growing in you. The marina was full of divorce; maybe it was in our water system. This summer there had been three different private investigators on the docks. One looked like a sheriff's deputy, maybe used to be one, fat and slow. One was thin and nervous and never took off his sunglasses. The Bounty Hunter, we called him. The third one—he was the real deal. Maybe from Raleigh or Charlotte. He was unremarkable looking, quiet and methodical in his snooping. I remember him from when the guy in the big Sea-Ray was fooling around. One time you'd see him with a woman his own age, a nice-looking woman with short dark hair, another doctor, they said. Next time it was a twenty-five-year-old redhead. She was there during the week, sunning on the deck. The quiet PI took his pictures from the parking lot and walked on the docks in cutoff shorts and a T-shirt, asking about boats for sale and jawing with the sailors. Next thing you know, the man and the redhead were gone and the ex-wife had changed the name on the back of the cruiser from *Wyld Ryde* to *Myne Now*.

As I swam closer to shore, I scared up a heron. It squawked away from the point, trailing its legs.

Myne Now had had its own wild times; the ex-wife paired up with a younger man and hosted parties for a new crowd of people. Dad didn't care much for the woman. I would have thought he'd sympathize, but maybe it was because she took up the lifestyle along with the boat.

It's not like I don't know about sex. Have known. I had had some idea even when I was pretty little, and learned a lot more about the *how* from biology books. But I discovered the *why* of it one day when I was rocking on the gunwale of a boat. I just kept doing it because it seemed to feel good, and then my body started shaking and I felt hot and sweaty. I figured it out, then, why all the perfume and clothes and hairstyles, why the seeking and cheating and lying and yelling. It was more than reproduction. More than what I read in my science books. Way before mandatory sex education, I had a real good idea about reproduction from reading about the life cycles of creatures. And seeing some of them. Once at Oriental, a sometime sailor had left his boat alone too long, so when he took the cover off the main, he disturbed a big nest of wasps. They came swarming out and he dove in the water, people on the adjoining fingers all swatting and cursing as the angry cloud spread out. Dad went down with Hot Shot and took care of the nest. He knocked it to the deck and broke it apart, spraying it with the killing stuff. When he threw it in the trash, I got a stick and pulled it up to look. The little cells had pupae and half-emerged wasps frozen dead in their places. I read about wasps and bees and how a queen lays eggs that can be male or female, as needed, and even different in forms and function, winged or wingless. I was fascinated by how life kept on being life. Fish that changed gender from male to female. Fish that brooded their babies in their mouths. Female mantises that ate their mates, once the deed was done, and spiders that did the same.

Reading was only half of it. Observation, that was how you really learned. Carl knew that. We lived in that boat shed for long enough for me to hear and see and understand. Once I walked into their space, not really a room, and they were stuck together like my pair of Valentine's Day huggy bears, and Dad just pulled the curtain closed and said to turn on the TV, it was all okay. So I tried to ignore it, but how much can you, anyway? And I think they didn't know that I understood what was going on. It became funny, then, hearing their noises. When they heard me laughing, that was the last time I actually saw or heard anything, except fighting. They took their sex elsewhere or elsewhen. But it was funny, this great compulsion, this need that made frogs hop and insects swarm and people pant and groan.

Myself, I think it would be much better to be self-sufficient, if you could take care of reproduction like frogs, no mate needed. Parthenogenesis. The sex part was something I learned how to take care of myself, once I had experimented with the motions and accepted the hazy thoughts that came into my head. Those got clearer and clearer and eventually became Fletcher. My boat cleanup duties earned me tips and gave me access to all kinds of stuff you'd think people would want to keep hidden.

Funny thing. I never had "the talk." Dad was too dog-scared to do it. And my so-called mother never really got beyond *you're becoming a woman* and some Kotex pads. And then she was gone. Sometimes I think about her coming back. About her answering one of Dad's letters by just showing up, tanned and beautiful. I know she probably looks like a model now, with money to make life easy. Or maybe she'd just know with a mother's intuition that I was in trouble, this mess with Charisse.

Crap. I gave myself an imaginary smack on the head. It was crazy to think like that. If my so-called mother ever did show up, it wouldn't be my needs she was here about.

You can cover a lot of ground, thinking. Or water. As far away as the shore had been, it was right there now, and I put my foot down and felt the slick mud under my water shoe. A few more strokes and my toes hit solid pavement.

This had been a state highway across the valley, before the lake was filled. It ran to the main highway, through a bunch of camps, then trailers where people lived all the year round, and ended up by the convenience store. Where the marina road branched off from it, we had put up a sawhorse with a sign "Road Ends" and a cable to keep people from coming down here, so the end of the old road was used only by us and the deer. Grass was growing through cracks in the asphalt, year by year encroaching from the crumbling sides, and now even in cracks and potholes in the middle of the road. The white line was fading but still visible down the center. Limbs and cones and trash lay where they fell, until a strong storm would pile them into windrows.

In low-water times, like now, the road disappeared under a long tongue of red mud that had been deposited in the spring. This was hard and dry now and it broke under my feet and sent up little clouds of dust. In high-water times, the old road made a natural boat ramp. I used to think it would be a great place for smugglers to bring their cargo down from Virginia, run it up in boats to the road, and meet trucks to take it on. Drugs, or something, though why it made a difference from Virginia to North Carolina I guess didn't make any sense. It wasn't like Prohibition or something. Still, this old road and its built-in ramp had an abandoned yet usable look, like a smuggler's cove. That's what I called it when I was younger. More recently, I used to think about meeting someone there myself. *Absconding* was a word I had come onto and I liked it—*absconding*, from what or to what I didn't know. When I was deep into the Fletcher thing, I used to imagine him beaching his boat there, and we'd walk into the woods where there was a totally secret, hidden place, my bower under the vines that I would show only to him. We would have been incredibly daring, and would have made love right there on the mainland.

I plucked my towel off the tree limb and shook it out—bark, ants, whatever—and dried off. I rubbed it through my hair that had grown out almost to my shirt collar. It was uneven, though, from the layered cut I'd gotten for years. I wanted to let it get long enough to have it cut straight across.

"Damn!" I smashed the mosquito that had needled the soft part of my arm. It left a streak of blood.

I draped the towel over my shoulders and started walking, my feet squishing in my water shoes. The road went up a little hill, around a bend, past the boat graveyard. We hauled boats out for people who couldn't afford the slip fees anymore but didn't have any place to take their boats, and left them there on trailers—or for ones without a trailer, lying on their sides. We charged them a few bucks a month. Boats came in, but I never remember one ever going back out.

The trees cast long shadows across the abandoned boats. It was just a sad place. We hadn't run the mower through since spring and the weeds were tall. The little bit of breeze stirred the rag-ends of sails and canvas covers. A halyard clanged.

I wondered how people could have a boat, love it even, give it a name and add the little personal touches in the cabin, and then leave it to rot at the storage dock, or even worse, on dry land. As long as it was in the water there was hope—but once it was on the hard, it was zombieland. Living death.

My skin started goose-bumping, even though it was still hot as an oven. I guess it was the air or maybe the miserable boats streaked with mold and bird shit, but I had this weird feeling and no reason for it.

I came to the cutoff path that we used to get from here over to the marina road, stepping from cracked pavement to sand and rocks. I had to walk slower to avoid the pointy stones that would jab me through the soft rubber soles. And it was really getting dark under the trees.

I heard the halyard clang-clang again. It didn't seem like there was that much wind. A bird probably, landing on a mast. I looked back but I couldn't see anything.

I began to whistle. Bird whistles. Then just noise. And then I realized what I was whistling.

So come sit by my side if you love me.

Do not hasten to bid me adieu.

Just remember the Red River Valley,

And the one that has loved you so true.

Stupid sappy song. I quit whistling.

Then I remembered where I'd heard that song. Dad had been singing it to my so-called mother, in the dark, in some shabby place we lived. He had been singing it to her after they had a fight—one of many fights. Maybe the first one that was the beginning of the end.

34

Big Paul sat down in one of the white plastic chairs. Carefully. It creaked, but held, and he grinned.

"No disaster this time!"

Big Paul wasn't really all that big, or not big in a fat way. He was maybe six foot two, but he was solid muscle, especially his arms. Big guns, and a strong, corded neck. But he didn't look freakish or anything. His personality was bigger than his body. Big Paul filled up a room with his huge rolling laugh.

He tore into the pair of chili dogs I'd fixed him (extra pickles, lots of mustard), pausing to chuck down some chips or a long drink of sweet tea.

"The water—that's something," he said, spitting a few crumbs as he talked about his latest paddling expedition. "On the one side it's black—tannic—and the other side is clear. They run side by side for a space and then they blend. And the trees—the trees!—cypress and swamp oak, the Spanish moss hanging to the water—it was like they could start talking to you, they're so alive and full of individuality."

"Were you by yourself?"

"Oh hell, heck, yeah. Last thing I want is someone's chatter. Scares the fish, but worse, it bores the crap outta me."

Of all the people who came around the backwater, I liked Big Paul the best. Top to bottom. He was one of the people you could count on for anything, but he wouldn't hold accounts on it and remind you that you were in his debt. Big Paul had pulled me out of a couple of scrapes with *Bellatrix*, but he never said a thing to Dad.

I pushed aside the college essay I was supposed to be working on and put my elbows on the counter and my chin in my hands. "So—I'm all ears."

"I'm gonna convert you to a paddler yet!" He threaded his

hands and turned his palms out, pinker and more defined than mine, and cracked his knuckles. "Well, I put in and floated the Lumber River down to Lake Waccamaw. I was drift-fishing and caught a nice stringer…"

I waited for the latest spasm to quiet on Channel 16. Stereo, too, between the store radio and Big Paul's.

"So, how many mosquito bites?"

"You don't count those."

"Right."

"You just count water moccasins."

I shuddered at that. I'm not really afraid of snakes, as long as I can see them, but the idea of a fat snake dropping out of a tree into my boat gives me the heebie-jeebies. And a venomous one, with that ghastly white mouth to show off the fangs.

"When are you going out with me on a trip? With the club," he added quickly. He belonged to not one but three kayak clubs: one for whitewater, one for sea kayaking, one that just fished and camped out. I'll bet he was the darkest guy in the bunch, and the biggest. At least from what I'd seen, kayakers were skinny white people. I wasn't sure what Paul was—he called himself "redbone" and said he was part Cherokee, and he did have a reddish tint to his skin and high cheekbones. But I think most people would just categorize him as Black.

"You tell me," I said, gesturing at the store. Weekends I was tied to the counter, weekdays I was in school.

"Maybe one of the school holidays."

"Maybe."

"Or even when school gets out. It's real nice in the winter sometimes, and no mosquitoes or snakes."

"Maybe." I didn't want to disappoint him, but I was a sailor through and through. Why paddle when you can catch the wind? "I think we're going down to the coast for a couple of days. Dad has to pick up a bunch of stuff he bought from a shop that went out of business in Beaufort."

"That's a good place to paddle too." Big Paul brushed the crumbs off his lap and tossed the paper plate and napkin in the trash. "Over to Shackleford Banks and the ponies, that's good, but I love Portsmouth Island."

"I heard that was way buggy."

"What's with you and the bugs?" He laughed, showing all his teeth. "Are you going girly on me?"

"I have a limit on itching."

He looked up toward the ceiling. Or maybe the sky, because he started talking about walking through the ghost town on Portsmouth Island, where the houses and church and all were still standing. "Now it's just the wind blowing through, but it seems like you can still hear the voices," he said. "Like the people are just out of sight, but not gone."

He was a mystical sort sometimes. It was kinda cool. I wondered if he believed in ghosts or spirits. Probably. He wasn't scientific like me.

"I like the beach in the winter. Good shells and no people."

"Yeah," he said, "he-heck, yeah!"

He gave me that look, his eyes full of mischief. "I bet you bring home bags of shells."

I blushed a little, because I used to. Every scallop, clam, even oysters, common as flies. I dragged them all home. One of several collections that I used to have, but I had to get rid of them during the moves.

"When I was a kid," I admitted. "But now I just like to see what the ocean brings in." I walk at the edge of the surf, where the water runs up and stirs the sand and broken shells. Minnows and mole crabs scoot back to the deeper water, and the coquinas endlessly upend and bury themselves only to be pulled up again. And sea lettuce, bright green, and weed with small bladders that pop, and dead man's fingers, all the stuff hidden under the gray-green waves. I always look for sharks' teeth but never seem to have any luck.

He wandered past the candy and looked at what we had for cookies. He grabbed a family-size bag of Pecan Sandies and plowed into them.

I wrote a note on the margin of the essay, reminding myself

to put in some stuff about the beach. It would be good—scientific and personal both. They wanted you to have some great story to tell, like growing up in poverty in Appalachia or belonging to a gang. I had only one dramatic thing to report in my life, and I wasn't going to write about that.

"What are you doing there? Homework?"

"Nah. It's my college essay. You have to write a personal essay as part of your application."

"Good girl! What you going for?"

"Marine biology."

"I love it!" The place almost shook. "You keep working hard. Don't be like me and blow it."

"It's tough sometimes."

He looked at me for a long moment. "Not just Charisse."

I nodded. It was like he could read my mind. None of them really knew about it, the adults, what went on in school. It wasn't bullying. What they called bullying, a hot topic these days. It was avoidance. And the remarks that came floating over the tops of the library bookcases, anonymous.

Ready for Homecoming?

Can't wait! I got my dress last night.

Just don't get around Maggie.

Like she'd even go.

Just saying—people around her end up dead.

Big Paul was looking at me, those bright eyes, and I had this feeling he could tell what I was thinking again.

"The kids are tough, sure, but what's tougher is when you let go, letting go of your whole life. Don't end up like me, a college dropout driving a towboat and pulling drunks off the rocks." His face got strange, like a little boy who'd just said something wrong. "No offense."

"Nope. It's all good."

Observations could fool you. Looking at Big Paul, in his bright yellow get-up and loud boat, most people would think he was all muscle and no brains. But it was like the protective camouflage that lets one creature look like another. Like a king snake that wears the borrowed marks of a dangerous viper. Big

Paul was gentle and reflective. We talked about everything under the sun. But he'd never before told me he'd gone to college.

"What did you used to want to be?"

"An elementary-school teacher."

Wow. I never expected that, but it seemed exactly right. The radio squawked some more. Who had fish. Whether the hot-dog stand was open at the new marina up in Virginia. The DER reporting in, and the Corps repositioning a buoy. It was busy anyway, but there was too much chatter. The VHF was for safety and emergencies, not socializing. That's one thing Dad taught me as soon as I was old enough to use the mike, what was proper radio use and common courtesy. It might not be life-and-death stuff here on the lake, but it could be on the ocean.

"You out of milk?" Big Paul asked through a dry mouth of cookies.

"Out of the bottles. We have half-gallons."

"Not that thirsty."

I went and got a carton and plunked it down in front of him. "Put your name on it." I handed him a marker. "You can have the rest—"

I was cut off by the radio, but this wasn't chatter. It was a woman's voice, tense but controlled. The boat's engine wouldn't start and they were drifting slowly toward the dam.

"Paul to the rescue," he said, but not before he took a deep swig, wrote his name in block letters on the milk and put it on the bottom shelf.

I heard the roar of those big twin outboards as the Sea-Tow boat hit the no-wake markers and headed up the lake.

The door opened and a pile of kids came in. Four of them, all ages. This would be a nightmare.

They headed for the ice cream and before they ever touched it I told them to leave the case closed till they had picked out what they wanted. They huddled over the top, breathing on it and smudging the glass with their fingers as they pointed.

"How much for the Nutty Buddys?"

"How much for the sandwiches?"

"What about the Freeze-Pops?"

I answered each one. Like they couldn't read—all the prices were written on a chart with color pictures.

I heard the case open and they rustled around. I was getting ready to yell at them when they closed it up and brought their treats to the counter. I scooted my essay to the back shelf—they were grimy and wet and had already opened the ice cream. A handful of sticky money later, and they were gone. *Bing-bong!* Thank God!

Quiet for an hour. I made a few notes. I stared out the windows.

Big Paul reported reaching the drifting boat.

I straightened the bills in the cash drawer.

A customer at last—Mr. Showalter.

I was happy to see him. He was one of the boat bums, always working on his baby, a bony old guy with a lined face and a goatee.

He squatted down by the shelves of boat supplies, the ones that mostly needed dusting. He turned over some of the brushes and found one that suited him.

"I'll take this." His fingernails were rimmed with amber-colored teak oil.

"Hard to believe you have anything left to paint on *Iolar.* Three dollars and sixty-eight cents."

"Prevention, my dear, prevention is the key." He extracted a five from his wallet. "For body and boat."

"Agreed."

He had a gorgeous old wooden ketch, not far up A dock. Shoal draft. I'd been inside it quite a few times—not to clean, because he never left it dirty, but he gave me the combination to the cabin so that I could check for bilge issues or put in some Damp-Rid canisters when he couldn't get down from Virginia for a long time. Sometimes I just sat there and imagined. The cabin was what you'd expect, nautical but not tacky, the brass polished, everything neatly labeled, stowed, and tied down. The word *shipshape* was invented for him.

"Thank you, Mister Showalter." I handed him the change and started to put it in a bag, but he held up his hand.

"I'm putting it right to work," he said. He stood for a minute and ruffled the bristles back and forth. "My wife tells me I should sell *Iolar*. That I'm getting too old."

"Never."

He grinned, showing long yellow teeth. I wondered how old he was.

"Never, never, never give up." He touched his cap in a sort of salute and went out.

35

D ad quit drinking.
He had gone on a real binge after our trip to the mall, cheap whiskey that was always the worst, that left him hollow-eyed and stumbling. He wouldn't eat, just sat at the table and stared at his glass, then refilled it slowly. I watched the store and handled everything, put off what I couldn't manage. Guillermo did whatever I asked, but he looked at me sadly.

Finally the binge burned out, like a wildfire running out of fuel. Then he couldn't sleep, and he had the shakes, and a couple of times I saw him put his hand on his chest, over his heart. I think it scared him. I know it scared me.

He had tapered off with beer until the shakes stopped, and then nothing. Two nights a week he drove up to the Methodist church for AA, though again he didn't really tell me that was what he was doing. While he was gone, I luxuriated in stretching out and reading without the radio going or him scratching away at a letter or talking about my so-called mother.

Surprisingly, he actually wanted to talk about me.

It was a Monday afternoon, when the store was closed. He said to hop in the car, we were headed to Norlington for dinner. I looked down at my sneakers and bang-around jeans. "Don't change, we're just going to the Burger Barn."

I didn't care if we split a Walmart sub in the park. I just wanted to see him normal, with clear eyes, at last.

We had burgers and fries and milkshakes and talked about little stuff, not any of the big stuff. But he surprised me when he asked about school.

"I haven't been keeping up very well," he said, "but I know you're planning on college in the fall—"

"UNCW. Yes."

He dropped his head at that. "I don't know about UNCW, punkin, at least right away."

My heart fell down.

"It's a lot of money, with room and board and all. Maybe community college, just for a year, till things pick up at the marina."

"Dad, I might be able to get a scholarship. For track. Coach said he can help me, even if I disappeared this past season, because I had a good year before. He's talking with the college and helping me apply, and with the FAFSA and all that." He nodded, and I saw how the lines had set into his face, as if he'd aged a ton in a few months. I wanted to be agreeable but part of me was desperate to get away. Away from London County, the backwater, away from him. While I still could. It made me mad when I came to realize, now that he wasn't drinking, how much responsibility I had when he was. It was as if I was his parent, and had to monitor him and work things out around him. I could see myself at Filliyaw Pointe the rest of my life, signing for deliveries and telling the crew what to do, while he sat at the table with a bottle.

"That's good, that's real good." He sighed. "I'm proud of you, if you can get it. Just don't set your heart too much on it, in case it don't happen. There's always London Community, just for a while. A year or so. Anyway." He balled up his papers and stuffed them in the milkshake cup and we cleared the table and headed home.

I watched his hands on the steering wheel, looking for shakes. I wondered how much of him was messed up inside, messed up so he couldn't heal. I worried that I would go that way too. I like wine, but not hard liquor. Yet. They say it's genetic. Some people at the marina drink a little bit and put it aside. Some drink with joy. And a few are like Dad. I don't know what's inside my cells. What one person can have, another can't, like an allergy, only worse. People think it's all the same—like if an animal eats something, then you can, but pokeberries and toadstools can kill a human. Alcohol is the same: some can have it; some it can kill.

Things were going along well—the AA meetings, and him taking care of projects that he had let slide for a long time. I let my guard down. Everything was smoothing out, with the drinking, with the Charisse mess.

Then the mail came one day, and there was the letter.

It was one of his letters, one he had written to my mother. He just held it, looking at it, then he looked at me and set it down on the counter.

"No more!!!" was written across the address. "Return to sender!!!" Three exclamation marks. Loopy writing. I guess it was hers.

Dad walked up to the parking lot and got in the truck. He roared off and I waited, hoping he wouldn't clobber a tree along the road. He came back and took a case of liquor out of the pickup.

So much for sobriety.

36

From Lachesis Lapponicus

Another subject of inquiry is why the Laplanders are so healthy, for which the following reasons may be assigned.

1) The extreme purity of the air, which seemed to give me new life as I inhaled it.

2) The use of food thoroughly dressed.

3) Eating their food cold; for they always let their boiled meat cool before they taste it, and do not seize it with avidity as soon as it comes out of the pot.

4) The purity of the water.

5) Tranquillity of mind. They have no contentions, neither are they over and above careful about their affairs, nor addicted to covetousness. Their lives are protracted to extreme old age.

6) Their never overloading the stomach, while the rustic of other countries eats till he is ready to burst.

7) Deficiency of spirituous liquors. Of these they rarely taste, and only in such quantities as to be rather beneficial than otherwise.

8) Their being inured to cold from their infancy renders them hardy.

9) Probably the quantity of flesh they eat may prolong their lives, as carnivorous animals are long-lived.

37

Observation: The Castle

What were surveyors doing back here? That's what I thought when I saw the orange flag sticking up.

I looked up the old railroad right of way, and then back down it toward the lake.

Just one flag.

I had a pretty good idea what it marked.

As I got closer, the construction emerged from the back side of a little rise. The surveyor's flag, pulled from somewhere legitimate, had been trimmed to a point to make a pennant and inserted in the top of the dome. It was the crowning decoration on a project that someone had spent a lot more time on than the earlier ones. The sticks were woven neatly. The bower was approached by a little roadway floored with white pebbles, and had a moat of pebbles around it. A castle.

I lay down flat on the ground and looked inside the pointed arch of the doorway. Pieces of moss had been pulled off trees and fitted together to make a carpet. A white stick had been placed at the center of the green floor. I reached my hand inside—carefully, in case there was some sort of trap—but nothing happened and I felt foolish for dreaming up scenarios. I touched the stick and rolled it. Light. Not a stick—a piece of paper rolled very tightly. I pulled it out. The paper had been tied in three places with twisted pieces of grass. I broke them and unrolled the paper.

It looked like a page pulled out of a book, thick and blank the way the pages are at the ends. A little brownish. I turned it over and found a drawing in pencil. A girl looking down at something on the ground, a flower maybe.

A girl that was me.

I dropped the paper and it coiled back up.

I turned over onto my back and looked up into the endless impartial sky.

Whoever drew that picture knew me. My pug nose and straight hair, my legs that were sturdy and not graceful. It was accurate, but not mean-spirited. You could see that it was drawn with affection.

I picked up the picture, thinking I would take it home, but then I put it back. I didn't want Dad to find it, or anyone at all to know about these domes.

Instead, I picked up a pebble from the moat, to keep. Smooth and white, quartz that had been rounded by water—you can find them in the gravel on the road and in the beds of old streams. I used to gather them when I was little. White and clear and pale yellow. I had made paths with them myself, and circles and labyrinths. Sometimes even now I would pick up ones that were especially perfect, round as pearls.

How would anyone know that? Not even Nat knew that. The only person who'd ever seen my little rows of rocks and shells was Dad. And Mother, too, I guess.

38

Dearest Angela
Miss you baby. I cant take these night all alone.
Maggie in her room and I sit here at the table,
no one to talk to.

I wish this mess w/Maggie was over. We're all in the
clear, her and me and the marina staff—some vagrant
or something, they say—but you still cant draw an easy
breath wondring if hes around. Maggie aint right. She
keeps it inside her but I know she's messed up about it.
To have her cousin killed and all. And the rumors. They get
worse ever day, crazy, evil.

I dont know where she got this stuff she made up,
all this Fletcher stuff, I guess some truth to it maybe,
someone she's had a crush on or something.

No one cares if I wake up tomorrow. I think it would
be better if GOD just took me off some night. I think
of you and hope you are happy with this life you have
made for yourself. They say money cant BUY happiness
but that's not true is it. Or at least its hard to look sad
when you got the WHOLE DAM WORLD. You sure feath-
erd yorr nest.

Not like us, Maggie and me. Maggie has got not a friend
in the world either. We're like at the end of the world, just
the two of us. She used to have those rejects she run
around with, but they've all gone off and she don't know
how to have a friendship w/ a girl. She lies and I think
she is like you in that, it's easy for her to just make up
something and then keep making it bigger and bigger until
its almost real.

Your only true lover Drew

Dear Dad,

You don't need to be sending this letter. You know how it ends up. So I'm going to answer you.

I need you to stop drinking and stay stopped this time, and be my dad. I will do my best to stay out of any problems and do like I should.

I am not like my mother. I make things up maybe, sometimes I have. It wasn't to hurt you or anyone else. Maybe I just felt like I could make the world work out more the way I thought it should be. If I could make up a story where she came back and loved you I would, because I know that's what hurt you the most and will always hurt you.

I love you. I care if you wake up tomorrow. You need her but I need you.

Maggie

PART III

"We must be our own before we can be another's."

- Ralph Waldo Emerson

39

You know how you know something is happening before your brain registers it?

I heard a metal gate rattle down hard and I looked out the little window to where the Pepsi truck was parked, in the turning circle right by the top of the walkway. I couldn't see Farley, so he must be around on the other side. I got up to prop the door open and clear a path to the cooler.

"Hey." That was Dad. He sounded like he was talking through gravel. I had thought he was still sleeping it off in the houseboat.

A voice came back, Farley's, I guess, kind of muffled.

"I told you a dozen times if I tol' you once."

Farley said something, but not as loud.

I peeked out the window again. Farley came around the truck pushing a load of cans. Dad was tailing after him.

"You're blocking my customers. Put the damn thing up in the lot."

Farley just kept wheeling, so Dad stepped between him and the walkway. Dad stood there leaning toward him, hands hanging by his sides. Farley set his dolly down and stood there with his elbows resting on the top, his beer gut hanging over his belt and hat tipped back, not looking too concerned about the whole thing. He was even smiling.

And then, BAM. Dad hauled back and hit him. Right in the face. But Farley was as big as a house and he didn't go down. Dad, overbalanced, stumbled forward and went head first onto the concrete.

Farley shook his head and swiped a hand across his chin. And then he laughed.

That would be a mistake.

Dad got up and I could see the blood running from his nose.

He rushed at the driver, who fended him off with his case dolly like a bullfighter with a bull, wheeling it around in a tight circle. Dad bellowed like a bull, too, and came rushing back, but this time he ducked away and sidestepped the dolly almost as neatly as if he'd been sober, and he flurried his fists into the man's face and stomach. And lower. I saw Farley drop to one knee, hands over his head, and Dad was pounding on his neck.

"Son of a bitch," he yelled. "Son of a BITCH!"

I ran to the counter and grabbed the phone, then dropped it. I couldn't call the police. I went back and saw that Dad was still beating on Farley. All sorts of cars up there, all the men in the marina, and not one to get involved. Cowards. I looked at the phone again, then grabbed an air horn off the counter and began to run.

"Dad. DAD." I blasted the horn. He stopped for a moment and looked around, but he wasn't connecting. He started in again, but he wasn't hitting as hard. Now I was afraid that Farley was getting mad, and he was so big. "Stop it! Stop it!" I kept blowing the horn, just automatic that I was hitting five blasts. *Help. Help. Help. Help. Help.* How you get help on the water.

Now Farley was getting to his feet, both him and Dad swaying, and I could see the blood on their clothes and the evil in their eyes.

"Shut the damn thing up, Maggie!" Dad glared at me. "Get outta here!"

I blasted again. But I had an escape route, always had an escape route. He wasn't in his right mind. His face was dark red and his skinned-up nose was swelling.

"Mind me for goddamn once!"

Farley had had enough. He reared back and unloaded one punch, and I saw Dad leave his feet and fly backward onto the grass.

"DAD!"

I ran up and blasted the horn right in Farley's ear. He grunted and stepped back. I heard Dad groan and saw out of the corner of my eye that he was getting to his knees. I headed for

Farley again with the air horn, but he just picked me up by the shoulders and set me aside. Dad was on his feet now, his hands balled up, but I could see his shoulders sagging. It was over.

I heard the siren before they did, wailing up the road, fast, and then the patrol car was in the parking lot and slewing around right behind the truck. The deputy jumped out and yelled for both of them to put their hands up. I saw he had his hand on his gun as he ran.

Farley had his hands up right away and was talking while bloody drool dripped out of his busted mouth. Dad's hands went up but started to drop, inch by inch, and he was bleeding hard and staggering.

"Just keep your hands up like I told you."

"He can't help it," I pleaded. "He's drunk. He's an alcoholic."

"Stay over there."

I walked closer because he had to understand that Dad wasn't really dangerous.

"Please. He's my dad. He didn't mean anything."

I heard a radio squawk and the deputy keyed his shoulder mike. "I got two men about kilt each other. Could use backup. And a' ambulance."

"He's my daddy. Let me take him home. He's just drunk."

The deputy didn't look at me. "You." He pointed to Farley. "Sit on the curb with your hands on your head." The Pepsi man sat down in a heap, his legs stuck out straight in front of him like an enormous doll. "You," and he pointed to my dad, "are going in the cruiser. And *you*, missy, just be quiet. You ain't too good to get hauled in too."

Dad had kinda folded up, and was shuffling along to the car, but when he heard him say that, it put the fight back into him.

"You keep yer hands offn my girl," he howled. "She ain't done a thang."

"In the car. Now."

Dad stiffened and stood. He snuffled and spat out a glob of blood. I should have prayed or something, because this was going to get really bad.

Another car came blasting into the lot, no siren, but a blue light was whirling in the windshield.

"Teddy!" Vann jumped out. "What's going on here?"

"Someone called in and said Andy was beating a man to death. Lucky I was right on the highway, 'cause I figure Farley was about set to kill him back."

"He's drunk! Can't you see? He can't help it!" I was crying, and so mad at myself for letting the tears come.

"This one—" the deputy said.

"I'll take care of her. You get this organized."

Vann took me by the wrist and led me back down to the store. I wanted to pull my hand away from him, but I didn't. Inside he sat me in a chair, pulled a wad of paper towels off the roll, and handed it to me.

I wiped my eyes that wouldn't stop leaking. I wiped my face over and over, even after I wasn't really crying anymore.

"You can put the horn down, I think."

I looked at my hand. I was still clutching the air horn in a death grip. "It was the only thing I could think of to do."

"Stupid to get between two men."

I shrugged. "I didn't want you all here."

"Yeah, I can imagine."

I blew my nose and wiped the tears and snot off my hands. I started to feel shaky, as if I'd been doing battle myself.

"You want something to drink? Water, Coke?"

"We only carry Pepsi," I said, a lame joke, but he smiled. "I think I'd really like a cup of coffee."

He gave me a thumbs-up (a plain wedding ring glinted) and went to the coffee pot. "I like sugar and creamer." He added the lightener, stirred, and handed it to me. It tasted terrible, but great too.

"What happened out there?"

"Dad's really drunk."

"I could see that. So why did he go after Farley? Bad choice, by the way—he played tackle at State for a couple of years."

I could see Dad in the back of the patrol car. He was slumped over, his head against the wire mesh, like a dog in a cage. Part of me wanted to go hug him, and part of me wanted to smack him silly.

"I've never seen Drew like this," Vann said, probing.

"He was trying to quit drinking. He did quit for a while. Then he got a letter back from my mother and he went and emptied out the liquor store. He's been pretty messed up ever since."

"Angela wrote to him?" He bent his head like he was trying to see around me.

"You know about my so-called mother?"

"A bit. But she wrote back to him?"

I sucked down some more coffee. There was a lot I couldn't tell him. "His letter came back with her handwriting on it, he said. The envelope."

"So was it her handwriting?"

"How the hell would I know?"

He held up both hands. "Peace."

I didn't mean to sound so angry at him, but inside I was just a volcano. Dad had completely quit drinking, for two whole weeks, but one piece of mail and it was like before. Worse than before.

"You calmed down now?"

I nodded, but it was a lie.

He went out, the doormat bing-bonging that happy little tune, and closed the door firmly.

I went to the window to watch. The deputy was sitting at a picnic table with the Pepsi man, taking a report down on a clipboard. Farley was holding his ear and it made me feel good that I got a little lick in the fight. Vann loped up and touched the deputy on the shoulder. They went to the cruiser and sat in the front. I could see by how they were turned around that they were talking to Dad.

I breathed in, until I'd filled all my insides with air, and then I breathed out until I felt like I'd faint. Again. *Take a deep breath, Maggie, and be ready for whatever.*

Vann got out of the car and the deputy stayed inside talking with Dad. The ambulance arrived and the medics brought out their bags. The detective waved them back and they stood, waiting. No major emergency here. Vann sat down with Farley, and at first I saw Farley shaking his head. Over and over. Vann kept talking. Finally the driver nodded, once, short, and then he nodded again. Vann motioned the medics to come over and he walked back to the cruiser. I saw the deputy roll down the window, and Vann leaned in. Finally, the deputy came around and let Dad out of the back seat. He stood up awkwardly and fell against the car. When I saw the handcuffs it just about broke my heart. How did it feel to have those metal cuffs locked on his wrists? Sobering? I wish. Cold, tight on his wrists. Even a little exciting in a weird way that I didn't want to think about too much. I wondered if he'd ever been handcuffed before.

The deputy led him over to where the medics were patching up Farley. I saw Dad, his head down, talking, apologizing, I guess. The deputy had Farley sign something, then he unlocked the handcuffs and gave Dad a pink ticket. One of the medics detached from Farley and started working on Dad. I didn't know if he was going to jail, but apparently not right at the moment.

I thought it was all over, but here came Vann again. He walked like a heron, long legs carefully lifted.

I went behind the counter and stared out over the lake, trying to appear as if I was absorbed in how the fuzzy mallard ducklings had transformed into adults, like their parents but a little smaller. They all swam around together and unless you looked closely you wouldn't know the real adults from the babies.

Bing-bong.

"Hey, Maggie."

I turned around. I was calm now. "I see you got a new ride."

"Oh. What? Yeah, the car. Nice to have air conditioning. It's going to be all right. I got Farley to agree not to press criminal charges, long as your dad made everything right with the doctor bills and his uniform."

"He didn't hurt him bad?"

"I think you did the worst damage."

I tried not to smile. I had been through scared and angry and past sad and was back to mad. I didn't want to let go of mad that easy. "What am I supposed to *do* with him?" Vann looked at me with those dog-brown eyes and didn't say a thing. "He's great, a great dad, but when he drinks he turns into something else."

"Are you afraid of him?"

Watch out. I could feel the trap in that. If I said yes, then they might arrest him or put me in some vile foster home like Geena Hibbs got stuck in.

"No. I know what to expect. He gets drunk and he cries and writes letters and then he goes to sleep."

"And you're okay with that? With living like that?"

Not really. But the alternatives were worse. Maybe even living at the Plantation and all that implied. I hated both Dad and my mother for screwing up their lives and mine along with them. I hated them with white-hot hatred. The volcano started boiling again and I felt my hands shake. Maybe that was how Dad came to pick a fight with Farley. That lava boiling around inside.

I looked at Drexel Vann, calm and quiet and sure, and I knew that, in spirit, he wasn't some beat-up johnboat or even a fast bass boat, but a sailboat. A classic daysailer, clean-lined and reliable, moving through tacks like an eagle riding the wind. He was the surest thing I knew in the world.

I stood up and dug in the watch pocket of my jeans. I felt the ring, thin and slippery, shifting around down there in the seams. I got my finger into it and pulled it out.

"Here. You should take this." I dropped it on the counter. Too late to take it back now, and I went shaky in a whole other way.

He looked at the silver ring, gleaming on the glass. The circle of it surrounded one of the little islands on the lake chart underneath. Then he looked back at me, and I knew that he knew exactly what it was, but he was going to make me explain. Part of me wanted to make something up, to tell a really elaborate, perfect lie, but I couldn't look into his eyes and do it. So I did the right thing. I told him about Charisse and the kiss and the old house, the lightning and thunder coming closer, the smell of flowers, and what she told me about the guy who tried to rape her, and the ring.

After I was all through, he picked it up and looked inside it for the inscription. He shook his head. "We've been looking for this."

"I know I shouldn't have kept it."

"It's pretty important."

"I couldn't tell you about it before."

"You know why it's important?"

I thought I knew, from TV shows, but I thought I'd best not be saying anything right now.

"We call it a trophy. Some kinds of criminals, sexual criminals, will keep things from their victims, so they can remember them and relive the crime. Often it's jewelry. We didn't put the ring in any of the reports. That's how we narrow the real suspects down from people who make false confessions."

I guess I looked strange, because he then said that people did that sometimes, people who liked attention or people who were troubled. He called them troubled, not crazy.

"We had an alert at the pawn shops and flea markets, for the ring. That's why Nathanael got caught; we also had the bracelet listed."

Poor Nat.

"I had it all along. She gave it to me. Really." I looked at him, wondering if I had just sunk myself after all. "You don't think…"

"You haven't made it any easier for us. Fletcher?"

I felt my face get red.

"But I'm happy that you finally came clean about this. Every little piece helps. Someday it will all add up."

He pushed the ring around on the counter. Then he picked it up and put it in his pocket.

I didn't want him to go, not yet. I knew I had to give him something more, something to keep him listening.

"Maybe…"

He stopped with his foot on the mat. *Bing-bong, bing-bong.* He took his hand off the doorknob and came back.

"Maybe what?"

"It's nothing. I think." He waited. "Last week. I was at the bathhouse, taking a shower. I always lock the outside door now, unless it's the weekend when we're busy. I heard the door rattle. I said to hold on, I'd be right there. I thought it was a woman, right?"

He nodded, his eyes dark and concerned.

"But the door kept rattling. I tried to look through the ventilation slats but the window is too high. All I could see was the top of a hat. I thought it was a man so I said the men's side was around the other end. He just stood there."

"Could you see his face?"

I shook my head.

"Anything else?"

I thought about *Law and Order* and what they asked people to describe. I remembered Dad standing by the door when we were painting the bathhouse and used that to estimate. "About six foot tall."

"That's good. *Good.* What was he wearing?"

"All I could see was the top of the hat, faded-out green or gray or blue."

"What happened then?"

"I wrapped a towel around me and grabbed my phone to call, but when I looked again, he was gone. I got dressed and waited till I saw someone else come, one of the regular boaters, and when he was leaving I walked out beside him."

"You had a bad feeling about this guy."

I nodded. Yeah, I did. One of those animal, instinctual feelings.

Vann came back to the counter. He put his hands on it and looked into my eyes, seriously serious.

"I want you to be careful. Even more careful than you've been. This may be nothing. But we still don't know who the killer is."

"You think it was him."

"I don't know." I thought he was lying. No, not telling the whole truth. "If it was, then I think we are looking for someone local, not a drifter who happened through and is gone. Someone living around here, maybe even someone you know."

I started to catalog every guy in the marina, in the area around. Too many to think of. This was the guy making the constructions, I was sure now. I wanted Vann to know about them, in one way, but I hadn't told Dad, hadn't told anyone. Who would believe me anyway?

"It could have been nothing." Reassurance, nice try, but I didn't believe it. "Don't fret over it, but be careful. Don't wander around alone. Okay? Will you do that for me?"

"Yes."

I looked at his plain, competent hands, the wedding ring and the flat little hairs on the backs of his fingers. The cheap Timex watch with a second hand that clicked around the dial.

"I wish Dad were more like you."

Vann stood back. Maybe he heard more than what I had said out loud, what was in my thoughts.

"Maggie, listen, I care about you, about your well-being." He let out a long breath. "But this is a case—a job—and I have to see it through. Whatever happens. I can't be your dad. Drew's a good man—"

"Even if he's *troubled*."

He bit his lip. "Maybe you could try to reach out more to him."

The detective turned and went out without another word. I thought about the letter Dad wrote, and the one that I'd written back. I never saw it again. *Yeah, reach out.*

I saw him and Dad meet at the top of the walkway. The ambulance was leaving. The Pepsi driver pulled away without completing the delivery. It was all over.

40

Turn on your chat whydontcha?
The email looked like spam at first, and I almost deleted it, until I realized the name made sense. NatHimself. Nat! I went over to chat right away.

You're hard to get hold of.

Guess so.

Yr Facebook is gone.

Yeah too much.

Sure. Instagram? Snapchat?

No way. Whatcha doing?

Using computers at the library. Cool place.

Where RU?

Greensboro. Like a palace. Got this big metal tree growing in the center of the rm. Nice.

Why Greensboro?

Y not?

Thot U'd be far away.

Far enuf.

U OK?

Yeah. Staying at Urban Ministry. Good 2 me.

Shelter?

Yeah.

Working?

GED then maybe comm. coll. Program fr homeless HS kids.

Good.

How's London Hi this yr?

Same. I'm getting stuff 2gether for college. Maybe scholarship.

Straight.

Yeah.

How R my parents?

Ok I guess. U don't talk?

They don't answer.

R U scared?

No. Are you scared?

No.

Good.

41

Mitochondria." Mr. Palko paused dramatically. "Mitochondria are membrane-enclosed—what—?"
A few ragged voices. *Organelles.*
"Organelles characteristic of the eukaryotic, or nucleated, cell. They are the Duke Power of the cell."

He liked analogies, metaphors, some of them pretty·weird for a science teacher. He always seemed to me to be somewhat like a small stalking bird, something fairly short-legged and compact. Walking quietly around the classroom when we worked, his yellowish eyes alert and probing, his hair a bit too long and hanging on his neck like breeding plumes. But I like him. He's smart and he expects us to be smart too.

He drew a thing like a cold capsule on the whiteboard, and filled it with dots and rippled things. "Mitochondria are semi-autonomous—they have their own DNA ribosomes, they can make proteins—they are in fact believed to have descended from free-living prokaryotic cells. They exist inside the nucleated cells of our bodies in a symbiotic relationship."

Mr. Palko began drawing organelles on the whiteboard in a weird purple color, like the color of cells stained on a slide. Maybe that's why he chose that color. The circles and rods and curly things proliferated. It was modern art, if you left out the labels printed in his square all-capitals style—GRANULES and CRISTAE—under each element.

It was a small class for AP Environmental Science, barely enough of us to allow the school to justify it every other year. We clustered up at the tables near the front. The same black lab tables used for chemistry and physics classes, with the sink and gas tap for the Bunsen burner. My partner was Marsha Bainbridge. I always hated that name—Marsha—instead of Marcia, the right way to spell it. Marsha—like something that came out of the swamp. But Marsha, despite her screwed-up name, wasn't so bad. Just a plain average girl, not pretty, not ugly. She was going to attend UNC and major in chemistry. She didn't talk much, but no one did in there, because there was way too much to pay attention to when Mr. Palko was lecturing, and so it didn't feel as obvious as the silence at lunch or around the lockers.

People don't know what to say to me. Some of them just don't say anything at all. I mean, what can they say? Sorry about what happened in the spring. Find any more bodies out there? Do you miss Charisse? Are you still a suspect? Whatever happened to Fletcher? Where's Nat?

It's just the way things are, that humans tend to form up into couples and groups and gangs, and in those groups people can talk to each other even if it's uncomfortable. When we were Portly and Aimless and Asshole, then we could talk about anything and everything. But once Nat took off, the group fell apart. Hulky stays away from me on girlfriend orders. Nat was the glue, the one that pulled us together, his skewed intelligence like a black hole that kept us spinning around together like planets that didn't belong together otherwise.

I'd felt pretty lost this past summer. The whole Charisse thing had busted us apart. For a while we were like survivors floating in the ocean, trying to hang on to a single piece of wood but cold and isolated from each other. Then Nat took off and it was just me and Dad. I thought I would really go crazy for lack of the others, but by the end of the summer, it was okay. I'd adapted. Successful creatures adapt. I worry some about Nat, because I don't hear from him much, and that's meant all sorts of scenarios working themselves out in my head. He's alone out there and I'm alone here. People always thought I was the capable one and Nat wasn't, but I think we both have learned how to solo.

I saw Mr. Palko give me a look and realized I was staring sideways out the window. He was talking about microbes.

"...ancient microbes live on inside our cells. At some point they became part of us, so they are immortal, invaders from the distant past which have found a way to hitchhike into immortality."

"Like *Alien?*" Forrest was always blurting out something about a movie or video game.

God! I thought about the chest-burster blowing open the guy's body, what was his name? And the creature sticking up out of the bloody hole like a toothy sock puppet.

"No, not really," Mr. Palko reflected. He would have seen the movie, sure. "That was a predatory process, a parasitical mechanism for reproduction. The host dies. Every time. Not really very efficient, is it? Here the organisms slid inside the larger cells or were incorporated or encapsulated, and they made themselves at home, helped out, found a task they could perform."

"Like my older brother coming home after he lost his job."

"Hmmmm. No, not that, exactly. He was already a part of the organism, the family."

"What is this, social studies?" Greg had no patience with thought exercises. He was a believer in statistics and probability, which meant he'd end up a math teacher or actuary, because you have to have an imagination for pure mathematics. As Mr. Palko says, Science is first imagination.

"I know! It's like a roomer. You put a sign out by the road, Room for Rent, and someone pays you to live in the spare bedroom." Everyone kind of looked sideways at Ranelle, wondering if that was what they were doing at her house. Her dad had been laid off forever and the cosmetics plant where her mom worked just cut hours and ended the third shift.

"Closer. I'll suggest this: A stranger comes along by night and you find him sleeping on the porch in the morning. He offers to cut the grass, to pay for intruding. And you let him sleep on the porch or over the garage, and pretty soon he's eating dinner with you. He becomes part of the household, helps out. He never leaves."

As Mr. Palko ended his speculation, I felt a buzz in my pocket. I peeked to see it was Dad, hit ignore, and tried to look studious.

The class ended with assignments for next week and reminders about projects. While Mr. Palko was erasing the board, I checked my messages.

U R coming right home after school right

About the same thing he asked every day, as though I had someplace to go or someone to go with. I guess he was just as lonely as I was. No wonder he was sort of drunk just about all the time. First my so-called mother, then me with the Charisse mess that dragged us both in and hurt business, too, though it was hard to say if the dock tenants pulling out and the lack of fishermen roaring in for gas could be attributed to the murder or to the drought that had pulled the lake down so low, or even to the new marina. We were watching for hurricanes, with anticipation this year rather than dread. A slow-moving tropical storm, not a Cat 5. We could use a big dump of rain. And for any storm there was always the anticipation and the preparations, walking the docks and making sure all the boats were double-lined and the sails and canvas secured. People racing in to pull the booms and foresails off their sailboats, and needing new line or bungees, and wanting to talk about the storm and what it was likely to do. The activity would probably bust him out of this whole depressed mess over me and the ongoing eternal Angela thing. He'll love her forever, just the way he writes in his letters. If that's what love causes, then I'll skip it. Love, lust, reproduction of the species, whatever. It was probably intended that creatures like me and Nat didn't pass down our genes.

"So, Maggie."

Mr. Palko was standing behind me. I don't know how he got there. Stalking behavior, yep.

"Sorry."

He waved it away, as though getting a mosquito out of the room.

"You need to be getting your college applications together. I hope you're on track for biology?"

I nodded. Still ashamed for zoning out in my favorite class.

"Are you still planning on UNCW? Great opportunities there—the Center for Marine Science—working out on the Shackleford Banks, the channels, Wrightsville."

Bang. I could see Wrightsville Beach, the morning all the Portuguese men-of-war had come in. Early morning, breaking day, and the tide returning. All down the beach, the crimped floats shone in the sun as it broke through the clouds. They were clear and iridescent, the tentacles a gooey magenta mass but still dangerous. One float, the top crimped together like plastic that had been heat-sealed, was inching a rubbery foot toward the water, still alive. The base of the float had a greenish liquid like a bottle that had been left with water in it and algae had grown and bloomed. Was the liquid a part of the organism, or a symbiont, or just dying organs? After hearing this lecture, I wondered if it was one of those fusions. Those men-of-war shining all down the beach had been like an invasion from space, innocent-looking things that were strange and deadly.

Mr. Palko was still rattling on about UNCW and the Bermuda program and the oyster hatchery and God knows what else. His long hair bounced on his neck as he nodded and gestured. I wondered if he had a wife or girlfriend to tell him when it got too long. Mr. Palko in love. It was a little strange to think about your teacher having a sex life, like penguins or elephants.

"How's the essay coming?"

That was one question I could answer. I'd been working on it in study hall, which wasn't the most conducive to real writing but better than at home these days.

"Here, I have a copy." I opened my notebook and pulled out the one I'd made for him.

COLLEGE ESSAY (draft)

If I were going to list one of my strongest points, it would be my sense of balance. You see, I grew up most of my life around water, and I sail. I also live on a houseboat at a marina. You learn how to feel how a boat is moving, even a houseboat, and you balance yourself automatically. That kind of ability to adjust is important in life because you never know when things are going to shift under your feet and you have to have the instinct to know where to jump. My strongest points also include the ability to observe. I spend a lot of time looking at natural things and I notice little things. I see deer moving in the woods and birds deep in trees. Most of my friends don't see anything—even something as big as a red-tailed hawk sitting on a branch beside the road. I trained myself to do this by following the example of my hero, Carl von Linne, also known as Linnaeus. He looked at everything, not just plants and animals but people, traveling around Finland and seeing what people did and how they ate and worked. He wrote books on nature and came up with the idea of classifying all life into Orders and Families and Genera and Species that we still use today. This was so that everyone would be able to describe the natural world by the same names rather than local ones. And you can see how things are related, like a family tree.

I have read his travels and learned how to see even how one plant grows tall in a patch of sunlight or in good soil, while the same one six feet away is impoverished by the place where the seed fell.

I believe that I would make an excellent student in marine biology because of these two strengths. I don't have any background in the sciences, so far as my parents go, but my father has taught me how to tear down boat engines and patch fiberglass. I've learned practical skills from him that would be helpful as well.

"Getting into the Parables, eh?" Mr. Palko said.

I didn't know what he meant, but I nodded anyway.

"Keep working on it. Your grades are fine but they look at all these other things. What about clubs?"

"I'm not a joiner, Mr. Palko."

"I know, Maggie, I know. I never was either. But you do belong to something?"

"Honor Society. Track. And your Ecology Club, of course."

"Of course. Maybe I can find us some other opportunities. Clean Sweep, even picking up trash with the Adopt-a-Highway looks good."

I wanted to include my real work, about the observations I'd made and the notebooks where I'd written about the natural life around the marina. He'd seen them and thought they were good, but then sometimes I thought outsiders would think they were childish. Maybe I could add something about my work with the paragraph about Linnaeus.

"This part about living at the marina is good. They like to see how your personal life connects with your studies."

"Okay."

I wondered about the people who made the admission decisions. Did they really ponder all this stuff? I wondered if I should get really personal and include something about Charisse, since everyone seemed to know about it. It seemed like it, but maybe not. Why would anyone at UNCW know about what happened in London County? But it wasn't that far, and maybe they would.

Or maybe I should look at going somewhere else. Leave the state. Go to Woods Hole or somewhere.

"Is there another college I should try, Mr. Palko?"

He fixed me with his yellowish stare. "Why? There are other programs, of course, but you'd be in-state at Wilmington, and you already know the coast."

Yeah, I knew the coast. I knew the inlets and islands, the wildlife. But it might be good to get really far away, like Maine or California, away from Dad, away from the backwater, away from everything.

I kept thinking about Wrightsville. We had been staying at this cheap hotel—more like cabins. The memory came up like jellyfish on the tide, pushed up to where it couldn't be ignored. I was walking on the beach at night, a windy starless night, and I was stumbling in the rough places and sandcastle digs, sand stinging in my face. Crying and walking. The salt wind and the blown sand and the roar of the waves that drowned out everything. I was walking toward the lights, the big hotel called the Blockade Runner, and people were outside dancing and drinking, and I wondered if there would be terrible fights in there, too, and name calling and things crashing and bruised faces, in those nice hotel rooms.

My phone buzzed again.

"You'd better be getting to your next class," Mr. Palko said at the same time.

I nodded and picked up my books and looked at the message as I walked out.

What's for dinner tonite I cn get something.

He didn't sound drunk but you couldn't really tell.

I needed to talk with him about college, about tuition and loans and applications and FAFSA and all of that. But even when he was pretty much sober, Dad always turned any conversation to questions about boys and sex and Nat and the mess with Charisse, all stuff I didn't need to be worrying about right now.

The hallway was getting quiet—I was late for history. Damn. I started walking fast and it seemed like I heard someone say "Fletcher," but probably it was only my imagination.

42

I felt for my pocketknife, slid it out of my pocket, and held it in my hand. It had only a four-inch blade, but it could do some damage. I thought about throat and eyes and the big artery in the leg.

I kept walking, just like before, kicking along the dirt track that ran between the machine sheds and the marina road, pretending that I hadn't heard the crunch of a footstep behind me, when I stopped abruptly to look at a green damselfly. It was so damn quiet, no sound of anyone working with the tractor or getting gas. Dad was in the store, I knew that.

I turned, my mouth set to scream, the knife in my hands as I thumbed the blade out to defend myself.

Someone was hiding, back in the trees. Movement, a flash of white.

"Who's there?"

"Me, Guillermo." He stepped out. "Do not be afraid."

"What are you doing?" My voice came out too loud and too shrill.

He hung his head.

Oh no. He *couldn't* be the one. Not Guillermo. Maybe Guillermo. No, not him. I kept the knife in my hand and started backing away. "What are you doing?" I asked, though he wasn't doing anything but standing at the moment.

"I am watching you."

Great. Creep. *Creep.*

"For your papa. He said, Guillermo, watch my little girl. So I watch."

Oh. I let my breath out.

He kept on looking at the knife.

"Do I have any other minders?"

He half-closed one eye and tilted his head.

"Anyone else following me around? Pastor? Mario?"

"No, I watch. I have—keep eyes?—keep eyes when I can, when I see you go walk."

I closed up the knife and shoved it back in my pocket.

"Crimony, you scared me sneaking around like that. You know?" I started walking toward the store, feeling a little like I was being herded that way anyway as Guillermo came up next to me.

I was going to give Dad some grief about this. And the detective, who must have ratted me out about the thing at the bathhouse.

It must have made Guillermo feel bad to get caught. Not so good at being a PI. Surprising that Dad hadn't hired one, come to think of it.

"So are you going to quit following me?"

"I do not want to do this, Miss Maggie." He must have picked that up from Pastor and Lawyer; Black people always said Miss or Mrs. "You father, he is the boss, so I do it. But it is not good."

He looked really uncomfortable, his face dark with embarrassment. "Please do not be angry."

I watched him walk away, fast.

And I figured that it must have been Guillermo, hoped it was him anyway, those times I felt that crawl-up-the-back sense of someone out there in the woods, watching me.

But maybe—those few wonderful moments when I knew I really was alone at last, free of it all, without anyone intruding on my world—this summer when I gloried in the sun in my secret hiding place, maybe I wasn't alone there, either.

Now I was ashamed, and I hung back until he was out of sight.

43

From Lachesis Lapponicus

…They do not, like us, compute time by the month, but by the course of their various holidays. They have also a name for every week. They are unable to tell when an eclipse of the sun or the moon is to be expected.

The Laplanders consult several natural objects by way of a compass as they travel.

1) Large pine-trees, which bear more copious branches on their southern side than towards the north.

2) Ant-hills, the south sides of which bear grass, the northern whortle-berries.

3) Aspen trees, whose bark is rough on the north side, smooth on the opposite part.

4) Old withered pines are clothed, on the north side, with the black Usnea, or filamentous Lichen (*L. jubatus*).

44

I was also shown the Agaric of the Willow (Boletus suaveo-lens Fl. Lapp. N. 552), which has a very fragrant scent. The people assured me it was formerly the fashion for young men, when going to visit their mistresses, to use this fungus as a perfume, in order to render themselves more agreeable.*

This page was yellow and torn at the edge, but it was safe inside the binder even on this dampish day. I was walking the remains of the railroad tracks, after the rain. This was a good time of the year for mushrooms, especially after a rain, and this part of the woods was the best. I had to bring Carl along, because he would have loved it.

The asterisk, by the way, referred to a long footnote at the bottom of the page.

*I must here present the English reader with a passage on this subject from the *Flora Lapponica*. "The Lapland youth, having found this Agaric, carefully preserves it in a little pocket hanging at his waist, that its grateful perfume may render him more acceptable to his favourite fair-one. O whimsical Venus! in other regions you must be treated with coffee and chocolate, preserves and sweetmeats, wines and dainties, jewels and pearls, gold and silver, silks and cosmetics, balls and assemblies, music and theatrical exhibitions: here you are satisfied with a little withered fungus!"

I think I liked this editor or translator almost as much as Carl. He was named J. E. Smith. I imagined that he must have been fairly young as well, from notes he wrote like this, and he had a sense of humor. Not an adventurer, but he wanted to be. Maybe he was sickly, or crippled, sitting at his high desk and dipping a pen in an inkwell to make notes and dream. When I tried to picture him, he seemed to look like Nat, hair falling across his high forehead, wearing a black coat and ruffled shirt. The soft rain that had filled the air for three days had stopped yesterday evening. Now everything was damp and quiet. The sky was still gray but the fog was lifting and the clouds were thinning. It would be sunny by afternoon. Boats would be out and then I'd be stuck behind the counter, so this was my time. Just me and the jays, the only birds bold enough to make a racket on such a gentle morning.

The big mushrooms were easy to see, huge white plates, but I liked to look closely for the small caps poking through the leaf litter. I had a list from last fall, what I had found. *Boletales*, fleshy and stumpy, or shaped like umbrellas blown out by the wind. *Agaric*s and puffballs and of course bracket fungi on the tree trunks.

This time I had a book with color plates, bought with my birthday money, not just the pamphlet from the university with drawings.

It felt good to be somewhat free again. The fear that had clamped down on the marina during the spring and summer had relaxed bit by bit. The police didn't have any more clues; nothing more had happened around the marina; I'd found no more stick huts. Everyone was starting to think maybe it really was just one of those things, a horrible happenstance of some drifter who had followed Charisse and maybe picked the lock on the boat or found it open. He was long gone, not coming back to the scene of the crime. Dad had let up on me, after I swore to be super careful, and today when I put an apple in my pocket and took a bottle of water, he didn't warn me about where to go or when to be back. I hugged him for trusting my good sense.

The land around the lake was mostly owned by the Corps of Engineers. They leased the marina property to Mr. Malouf. Some people had land that went down to the water, but they could build only so close because of the fluctuations, so you couldn't see any houses except when the leaves fell. People used to live here, of course. Farmers and plantation owners back in the day. The government bought them out and what they left behind was flooded, burned, or let go to rot in the woods. There were old fences, chimneys, cellar holes, even wells. You could get into real trouble if you went wandering around and didn't watch where you put your feet. This raised path was an easy walk. Straight, no holes or tangles of barbed wire. It had been the bed of a railroad that hauled out timber. At school, right in the entrance, is a picture of the trestle that used to take the railroad over the valley—so deep that the bottom of the lake is eighty feet down in the channel. It was called the Queenshope Trestle, after the cross-roads they thought would be the county seat but that withered away when the trestle burned and the trains stopped. It was all long enough ago that good-sized trees are growing in the middle of the tracks.

I saw a yellow cap and stepped down to get closer. I took out the book and checked the plates. *Amanita gemmata*, yellow now, but it would widen out into an orange flying saucer eventually. I hoped I'd find chanterelles or a *marasmius*, the handsomest of all, fluted red like a parasol, pure white on the underside. Puffballs matured from ping-pong ball to tennis ball to softball and bigger, until at last they would exhaust their smoky spores and collapse. They weren't the strangest. Jelly fungi looked like peach preserves gone bad, and weirdest of all, slime molds existed in a place somewhere between plant and animal. They could move, crawling along in search of damp rotted wood, sometimes raising themselves to let loose a cloud of spores.

The jays screamed, and wrens set up a racket, but otherwise the woods were as quiet as a blanket pulled over your head. I almost started to whistle. I sat on a tree trunk and ate my apple, looking deep into the woods to find shapes that broke the pattern, or a bit of color.

A squirrel chattered, and then another. I watched to see what had them alarmed.

There was no wind, but across a space of fallen trees and tangles of grapevine, a branch moved. I froze and watched. A deer, probably, or maybe turkeys foraging. I wondered what I'd do if a bear came out.

The squirrels had fallen silent. Another branch moved, on a holly that was thick and green in the yellowing woods.

A spot of white.

Damn Guillermo, already tailing me again!

And then the pattern resolved out of the background. A man's face shadowed by a faded hat. Just a glimpse of open mouth and beard and deep-set eyes. Not Guillermo. Then the face was gone, with the crash of brush, going the other way, and I fled down the rail bed, the fastest way to the road. I left my apple and water but not Carl, never Carl, not unless he was the last thing between me and whatever.

45

Saturday, and the Filliyaw Pointe Yacht Club was assembling for a round-the-buoys race and cookout. I stood pumping gas into a speedboat, watching the boats turn to the wind, one by one, cut their power and hoist sails. They became new creatures as they heeled to the force of the westerly, no longer wallowing along on the push of a propeller. *Bellatrix* pulled at her lines, as though she, too, could see the procession of boats dipping and galloping over the chop.

"Soon, baby, soon," I whispered.

The man in the speedboat turned his face up, quizzical. I looked far away, toward the sailboats and the islands.

"Eighty-two fifty," I told him.

"Credit card?"

"My dad's inside and he'll ring you up."

I put the nozzle back on its hook and watched the last of the big boats, an old Catalina 30 called *Windrift*, catch the breeze in her worn sails. I could have raised my arms and taken off just the same way, I was so full of the urge to fly. Instead, I was stuck at the store, frozen to the dock like the late mayflies clinging to the lights and the cleats. Amazing creatures, soft as butter, variable in green and beige, but the nuptial flights they made at night left them clumsy the next morning, hypnotized by the sun. On land, I was about as stuck. The only time I had wings was on *Bellatrix*.

A black-haired woman much younger than the boat driver sat on one of the cream-colored benches facing aft. She ignored me as if I were a piece of equipment. When the driver came out and started the engine and I cast off and tossed in the line, he gave me a cheery wave—but as the boat turned and her gaze crossed my path, there wasn't a flicker of interest. It seemed like that was her permanent expression, boredom. Maybe she was just Botoxed too much, I don't know. I wondered if that's how my mother looked, riding around on her giant yacht in Miami. Didn't seem like it was worth it.

I took a rag and wiped the bird poop and cobwebs from the throw rings mounted on either end of the gas dock. From the farther end I could see the race going on. It looked like a triangle course. They didn't set rounding marks, just used the Aids-to-Navigation buoys. Unlike a one-design race, where dinghies were matched against others that were just the same, Blue Jays or Lasers or Flying Scots, the big boats used Portsmouth Handicap ratings. More like golf. You could have a slow old tub and still win the race, once the times were computed against the handicap.

"Hey, punkin." Dad was leaning out the door. "I can cover this," he said. "Why don't you knock off and take your boat out for a while?"

"Yessss!!" I pumped my fist and he grinned. He was really trying these days, his drinking down to mostly beer and not too much liquor. We were both feeling better, but it wasn't something we talked about. Like the letter I wrote back to him. I was sure he had read it, but he'd never mentioned it. I was afraid to wake up the booze monster so I walked pretty light and tried to be a good kid. I didn't expect it to last, but for now, it was okay.

I stowed the rag in the bin and ran up for a quick pee, hoping that a crowd of boats didn't come in and cause Dad to change his mind. But the dock was clear when I got back, so I waved at him as I walked by the lakeside window, and within minutes I had the mainsail cover off and the jib hanked on, and I was ready to cast off. My hat, sunscreen, PFD, trimmer's gloves, everything I needed was already in the boat.

I raised the jib and let the light breeze take me out of the slip, then turned the tiller and trimmed the sheets until the sail was full and the telltales lofting nicely. Once we were away from the marina, I hauled up the main. As we came around to just forward of a beam reach, *Bellatrix* heeled and took off. I leaned back to balance the boat, and looked up into the white sail, like a cloud against a perfect clear blue sky.

A single monarch butterfly floated past, headed south. "Hello, sister," I said.

I came up on the bottom leg of the racecourse. Most of the boats were flying the FPYC pennant from their mastheads, although I saw several without and a couple that showed the red burgee of the club near Clarksville. As I sailed to the lee of the racers, each of the helmsmen waved in turn—*Bonny Gal, Angelfire, Peregrine, Gail Force, Olyve Oyl, Sunrise, Driven, Son of a Sailor, Blue Eyes.* I counted nearly all of them as customers and some of them as friends.

Water burbled past the centerboard and tiller, a merry tune known only by sailors. I pitied people who'd only ever been out in powerboats, their experience of water and wind erased by the roar of the engine and the stink of gasoline. Like driving a Hummer up a hiking trail—you get there faster, but you haven't gained a thing.

Along the shore, tickseed was blooming bright yellow in the waste places. Where old roads and rail beds showed in the forest, patches of the flower made golden inlets among the trees.

I heard the jib begin to flog and realized I'd been easing the tiller as I studied the trees. I fell off until the sails were drawing well. The west wind was steady, even if my hand wasn't. I could reach all the way up the lake on this breeze. That's why fall sailing was the best—the winds tended to be more even, not gusty like spring, or dropping off to cat's-paws and dead calms like in summer.

The Society Islands grew from green blobs to red-rimmed hillocks with rocks and the broken trunks of dead, drowned forests showing between. Some of the channels that I could blow through when the lake was at full pool were chancy now unless I raised the centerboard. With the lake so low, you had a better sense of what this area looked like before the dam: rounded little hills, with creeks flowing in narrow valleys into the river.

On the point opposite the islands a pair of bald eagles had built a giant stick pile in the top of a dying tree. Two young eagles had fledged, wearing brown feathers like a golden eagle, without the "all field mark" white head and white tail of the adults. They circled the water in front of the point, diving and flaring their talons and then screeching away. I didn't see a fish caught. They'd keep trying until they learned, or starved. I dropped the main, raised the board, and let momentum and a loosely held jib carry me onto the beach at Bora Bora. It felt weird to be back. I had sailed up a couple of times since the spring, but never landed, just sailed around. I saw a small copperhead in the water as I stepped out. I dropped the sails, tiger-tied the main to the boom, and fixed the painter to a sturdy tree.

Maybe I was wrong, but it seemed like the area was much cleaner. Had the partyers stayed away with the low water? Or had a better class of people begun taking their good times away with them instead of leaving it all on the beach? A few beer cans, a bait container, not much. The remains of a dead carp lay beside the Y-sticks of bank fishing. Ugly things, carp, water-fouling creatures with coarse scales and vacuum mouths. They weren't native here anyway but brought over from Europe. Carl had made detailed examinations of the carp he found in Lapland. Genus *Cyprinius*. He called them "nondescript" but he still wrote down every detail—body color, spots, the shape of the nostrils and tongue. He noted that they did not have teeth, and that the tail was forked. There was not a gray bug or clump of grass that seemed to be beneath his notice. I tried to be as observant. A light-brown caterpillar humped along a twig. A blowfly buzzed the carcass but didn't land—apparently too dry for its purposes. Carl must have felt just as free, far from the schoolrooms of Sweden, away from the stuffy priests and townspeople. He was among people who slept naked and lived healthy lives. He could think and write without someone telling him how to do either one. Here in the Society Islands, I could breathe. No one was watching me—not Dad, not Guillermo, not Vann. Not the weird face appearing in the woods. True freedom. If this were a real island in the ocean, I could be as true to myself as Robinson Crusoe, inventing my own way of living.

I walked up one of the hills at the center of the island. The oak trees were still covered in dull green. The grassy bowl where I'd found the campsite, and where I used to dream of lying beside Fletcher, was as inviting as ever, sheltered between the two hills.

But I knew where Fletcher had come from and I didn't dream anymore. I didn't want there to be a Fletcher, real or imagined. I didn't want there to be anyone that I had to be accountable to or take care of. I wanted to be free. Like Rima. I took off my shirt and the air felt sweet. I took off everything and didn't feel like it was a sin or anything, just took off all my clothes and lay honestly under the sun. This was the last free place I had, the lonely woods and the secret place that had been mine no longer seeming safe. This was a place where I didn't have to hold my breath.

I had intended to do a lot more sailing and head for home windburned and shoulder-sore. But the sun did its thing, warm and soothing as a blanket, and I napped and dreamed about living on a boat. The boat was small as a Blue Jay when I was in the cockpit sailing it, but long stairs went below into a huge living space. It was an old, old boat inside, planked wood, teak, brass fittings on portholes. The boat was anchored in a creek mouth, and beyond, I could hear the surf crashing on a beach.

I was an eagle, flying up and down the coast, out of my nest, always on the move.

When I woke, I was curled up in the shade. The air was cooler and the sunlight slanted through the trees without much warmth. This was a new kind of secret feeling—not like the sense of being watched, which made life so unbearable around the marina, but a new feeling of being alone in the world. Untethered. It was so quiet it seemed as though everyone had disappeared while I slept. Or I'd lost my hearing. Finally, I heard a kingfisher rattle, and I let out a breath because even the impossible seemed for a little while as though it could be real.

I pulled on my clothes, feeling stiff from sleeping so deeply on the hard ground. I walked down to the beach and was almost surprised to see *Bellatrix* at rest. It seemed as if the boat from my dreams should be there, gray with sea-storms, riding at anchor. I could see the cell tower past the marina. Boats in their slips. The race was over. Everything was normal, but now seemed somehow dislocated, foreign.

Another monarch butterfly sailed over me, flapping and then gliding. Headed to Mexico, I've read, to winter in the trees and lay eggs so another generation could hatch and fly north. Hard to believe that such delicate creatures could persevere, could survive so much and fly so far.

46

I woke up to a skittering, scratching sound. I lay flat, still in my chilly bed, and waited. In my dreams it was the claws of something terrible on the roof, tearing its way inside.

The scratching began again, something hard, but random, not the sound of a bird hopping. The sound of nails dragged across the metal.

I heard waves slapping against the pontoons. I remembered waking in the night to the windy edge of a thunderstorm. *A cold front is approaching from the north*, NOAA radio had intoned yesterday afternoon. I listened for a while but didn't hear Dad snoring, so I got up and pulled my XL hoodie on over my pajamas. I walked aft, gently, balancing on my bare feet to keep the boat level. His bed was slept in but empty, the pillow bunched in a ball and the covers flung back. The ship's-wheel clock read 7:25 a.m. and it was light.

The door squawked a little when I opened it, and I winced to think of what might be alerted, but right away I realized what I'd heard earlier. The deck was littered with giant sycamore leaves, brown and curled so they stood on their points and stems like tarantulas. They were sturdy enough to skitter noisily across the roof rather than just blowing clean like the thinner, smaller leaves. One mystery solved.

I wrapped my arms around me; the air was much colder than yesterday. The sun was a yellow ball shining through a thin deck of southeasterly clouds, and steam was rising off the lake and blowing away, the water warmer than the air. Dawn glowed in the vapor, making it rags of the dead, shrouds, spirits.

I heard a truck engine and saw the lights swing through the lot and then around as Dad pulled into his parking space. He came down the ramp swinging a brown paper bag. And whistling.

I went back and pulled on my sweatpants. He yelled, "You awake yet?" as he stepped aboard.

"Yeah. Making coffee."

I was hit by the smell even before he opened the bag. He had gone down to Angler's Rest, the bait and tackle and gas and ice and beer stop where the marina road met the highway, and brought back fresh sausage biscuits for breakfast. We tore into them like wolves, the biscuits thick and crumbly, the sausage a little on the hot side with red flecks of pepper showing in the meat. They were about the best things you could get, and I dabbed up the crumbs with my fingers and we didn't leave anything when we were done but greasy papers.

Dad was quiet, but he wasn't hungover. He had had a couple of beers after dinner but I knew the bottom cupboard was clean. No bottles. Lately I had not smelled the sticky scent of rum or the hot sting of whiskey, and that had me hopeful when I was afraid to let myself feel that way. He might be getting sober. Or he might blow up again. I felt like one of those bomb-disposal people holding a sealed box, and inside was something that went tick-tick-tick. Today he had a big job ahead replacing rotted planks on the storage dock, and I guess he wasn't wanting to cut his fingers off.

"Good breakfast?" He grinned that whiskery pirate grin and I felt like I was eight years old.

"The best!"

"Should hold us till lunch, I expect. I'm going to be back on the storage dock all morning. Get yourself around quick, now?"

I knew he meant for me to shower here and stay in the office, without him having to spell it out. He grabbed his hat and took off, pulling out his cell phone to make sure that JM&J were on the way.

Showering in the nasty little cubicle was no pleasure and not much toward cleanliness. The walls were beige plastic that gave when you leaned against them, and the edges were black. The water didn't stay hot for very long. It was get wet, soap up, rinse, and get out. But I wouldn't get naked in the bathhouse alone, not in the empty days of fall, not even with the door locked.

I cranked open the little window to clear the steam. Somewhere to the west a gunshot, and then two more. Cool air whistled in and goose-bumped my wet skin. In the little mirror over the basin, distorted and streaked, I saw my nipples rise and thought about how my daydreams caused the same thing. The body had only so many responses to stimuli, even ones from very different sources. I put on some of Dad's Right Guard—I needed to get to the store sometime, and I was due for a driving lesson, as much as he hated the way I zoomed and braked. Driving was no way as intuitive as sailing. I pulled on a sports bra. My summer tan was fading, the darker shade ending at the blurry overlapping tan lines from T-shirts and bathing suit. I was returning to my ground color. Teeth brushed, hair combed, sweats, Nikes, ready for business. And it was not even nine.

The oversize wing nuts holding the window shutter/signboard—lettered CLOSED on the underside and OPEN when it was dropped down to be visible to boaters out on the lake—were balky this morning. Then the door lock stuck. I gave it a good pull and it opened anyway. It was like the door on the *Annamariner*, a cheap kind of trailer door that didn't fit right in the frame. I went to plug in the coffeepot and had the prongs the wrong way. Everything seemed to have a personal grudge against me. I got the coffee started and checked over the quarts of milk and bologna in the refrigerator case. The FedEx guy delivered a package of parts for one of the boat bums. A fisherman filled up his tank. The radio offered sparse traffic. Same old, same old. I propped open my English book and tried to get some homework done, but I kept staring out the window. The storms had swept the sky clear of humidity. It was bright, bright blue, with the last bits of cloud exiting to the south. The lake rippled like a horse's hide with gusts of wind that darkened the water and then faded. I hadn't taken *Bellatrix* out in a while, but this wasn't going to be the day.

The morning passed. Dad came back for lunch, last night's spaghetti reheated, and told me the job was finished. He let me off from store duty and I promised to keep within shouting distance.

I picked up my journal and headed up to the picnic shelter to write. I had a story brewing, about a young woman who wears men's clothing so she can go out and explore. It was a story I really wanted to tell, I just didn't know what place or period. When would women have had enough education to do what Carl did, but not be allowed to do it? Eighteenth century? Nineteenth century? What if one of the men on the Lewis and Clark expedition was really a woman? That gave me a whole different kind of excitement, the sense of discovering something that no one else knew, something that might be real, could have been real. Of course there was Sacagawea. But we already knew about her. No, she would find out that the soft-spoken young paddler was really a female, and she'd help keep the secret. Women were better at keeping secrets than men, no matter what men said. I made notes about things I needed to look up. Research. Lots of stuff on that expedition so it would be pretty easy. I imagined myself in deerskin leggings and boots, carrying a rifle, one of the assistants. They would tease me about my lack of a beard, but people started working when they were real young back then, because they died so early. Like Carl going off to rummage around in Lapland when he was basically a college kid, and changing the whole world.

The wind was shifting. I felt it in the hairs on the back of my neck. First it blew the smell of water, backwater, and then it was the crisp brown smell of the woods and the fallen leaves. It pulled me right out of the imagining and into the real. My feet itched to wander.

I slipped away.

I went skittering like the leaves, cut free. I was tired of the docks and the uneasy footing of boards laid down above water, the smell of dead fish and algae. But I would stay close enough for a holler to draw help. That was not really breaking our agreement. I could hear Pastor running the string trimmer around the fence posts along the road, and I could see JM&J working on the cleanup barge along the water's edge, pulling up bleach bottles and wandering boat fenders that had lodged in the brush.

Summer into fall into winter. It was a slow process, from the thickest green of late spring until the understory started to fade after the bloom and fruit were gone. Green subsiding to yellow and then brown. We'd had no frost yet, but the black walnuts were bare, the pinnate leaves falling earliest and then coming apart on the forest floor. The dogwood, red maple, and sourwood had reddened. The oaks, of course, would be last, hanging on to their leaves until next spring along with the beech trees, those copper-silvery leaves. Squirrels and jaybirds and chipmunks were busy. The shavings of nutshells made by rodents' teeth were everywhere along with opened nuts. More nuts came flying out of the tops of the trees, cut down for retrieval and burying. The noises of this season were falling acorns and the harsh call of jays and crows. The songbirds didn't much sing anymore, with breeding season over.

I walked in sight of the road, able to see farther into the thinning woods in the clean light of October. On the other side of the road a tobacco field showed through the line of trees, the plants stripped of their leaves and reduced to stalks that would be turned under and the crowned rows readied for spring.

And there they were.

The white doe and her fawn stood just inside the edge of the woods. Regular deer would have been invisible, except when they switched their tails, but these two were like neon signs. The doe was chewing, slowly, contemplatively, and looking at me. The wind was in my face so they couldn't smell what I was; so as long as I stayed still, they wouldn't spook.

A day for spirits. The mists on the lake, the white deer standing and flicking their ears. It seemed like an omen, but I didn't know if I should consider it lucky or unlucky. The Indians thought that "ghost deer" were good luck. I thought it might be the other way for me.

When they showed up, things happened.

The lightning had cracked again, and the thunder rolled, and

I heard her yelling, *Maggie, don't leave me.* The rain had started, a hard spatter, and more coming along with the lightning. I ran the long lane from Wisteria Lodge out to the road, huge cedars on each side making a tunnel. I heard something, turned and saw something pale and thought that Charisse had somehow caught up with me, but it was a white deer bounding along like a ghost fleeing hell. Now I thought back to how the deer had made a pivot—when I turned it had been running perpendicular, crossing the lane, and then it made a right-angle turn and ran past me.

Something had been on the other side of the cedars, someone who had made the deer cut and run along my path, Charisse's path.

I watched the deer and they watched me back. The yearling was not smart yet. It put its head down and started to graze again. I could see that they weren't really albinos—they had dark eyes and noses and hooves, not pink. *Odocoileus virginianus*, the white-tailed deer, the local ones being *O. v. virginianus*, the Virginia white-tailed deer. There were lots of subspecies but of course no special class for albino or melanistic or spotted. The fawn had a trace of brown on her rump. I guess it was a she. Seemed like the white deer were mostly female. Maybe the bucks got killed. I don't know.

There were always a few around the lake. Some people wouldn't hunt them even though there was no law against it, just superstition—a man from the Soapstone community killed one a few years ago and the next week his house burned to the ground. It was because of an electrical fault, but that didn't change anything. Some people had even posted their land, which wasn't popular hereabouts, so that they only let in hunters who said they wouldn't touch the white deer. Something about curses or Indian princesses.

I had looked it up. Thank God and all the little angels that the internet had reached the backwater. I read the whole spiel about the Lost Colony and how Virginia Dare was born as the first English child in the New World. And then the settlement was cut off for three years because of bad luck and war. When the supply ships finally got back to Roanoke Island, all they found were empty buildings and the word CROATOAN carved on a tree.

This legend now was some weird old stuff, with a princess called Winona and two men who were both after her. One was a shaman, and he turned her into a white doe out of jealousy. The other guy wanted her back as a girl, of course, so he went to a different magician and got a magical arrow to do that. There was a hunt, and a third guy (not sure why he's interested) had a silver arrow that would kill a magical deer. Anyway, her lover and this guy shot at the same time, and one arrow turned her human and the other one killed her. Later a white deer appeared to the grieving lover, and those deer have been around ever since.

We aren't close to Roanoke Island, but close enough. Like the books in Old Trinity, and the names on the gravestones, we were part and parcel of the English settlement. If you asked anyone if they believed this romantic Legend of the White Doe stuff, they'd laugh at you, but there must be enough of the superstition to keep these deer alive year after year. Maybe way up north their color would have been an adaptive mutation, something to help them survive where there was more snow. Down here, where an inch of snow shuts down everything until it melts, their color is a death sentence. If it's not hunters, it's dogs or coyotes or something. "Survival of the fittest"—and the fittest were dull brown.

The white deer that ran beside me and Charisse that night could have been an omen. But it was more of a warning. Someone else had been in the woods that night and had frightened the deer more than the storm and more than Charisse and me had.

Vann had told me something that really gave me the willies.

He hadn't been around much, not since I gave him the ring and showed my feelings too much. He kept his distance. But last week he had stopped by to talk with Dad, and I'd spoken to him and tried to let him know I didn't hold a grudge.

"Any news?" I asked.

"Very little." He gave me that look. "Are you staying close to home?"

"Yes, sir." Not entirely true, but more since the day of the mushroom hunt, which I had told Dad about, and he had surely told Vann. "And no bathhouse alone. It's your fault if I smell like mold."

He tilted his head.

"From the crappy shower in the houseboat. Yuck."

He laughed, and I just couldn't be mad at him anymore.

"So when do I get off probation? I feel like I have a house arrest bracelet locked on me or something."

"Wish I could give you a date, Maggie."

"Maybe I should just go back to living normally." I guess I wanted to see his reaction. And I got one.

"No." He seemed to get bigger, darker. Like a cloud that had passed over the sun. Different, for sure. "I am not joking about this, Maggie. Your father knows what my concerns are, and he's looking out for your welfare."

"You tell him things you won't tell me." I was a little angry, but not as much as I put on.

"You're a juvenile."

"Not in my *brain*."

He sat back and sank into thought.

"You still don't trust me."

"Maybe it's better sometimes not to know everything."

"If it's about me, then I have a right to know. I can't stay away from the things I don't know about." I was getting passionate for real now. I hated to be treated like a child, someone who couldn't make her own decisions. "That's like sending me out without a map. That's not fair."

Vann tented his fingers, then interlaced them. I had the weird feeling he was going to start *here's the church and here's the steeple*.

"Okay. Nothing but the truth." He held up the Boy Scout sign, not the raised palm of the court witness, but I knew he meant it. "Lots of loose ends to this. Too many to make sense of it yet. It may just have been one of those random things.

Someone grabbed Charisse. Maybe a man off the highway or the railroad, a vagrant who was in the woods that night. But I believe that *you* might also have been a target, Maggie. And that he's still around, and you are still in danger." His eyes watched me from behind his glasses. I didn't want to go all girl on him so I kept my face still and expressionless.

"You think he was watching me? Is still around here?"

"Yes. Too many sketchy reports of a man in worn clothes and a weathered ball cap, seen where no one's expected. Thefts. Break-ins. What you've told me, and what you *haven't* told me about."

I must have blushed at that, because I had kept things back. I always did. But how can you count noises, or shoe prints going into the boneyard that were probably from someone stealing parts, or the smell of a cigarette that might have just been a fisherman's, or a pair of boxer shorts crumpled up beside the path? It would be like crying wolf. And what could you say about strange stick-things built out in the woods? That was another secret I held close, close as my skin.

"Personally, I think he is from around here. One of your neighbors, even one of your marina tenants. We didn't lift any usable fingerprints other than the expected, and the fact that we couldn't get a hit on DNA only means he hasn't come into the system before. The worst dangers are the ones that hide in plain sight."

It was like finding out that Guillermo had been watching me the way I observed the creatures of the woods, that someone else might be regularly watching my comings and goings, charting my courses, trying to understand my behaviors.

"You think he—wanted to—?"

Vann didn't answer. Maybe it was too hard for him to say that this man wanted to attack me. All the romantic ideas I used to have about sex on a mossy bank or a hidden beach just shredded, and I saw myself lying dead like Charisse. Everything inside me clenched at the thought.

"I think it was just Charisse's bad luck, and your good luck, that she was running after you that night when he was waiting for you to come over the back way from Old Trinity to the marina. He knew your path, Maggie. He knew where you were and where you would be going. Charisse just happened to put herself in his way." Vann's face had become more and more strained as he watched the knowledge sink in.

Maybe he had come to doubt the wisdom of telling me all that.

This information has made me jumpy. Wild, like a deer that knows the hunter is around. Not like the simpleminded white deer, protected by superstition. They were still standing at the edge of the woods, watching me, with grass hanging out of their mouths.

"Hi-up! Get outta here!" I clapped my hands and the deer jumped straight up, then leaped away into the tobacco field with their white tails flaring behind their white bodies. I could see them run for quite a way.

Charisse was not wild enough or strong enough, her beauty like a white coat in brown woods. Bad luck. She was the white deer—too fine a target. She was taken while I fled like the plain brown creature I am. The arrow meant for me had turned aside to take her.

47

Hartner Progress-News

Fall has returned. Homecoming is this weekend. Some six months ago, the students of London County High School were bubbling with anticipation of prom night. Corsages had been ordered, best shoes shined, perfect hairstyles created.

By the end of that weekend, an innocent and joyous rite of passage had been tarnished by the discovery of Charisse Swicegood's body under circumstances that can only be described as mysterious at best, and at worst as a cover-up.

It seems there has been no progress on this dreadful case that took one of our community's brightest stars. So many questions remain unanswered. Where had Charisse been that night? How had she come barefoot and tattered to the deserted docks of Filliyaw Pointe Marina? What brought her there? Who is responsible for her terrible demise?

This case has shaken our community to its core.

We urge the authorities to involve the public in solving this crime. A close-mouthed approach may be the general choice, but here it seems we suffer more from a lack of information than by too much information.

America's Most Wanted has announced it will produce a segment on this heinous crime. Good! This show has proved that John Q. Public can be the criminal's worst nightmare. Put us to work, here and across the nation! Let us know more so that we can bring the perpetrator or perpetrators to justice!

48

Damned golf-cart people.

I heard it before it hove into view—a cheap electronic trumpet repeating "Dixie"—probably someone drunk at the controls. Or just crazy. The people who lived in the trailers along the road scooted back and forth in these carts, some of them painted up with flames and shark's teeth. The one with the horn had a Rebel flag for the awning and was driven by a middle-aged man and woman who were regular participants in the low-rent hootenannies. Cart people laughed and carried on and stayed drunk a lot of the time; for some of them, a Club Car was the only way they could get around because of DWIs.

The cart skidded into view around the curve, moving as fast as its battery allowed. I leaned on my rake and got ready for a good laugh.

"Help!" the woman yelled. "Help!"

Her streaked hair straggled off her head and her mouth was open wide and red as a cartoon. She was wearing a pink shorty top over turquoise Capris, and her tummy rolled out over the waistband. She was half out of the seat as she drove, the cart weaving and bouncing.

"Help me, please!"

I dropped the rake and ran to her, and saw Dad coming the other way from the machine shed.

"What's the matter?"

"Oh God, he almost got me." She stopped and put one leg out as though she had to steady the cart from tipping over.

Dad hunkered down beside her. A long hank of hair hung where it had been pulled out of her scalp, and bloody scratches marked her arm. She kept turning around and looking behind her.

"Who? Who did this?"

"I was running back to the house from the picnic. We forgot the bean salad." Her mouth hung open as she finished each sentence, as though she might start howling again in pure panic. "I was going up the road, past the place where you keep those boats, when I saw someone."

The boneyard. Last chapter of lost jobs, divorces, and sickness, most recently, Mr. Polozny, whose pontoon had been dragged there after he had a stroke and was put in a nursing home.

"I saw someone run between the boats. And I turned the cart up into the lot to chase him. I thought it was Kenny with a Super Soaker. He got me with it the other day, and I was going to make him pay for it. But it wasn't any Kenny. I got up there and didn't see no one around, so I was going to sneak around behind and give him a good scare. But I'm the one got blindsided. Knocked me off my feet."

I caught Dad's eye. His face was white.

"I kicked and yelled, but they got the music going down there and no one to hear. I was on my own, ya know? I kicked and caught him in the shins, and then he grabbed my hair and tried to drag me thata way." She reached up and felt her head, and I saw blood on her scalp. She pulled the hank of hair out of the tangle. "Shit."

"And?"

"I pulled away and lost my hair, that's what. And I kicked him again and this time I got him right in the knee."

"Hurt him?"

"Damn straight. *Damn* straight. I heard it crunch and he let go of me."

Dad pulled out his phone and called the police. He told them about the attack, that this must be the man who killed Charisse. I just stood there feeling a little sick. I'd walked past the boat graveyard a hundred times, usually thinking about something and not paying any attention. This had to be the man who'd been watching me all along. The one I'd started to think was like Fletcher, conjured out of air and gone back into it.

I remembered the halyards clanging that day for no reason, back in the summer, the day I went swimming.

"They're on the way, Donna," he told her. "It's okay now."

She made a little face, sort of a grin. "I think I got him good. I don't think he's walking real good right now."

"I'm proud of you," he said.

She pulled her fat leg back into the cart and sat straight, like a soldier; then something must have sunk in because she began to sag back in the seat, and looked like she'd gained ten years in those few minutes.

"I was running back to the trailer. We forgot something. Last picnic for the year, we said. I was going past the graveyard when I saw this man. I thought it was Kenny. Swear to God I thought it was just Kenny. I didn't see him good, but he looked familiar, I'll tell you that." She looked at Dad, and at me, as though the story had to be repeated until it was believed.

It wasn't long till we had the whole of London County civil authority there, it seemed like. Ambulance, sheriff's department, volunteer fire department, even the town police from Hartner. It was the kind of CF you'd expect. The paramedics were trying to treat the woman when here comes the sheriff's deputies and said not to touch her because they had to get a rape kit done, and Donna said he goddamn well never got in her pants, but they were putting bags on her hands because she might have scratched him, did she remember if she scratched him any time? Visible bruises started to pop up on her arms, the imprint of strong hands.

A search party was put together, Dad leading the way, and I sorta tailed with them because I didn't want to be alone over at the marina. Nobody was really thinking about me, so I had to watch out for myself. And Vann was going to show up soon, I knew, and he'd be where the action was.

In the late-afternoon light, the boneyard looked as bad as its name. Boats on flat-tired trailers, others tilted and lying on their sides, and all of them streaked with weather and crusted with mud-dauber tubes. Parts had been ripped off, stolen or vandalized. Tarps put up with good intentions were just rags.

One pretty dinghy had been decaying for years; the sticker for a Tampa yacht club was barely visible now. The teak was splintered gray, but the forestay still held and the mast stood straight.

The woman said that the man had tried to get her onto a big cruiser. It had to be the Carver, square as a house, which had been sitting there for years. A deputy took her aside and began to take her statement.

Several of the men milled around the Carver, keeping it under guard, although she'd told them the man had limped off into the woods after she kicked him. You could see a long way into the bare November woods, but so far as the search party finding a trail, I didn't think they'd have much luck with the dry leaves. The sheriff arrived and sent some of the deputies on foot in the vague direction she'd indicated, while others went back to patrol along the side roads and the highway.

Vann pulled up, looking a little frantic. "Anyone been in there?"

"No," Dad told him. He'd stopped one of the volunteer firemen from climbing up to "flush the bastard out."

Vann nodded. He was ready to detective. He had an evidence technician with a camera and rubber gloves and a black tackle box and the whole CSI thing. I stayed back, at the edge of the activity, between the police and the gaggle of golf-cart people who'd rumbled up from the picnic to watch the goings-on. Donna was telling her story again, now with gestures. I heard the hiss of beer opening.

Vann called out and told the man that the police were there in force and he should come out with his hands up. It sounded too much like a bad movie. But no sound, no movement. Vann walked around the boat several times, and the technician came and took pictures of the outside of the Carver. They looked at the ladder. They looked under the boat. The lower units stuck out, caked with corrosion. The technician did the fingerprint thing on the railings, and it seemed like it took forever until Vann swung himself up into the cockpit. I saw him unholster his gun as he moved past the wheel and through the shredded cover to the cabin.

The cabin door was open. Vann shone a light around inside, probing into the corners. Finally he went down, disappearing into that black hole. I had a little stomach flip. What if the man had actually come back and was hiding? He might be behind the door or in the head, silent, waiting to ambush Drexel. Didn't they have a dog or tear gas or something? What if there was another dead girl in there? I tried to wipe that image out of my mind. Sometimes the dead girl in my imagination looked like Charisse, and sometimes she looked like me.

It was dead quiet, no more sound than the flashlight beam. I saw the boat rock a little as he walked forward. A soft thump of a foot hitting something, or a door closing.

At last he came back up and called for the technician.

I let out a breath, relieved. I think everyone did.

A deputy was putting up Police Line—Do Not Cross yellow tape around the Carver. As he finished, he told the golf-cart people they'd best pack up their stuff and get home, no telling where this guy was now, and it seemed to dawn on them that they could be in danger and not just watching a *Lifetime* movie. They made like bees back and forth, hauling the beer and tents to where they could party in safety and honor Donna the Warrior.

It was a slow process. I could see the flashes as the technician took pictures inside. Then things started to come out, bagged and tagged. Evidence. A stained blue sleeping bag with the stuffing coming out of one corner. A lantern. Bag after white paper bag sealed with tape, whatever was inside protected from dirt or anyone seeing it. He had a whole little camp in there, who knows how long? Jesus-creeps.

Vann came down the ladder with one last bag. He saw me, still lurking around the edges. He nodded once. He didn't have to say, "I told you so." He was right, and Dad was right. More right than they would have wanted to be.

49

Observation: Box Turtle

I saw what looked like a hump in the water, the broken end of a dead tree floating along. But it was weird. Something—it was too rounded. It didn't look right.

Then I saw that it was moving, not with the wind, but in the other direction.

I watched the hump get closer. Finally I could tell that it was a turtle. And not a water turtle—they are flatter, better shaped to move through the water. This had a rounded carapace, dark with yellow patterns. A box turtle, meant to stay on land.

As it got closer, I could see its clawy feet pushing out, left front right rear, right front left rear, trying to walk that big upside-down bowl of a shell across the water. The little tail stuck out straight behind.

Brave little thing, it had no business being out there. It was barely able to get around on land.

It seemed tired, but that's hard to tell. It submerged its head sometimes and seemed to pick up speed, then it would raise its head out of the water to breathe. Or look for land. Then down again for a few more strokes.

I looked into its red eye as it labored past.

I almost went over to A dock to fetch a long-handled net. I would have given it a lift, because it did not seem like it could make the shore. The last yards were slow, slower, and then it was at the edge. Did it have enough energy left to crawl up a slope? I couldn't tell, because the shoreline was thick with weeds.

It didn't seem right that a box turtle should be swimming across a wide stretch of water like that. I looked it up on the web. Some sites said no, box turtles will drown. I found others that were more authoritative (*Reptile Adventure*) that said they could, and may even have made it west by swimming across the Mississippi.

I hope it made it wherever it was going. So brave, to keep swimming and swimming and swimming. So stupid to be out in that water.

50

Angela dearest-

I am writing this tonight and you will be happy to know that I am stone cold sober. Can't promise it will last forever but right now, I'm doing one day at a time as they say.

We know who the man is, the one who killed Charisse. A few days ago he tried to get one of the women going by on a golf cart. We found his nest in one of the stored boats. Looked like he'd been there for quite a while, sneaking in from the woods. The police did their fingerprinting and came up with a name, which knocked me over because I should have known all along. I should have remembered. Now I feel like I'm someways responsible. It was that Ledsome fellow—Orville and Patty Ledsome's kid, the no-account one, Alan. Not Junior but the other one. He was here late last fall to do a repair, not one of the regular carpenters but a fill-in. He was only here a couple of days so when they asked about workers he never came to mind. He was a temp for Grover—you remember Grover, he helped put in the fence at your parents' house? Grover went down with kidney stones.

Anyways, Alan washed out of another of his sure-fire deals and come home, but his parents got sick of him laying around like before. I guess he remembered the boats and figured out that was a place he could camp. He was living right under our noses the entire time. Watching Maggie who is just innocent as a lamb and wanders around never thinking about the bad in men's hearts. I got down on my knees and I prayed thanks to God when I learned how close we come.

Nobody remembered him but I know he was in and out

of the office and the storage dock because he did work over there.

Maggie even saw him once, but not enough to recognize. He was lurking around the bathhouse. Many a time I thought real strong about having her stay over with your parents, but when I mentioned it she said she'd run off first, like that Nat character. You can believe me that I have kept her on a mighty short leash.

And I blame myself for not remembering. Vann said that poor Charisse was tied up with left-handed bowlines, which is interesting but not exactly the lead pipe in the library kinda clue, right? But it all fit together. I saw him sweeping up after he drilled, and he was left-handed. Angela, I should have remembered. And I had to teach him how to tie up boats when he was moving them around, he was making granny knots and we lost one, and I had to show him a bowline. If I had a brain I woulda remembered he done it backwards then. All those clues and me without any sense to put them together.

Well, water over the dam or under the bridge or whatever. We got a name and a face and they'll catch this guy soon. He'll walk into a hornet nest if he comes to bother me or mine, I promise you.

I stuck my head in a bottle all these years, dreaming we could be a family again. Maybe its shock therapy, this whole thing. I see that hoping won't make it so, not with all the hope on one side.

I don't expect I'll be hearing from you, but time I quit expecting that. Or writing to you.

Drew

51

Observation: My Bower

This was my most private place.

A long time ago, a giant tree had fallen and lodged a few feet off the ground. Grapevines and honeysuckle had grown up around it and then over it, enclosing a space cleared by their deep shadow. One day when I was wandering, I saw a rabbit, pursued by a hawk, come racing across the woods and dive into the thicket. Of course I had to follow. I circled the mass until I found a place where the vines made a curtain instead of a wall, hanging from the tree trunk but not rooted. I bent and crept inside. The rabbit was gone, but I found a space like a natural tent. A small opening at the top, like the pupil of an eye, let in a circle of sky. A sanctuary, that's what it became, a special place visited only when I was bursting full, overjoyed or in despair.

Like today.

I didn't mean to fight with Dad. He had been holding it together so well, not drinking, going to meetings and even church a couple of times. But that didn't mean everything was smooth. He had a lot on his mind, I knew, but that didn't stop me from being a normal shithead teenager this morning and getting into an argument with him. We both ended up with our voices raised and hands shaking.

I had to get away, somewhere, and here was where I used to come whenever I was jangly with more emotions than I could name. This secret place that only I had seen. Mine. Although I had not been here in so long.

The sun broke through the cloud deck and flooded the woods with light. Beech leaves, pale and translucent, caught the slanting sun and glowed like stained glass. These gentle slopes running down to a sometimes stream, the beech trees with their smooth gray bark, surrounded my place of peace.

You would think that in winter the green shelter would be bare, but the grapevines twisted in a heavy mass, making a skeleton for the living skin of honeysuckle. The leaves of the honeysuckle were evergreen, and dead leaves had piled on top of it all. I stood a little distance away and listened, watched. Breathed. That was how much things had changed. I was always listening now. Yeah, I wasn't supposed to be out here alone. Yeah, I'd promised. But Dad had that stretched look, and I knew that one more word might be the one that sent him back to the bottle. There was something inside me that might have said that word.

The only sounds were the rattle of dry leaves on their stems and a distant drone of a small airplane. I walked around to the back side, parted the vine curtain, and ducked inside.

I almost passed out.

One of those stick things had been built right in the center, under the sky-eye. A bower *inside* my bower. In my most secret and hidden place.

I froze, listening as far as I could, demanding that my ears hear what wasn't there to be heard, the crunch of Ledsome's feet, the sound of his breathing.

A flat ribbon of dried-up leaves led to the bower's entrance hole. I poked at it. The thin leaves were dull purple underneath, not leaves but petals from wild aster blossoms. They were completely withered, put down a long time ago. Some oak leaves had drifted over them.

I felt my skin prickle. He might still be watching. I got down on my knees, almost feeling the point of a knife in my back or the rope on my throat, but I had to know.

I looked inside.

The floor was made of moss, like before, and on it, MAGGIE had been spelled out in white stones. Behind my name was a brass candlestick from a church, and I knew what church, and when and where it was taken, and the source of that piece of heavy brown-edged paper that he used for his drawing.

A shard of mirror had been suspended from the top of the dome. It turned and showed my face, turned the other way, turned back.

52

I was walking along the marina road, headed back after checking out the campground, when I heard a car coming and I moved over on the gravelly edge. I turned to check who it was, just standard these days, and saw that familiar white Chevy. Drexel was peering through the windshield at me and he didn't look pleased.

The passenger window came down. "Hey, Maggie."

"Hello, detective."

"I guess you figure I'm here on official business."

"I figure."

I kept walking and he kept pace with me. I saw he was wearing a suit, very conservative navy blue with a white shirt and a striped tie.

"You're all dressed up."

"Court. While I was waiting to be called, I realized there was something I needed to see in the boat storage area."

"A trial?"

"It was."

"Sometime, I'd like to see the courthouse," I said, "and the jail. Would you give me a tour like they do the bad kids?"

"It's not a place you want to see, Maggie. Just misery. The day we don't need jails would be the happiest day of my life." He stopped the car. "I thought you promised that you weren't going to wander around alone anymore."

I pushed a big branch away from the road with my foot. He waited. That was his strongest point.

"I'm right here in the open."

"And so that's safe?" He stopped the car. "Hop in."

We drove to the marina, but instead of letting me off and going back around to the boneyard, he parked and turned the car off.

"My dear Maggie," he began. That sounded ominous. "And I do mean that. You've become important to me, in a professional way, and I don't want to see you come to harm because of your cussed stubbornness."

"I come by it natural."

"I'll agree there. And something else. You like to push the edge, do things that are reckless. Even dangerous. If that's the way you assert your independence, it's not a good one." He rested his hands on the steering wheel and did some more of that silent waiting. I could wait right with him. It was interesting to see what was in his car, the radio and the blue light, a box of files on the floor that I had to tuck my feet around. And a picture of his kids on the dashboard, both of them wearing glasses. Genetic.

"I did not want to tell you all this, but if this is what it takes." He focused his owly eyes on me. "I told you before that I thought this man was after you. You, specifically. That was more of a hunch at first, but it turns out I was right."

I shifted in the seat. This was getting uncomfortable.

"When we found his hiding place, there in the boat, we took out a lot of stuff."

"Yeah. I'll bet it stank."

He laughed a bit. "Yes, it did. But that aside, do you remember the white bags we took out, the sealed evidence bags?"

"Sure."

"You should know what was inside them. Rope. Explicit magazines. I don't think I have to say more."

"Did you find stuff from a church?"

He seemed to hold his breath. I could shock him too.

"Yes. How do you know about that?"

I spilled the beans, finally, about the bowers. But I didn't tell him *when* it was that I found the candlestick. Or that I knew it came from Old Trinity.

"And you wandering around out here. Maggie!" He had this dad quality of exasperation. "Anyway, that's not all what I wanted to tell you. We found pictures. Of you."

"Pictures?"

"He had been drawing pictures of you, Maggie. Including a nude picture."

I glanced sideways and saw that he had turned his face away, looking out the window.

"Do you understand me?" he said, turning back, his face no longer showing whatever emotion had broken through. "A picture of you naked, out in the woods."

Damn and damn. I had only been naked a couple of times, once on the island, where he *couldn't* have been, and a couple of times on shore, when I was absolutely sure I was hidden in my bower. In the place that *no one* knew about. Well, that's what I used to think. But no one could see inside there, not without being so close I would see them, hear them, so he couldn't have seen me. He made it up. It was even creepier that he had imagined what I looked like naked. He was a fictionalizer too. Was the naked picture sweet, like the rolled-up piece of Carl's book, me with a flower? Or my face stuck on a body like the ugly drawings in restrooms, giant hairy vaginas, saggy breasts? Either way, I wanted to vomit.

"You know it's me?" I couldn't look at him, because he'd see that I wasn't surprised, that he had told me something I already knew.

"He had good likenesses of your face." He started the car. "I don't want anything to happen to you. Not like Charisse."

I nodded. I just wanted to get out of the car. Now.

"You're on my watch, okay? Don't make me have to take you out of someplace like that."

From Lachesis Lapponicus

> Several days ago the forests had been set on fire by lightning, and the flames raged at this time with great violence…(this part was torn and smeared with mud)… nearly extinguished in most of the spots we visited, except in ant-hills, and dry trunks of trees. After we had travelled about half a quarter of a mile across one of these scenes of desolation, the wind began to blow with rather more

force than it had done, upon which a sudden noise arose in the half-burnt forest, such as I can only compare to what may be imagined among a large army attacked by an enemy. We knew not whither to turn our steps. The smoke would not suffer us to remain where we were, nor durst we turn back. It seemed best to hasten forward, in hopes of speedily reaching the outskirts of the wood; but in this we were disappointed. We ran as fast as we could, in order to avoid being crushed by the falling trees, some of which threatened us every minute. Sometimes the fall of a huge trunk was so sudden, that we stood aghast, not knowing whither to turn to escape destruction, and throwing ourselves entirely on the protection of Providence. In one instance a large tree fell exactly between me and my guide, who walked not more than a fathom from me, but, thanks to God! we both escaped in safety. We were not a little rejoiced when this perilous adventure terminated, for we had felt all the while like a couple of outlaws, in momentary fear of surprise.

53

An outbreak of doodlebugs filled the area behind the gas line boom.

Doodlebugs—water boatmen—oar around with paddle legs. A few could usually be found making their rounds near the dock, twirling and zipping. But this was massive, a dark horde of boatmen. I couldn't begin to count them. Such fertility! Just too many at one time in one place. The more vulnerable you were, the more you had to breed, to make up for the whole world making its living on you. Giant tortoises and whales could afford to be slow about reproduction; they were big and long lived.

I saw a film about corals spawning, billions of eggs and clouds of sperm, the entire ocean turned to milk. It was appalling. The individual doesn't matter at all, it's about the continuation of the species. Whatever small differences existed, from one water boatman to another, disappeared in the whole. I wondered if aliens came to earth if they would notice any difference among the humans, in our billions, these creatures walking around on two legs and breeding more than necessary and eating up more than our share of the world. Maybe they'd see us as we see bugs, just a swarm.

I love nature, the needless beauty of it, how the damselflies are jeweled and skinks have neon-blue tails. And how much we're given, nuts and berries and apples in abundance, too much there, too, I guess, but sometimes the natural world can be just scary. I've seen the *National Geographic* shows, read a thousand books. Watched catfish swirling like giant globs of mucus waiting for a handout of dog food. Maggots in a carcass. Maples spewing seeds until they pile up in drifts. Spiders hatching in a seethe of tiny legs. Kudzu and mosquitoes and ticks. All of this feeding and breeding and dying and starting over again. These water boatmen were innocuous enough, not like giant water bugs that will bite like fire if you're stupid enough to handle one (I was, just once), but water boatmen only graze on algae and whirl around. Until they erupt into a swarm like this, and it gives me the shivers at the thought of being in the water among them.

I didn't like the direction my thoughts were heading, as dark as Nat's imaginings. I should do something, something physical or something that demanded attention. The lake was flat calm, so no sailing. I popped inside and asked Dad if I could take the truck up to the Pizza Annex to play some games.

Dad wouldn't let me walk alone anymore, anywhere period, and that was okay. Now I was in agreement with Vann and him. He let me take the truck around the marina and, in the daytime, up to the convenience store or as far as the crossroads. Sometimes I've gone a little bit beyond, but I don't push it. Not as far as Norlington or anything.

The state had put down fresh tar and stones on the road. Loose rocks clanked up underneath and I slowed down so as not to slew around on them. I passed the trailers and little cottages, some of them summer places but most of them year-round homes. I wondered where Donna, who almost became one of Ledsome's victims, lived. One old guy keeps a sign by the road, Fire Wood $4, and I guess he sells some of it to the campers and hunters. Golf carts and bass boats sat in the yards, and a couple of sad mothballed sailboats with their masts lashed down across the cabin tops.

I saw where a whole big patch of pine woods had been slashed down. For pulpwood, must be. A few goats that used to pasture there looked forlorn without anything but stumps around them. As I got close to the main road, the camps gave way to crop fields: dry soybeans, scabby pastures, turned-over dirt that was gray-brown. A few of the bigger fields had been planted in a cover crop. Bright green, it looked like April, like spring and Easter grass in baskets of eggs.

At the highway I waited for a log truck followed by a chain of cars. The signpost on the other side of the road, narrow white boards painted with a black arrow at one end, pointed to CORBIN and QUEENS HOPE, towns that didn't exist anymore spelled out in black letters.

I thought I'd get a snack and maybe play some of the games, but as I drove past Old Trinity, I slowed down, then turned and parked where Charisse had pulled over the Jaguar that night. It seemed like a million years ago. I hadn't been there for a long time. Not with memories of Charisse to spook around the graves, and then memories of Nat, whose absence felt like a death too.

The stone wall was open by the parking spaces, with two steps up to the level of the graveyard. I walked around in the shade of the cedar trees, reading the gravestones and thinking about Nat and Charisse and Hulky and all. I guess I was meant to be blue on this blue day. I read the inscriptions and looked at the carvings. Garlands. A lamb. A broken tree. A butterfly. A toothy skull head with angel wings. Praying hands. Something that looked like a ghost, with a long gown.

Maybe we were all ghosts. What we thought was living and breathing was just in our minds, or someone's minds. We were dead and in a ghost world somewhere, or maybe just the fantasies of some greater mind. Ghost Fletcher and ghost Ledsome, as if they had come from Heaven and Hell, and ghost Maggie and ghost Nat. Ledsome a bad angel who had to land somewhere. I wondered how he could live in the woods or in one of the old slave cabins fallen in behind the great houses, most of them, like Wisteria Lodge, fallen in too. The rich people and the slaves equally dead, and the places they had lived equally decrepit—so much for getting ahead in the world. All of us ghosts, or angels, or figments, bright angels and dark, two sides of the same thing just as the devils supposedly were bright shining angels that burned by being thrown down from heaven.

At night I'd have sat on a tombstone, but that seemed cruel in the daylight, so I sat on the church steps. The door behind me was safely locked, but once it had been open.

Big monuments and little ones stuck up from the thin grass, even tiny plaques that just said Baby. We all ended up here regardless, if you were beautiful or ugly, a baby or a young woman or a strong man, or old and curled up like a leaf—it didn't matter, what mattered was the species continuing. That was what the urge was, the drive forward. Sex. Sex and reproduction. A few didn't care at all, like Nat, or cared too much, like Charisse and her father, and some of us wondered if we belonged anywhere. Still, the whole thing was doodlebugs just making more doodlebugs. Sex and kids and families and grandkids, the next generation pushing you out, *Get out of the way, let me through*. I tried to imagine Dad bent over and gray-haired, but I couldn't. Not yet.

Eve bit the apple and then there was death, according to the myth, and sex became something to be ashamed of. It seemed like there had to be a way to avoid the whole thing.

Eventually I drove home. I didn't feel like games or pizza or the sight of other people. The sky was intense and blue over the calm water, the lake darker blue, thoughtful.

I walked past a kid, maybe in junior high, skinny and with his hair sticking out all over. He leaned against a rusty Toyota by the bathhouse. His eyes were closed and his head bobbed as though he were listening to an iPod, but there weren't any earbuds. He sang in a repetitive drone, the words unclear but the sound menacing.

54

I watched the mail pretty closely these days. Dad used to grab it right away, to look for a letter from Angela. But he's stopped doing that. I wasn't going to claim credit but I was happy that he was letting go, whatever the reason.

I was the one grabbing the stack now, to look for another note from Nat. We'd exchanged some short messages on the internet, stuff about his studies and where he was living. Then those stopped coming for a long space. I'd check to see if he was on chat; nope. Sometimes I sent him an email but never got a reply. I thought of him alone in Greensboro, a big city with lots of street crime, or at least that's what we saw in the local paper, reports of murders and dead babies left in dumpsters. Nat may not have been meant to live in London County, but I don't think he was any better adapted for urban life. Finally I got a postcard. Talk about retro. It had a cartoon owl on the front. The postmark said Pfafftown, which turned out to be near Winston-Salem. He wrote that he was enrolled in a filmmaking class and sharing a house in the country with some other students. *More ltr*, he'd written.

Not today, apparently. I shuffled through the catalogs and Publishers Clearinghouse envelopes with their official-looking seals. Two replies to our annual reminders about dock rent. I was afraid to open them after seeing how many had come back marked *not renewing—boat sold—pulling boat—moving*.

One of them was a renewal. It was for *Highland Fling*, a beautiful Tartan with a deep red Awlgrip hull. The other had a note written in clear, square letters: "I'm sorry, but for my family's safety I cannot renew at Filliyaw Pointe. You have been very kind but circumstances dictate that I move our boat to Moonlight Bay."

Damn. Another one.

Moonlight Bay—and wasn't that some goofy-ass name for a marina?—had opened on the Virginia side. It had been talked about for years, but when it finally happened it came through quick and with a lot of buzz. It was too long a haul for the locals and people from Raleigh and points south, but it was siphoning off the Virginia crowd. And it had a travel lift and a restaurant with big windows looking out on the lake. Dad didn't say much about it but I knew he was worried about the concession.

I set the forms and a letter from a paving company in his basket. With the renewal on the top.

There was no reason to keep the store open today except that it was Saturday and we were supposed to be open, and to get deliveries. No one was going out on a raw day like this. So, with the mail sorted and the floor already swept, I turned to dusting under the counter and lining up the fishing reels, the one VHF radio, one GPS unit, and one fancy wind gauge we kept safe behind the glass. *Avoid the five-finger discount.*

Dad was on a supply run, and I was expected to keep the lights on and the door open. I guess he thought the store was safe enough for me, with the guys working around. It was still creepy though.

I hoped they caught Ledsome soon, handcuffed him to a chair, interrogated him, and sent him to prison. I imagined Drexel Vann looking at him through his big glasses, waiting for an answer, waiting like he did so well. In a little room with black plastic chairs and green walls. Why green? That's just how I saw it. I could make things real in my own mind, imagine things so clearly that I didn't need to know a lot of details to have the whole thing spring to life. Like how they found Charisse, dead on the crushed velvet sheets, the cheap red comforter I'd fluffed while cleaning. Posed like a woman in one of the magazines they found in the Carver, her knees bent one way and her head the other, her wrists looped with weathered yellow polypropylene rope, rough and hairy, that was tied off with left-handed bowlines. Her mouth was filled with something. Some people

said it was her underwear. It would have been peach. Charisse
was like my mother; her things were always coordinated.
    I began to construct a scenario, how he got her. She had
been running after me. The rain and thunder. The closed-in
lane leading from the old house. Did he catch her there, after
the deer spooked? No, I could see her running toward the marina, the ground dissolving under her feet as it was under mine,
except hers were bare. She would have slipped on the slick clay.
Soaked with cold rain, and her feet sliding. The marina was
to her left; she could see the glow of two lights. I had disappeared as I headed for home. She struggled with her sopping,
heavy dress.
    I imagined Charisse would have fought. She had fought off
that college guy. But maybe she had no fight left, with the running and all the chemicals in her body. I imagined him carrying
her over his shoulder, knocked out or passed out, her arms
flopping. I wondered if she woke and struggled as he tied her
up, or if she was comatose. Did she try to scream when he cut
her dress off her? Did she kick or just lie there, accepting her
fate?
    I could taste the vomit from her lips and imagine it rising
again and how her mouth would have filled behind the gag.
    It was so easy for me to picture things, to see them take
shape and become real. Maybe someday if I don't become a
marine biologist, I'll write stories to publish. The world in my
head was as real as the world outside, as real as Carl was to
me. I could read his journal and see his pale face darkened by
weather, straight nose and long earlobes, his stained Finnish
garments. With bare hands he caught a ptarmigan chick *upon
which the hen ran so close to me, that I could easily have taken her also.*
He had a tender spirit, even if he was a scientist, and would not
deprive the young ones of their mother.
    If the world were a fair place, then we would have been born
in the same time and not hundreds of years apart. We would
have had a lot to talk about. I could have helped him gather specimens. We might have been partners, or even married

people, though when I think of it, women back then just had babies, so I would have been stuck in a house somewhere in Sweden while he had adventures.

It was nearly closing time when Dad made it back. He had food and supplies for us and some things for the store as well. He gave me the groceries to take to the *Annamariner* and stow in the galley.

I was going to try again tonight.

The sheriff and Drexel Vann kept saying they would get Ledsome, now that they knew who it was, now that he had lost his nest and was out in the cold. Only a matter of time, they said. But that wasn't really reassuring as the season got late and the marina got empty. Vann and the rest of the police were a long way from the backwater. I had asked Dad more than a time or two about getting a gun for protection, and he always put me off. *I don't do guns, punkin.* And that was it. Even if the whole rest of North Carolina was armed, we weren't.

I didn't know if a gun was *the* answer, but it sure could be part of the answer. I felt so helpless sitting in the store, watching the parking lot, analyzing if every person meant to do harm. I never used to feel like that. And it would be a powerful reassurance to have that little piece of destruction close by. I tried to imagine Ledsome, but his face would never come clear. It was a shadow, an open mouth and deep-set eyes glaring out from the woods, not like his picture in the paper, the guy I'd actually seen around before, a clean-shaven average guy with dirty-blond hair. I tried to imagine him better, but for some reason he wouldn't come into focus. Not like Charisse. He was thin and flimsy, someone else's story. I imagined this shadowy man in a doorway, and me pulling the trigger, and that was real. I could smell the smoke and feel the gun kick against my hand. But whether I could actually do it, shoot someone, I didn't know.

When Dad closed up the store and came to the *Annamariner*, I had the hot dogs in the pan, mac 'n' cheese in the micro, and the computer on.

"Dad."

"Uh-huh."

"I'd like you to look at this."

I turned the screen around and showed him the page about the best handguns for home defense. Pictures of Glocks and Lugers and Colts. I'd read up on all of them. "We should have something to protect ourselves, and the store. Or if there's a rabid animal or something."

He looked at the screen without saying anything. I kept talking. I'd read up on it all, the difference between a pistol and a revolver, the different sizes of bullets. Just like with living things, there were orders and families and genera and species. I'd decided that what we needed was a double-action revolver. The experts said it would be easier to work and less likely to jam up.

"I think we should get a .38-caliber revolver. That won't be too big for me to handle." I pointed to the snub-nosed Smith and Wesson.

"They look all nice and shiny." Dad was giving me a look not quite like anything I'd ever seen. "Thing about guns is, they tend to turn on their owners."

"But we're just all by ourselves out here." Stuck at the end of the road, between the woods and the water, and no one around closer than the camps on the marina road. What seemed to be a paradise a long time ago now seemed like a trap.

"Let's take a walk."

I thought he'd lost it, but I turned down the heat, put my fleece jacket back on, and followed him up to the end of the dock.

We stood there and watched the lake under the moon. Dogs were barking far away, not just mutts but hounds, on the trail of some animal.

"I don't know if you paid it any mind, back when we went up home, but you didn't see any guns at your uncle Philip's house."

I thought back to the trip. Fishing tackle, bows and arrows. No guns.

"My family ain't no different than most in West Virginia. It's a gun culture. Comes natural from the time when the mountains were inaccessible and you had to take care of your own, on your own. My people liked guns and bought guns and traded them around. It was a normal part of growing up."

What would my life have been like if I had grown up around the Bear-Hairs? It wasn't something I wanted to think about.

"My pap had guns, and all my uncles. Just normal, like I say." He stopped, but I could sense the tension.

"I had this cousin, Eli. He was a year older than me. We were almost like brothers because of our ages, and because we both had this desire to roam around and get into scrapes. Now Philip, who wasn't but eight at the time, he's always been a law-abiding sort. Boy Scout, all that. But me and Eli, we was hellers. So I was staying with Eli. He was fourteen, I was thirteen. After the family was all to bed, we snitched some beers from the fridge and took our poles and went night fishing. It was a moonlight night like this, but in the summer. Hot."

Dad was a pretty fair storyteller himself. He had these pauses to let things build up, so you were itching for the rest.

"Well, we caught some catfish and finished off the beer and were pretty proud of ourselves, all in all. We was gonna surprise everyone with catfish all dressed out for breakfast when they got up. We had snuck out through the bedroom window and didn't think to unlock a door so we could get back in. We were out on the porch, whispering, though I imagine we were pretty loud, and then we pushed up a window in the kitchen."

He took a deep breath and let it out in a long, whistling exhale.

"Eli went in first. He was halfway inside when I heard the gun go off. The shot pushed him back out the window and he fell on top of me. I was screaming his name and crying, and feeling him twitch. I pushed him off me and ran off into the woods. I ran all the way back to the river and jumped in to wash off the blood. I threw away my shirt and scrubbed myself raw. Then I did it again. Didn't come back till near noon."

"Was he dead?"

"Yeah. Hit in the chest, never had a chance to say anything. That's what his father kept saying: 'Eli didn't forgive me, Eli didn't forgive me.' My folks grabbed me and hugged me to death for coming home and being alive.'"

I felt this hard lump in my chest, even though I never knew Eli.

The damp cold had seeped into us. Dad put his hand on my shoulder but didn't have anything more to say.

We walked home over slippery dock boards instead of most people's normal grass and pavement. Past the dock lights that didn't all work. The dogs had quit howling and somewhere on B or C dock, a bilge pump was running. The lake smelled different as winter came close—still a little fishy, always that because of the otters spitting up shells and bones, but cold now and dead-tree like.

I couldn't tell Dad about the sense of dread that had come down on me. He thought he could keep us safe through the long nights. He had a baseball bat in the houseboat. That could do some damage in his hands, but it wouldn't be as effective as a gun. Something I could manage.

I did feel somewhat safer because Dad wasn't drinking now. It can be real lonely when the only other person in the world, it seems, is passed out.

Warm yellow light showed in the ports of the big Beneteau on C dock. Someone was spending the weekend. The boat had heat and air, a tricked-out galley. It would be like a cabin in the woods, snug and warm. People sitting around a table with wine in glasses or maybe hot chocolate in mugs.

We stepped onto our houseboat. It wasn't so elegant. The doors were warped and the plastic trim was cracked around the sink. But we turned on the lights and they were warm and yellow too, and they spilled out onto the black water the same way they did from the yacht.

55

The bright idea was that, like a deer drive, the posse could sweep from the highway through the woods and fields toward the marina, and that Ledsome could be pushed out and captured from wherever he was hiding. If he was still out there somewhere, which didn't seem likely now that the cold had settled in.

It sounded good on paper.

The posse rode out of the woods looking worse for wear than their quarry. I imagine they'd had a time with the catbrier and deadfalls and maneuvering their horses around old fences and the like. The wet day that was supposed to let them approach more stealthily had slicked their faces and raincoats. They took off their hats and wiped their faces and put their hats back on. They slumped in the saddles.

No better luck than when they had been out looking for a lost girl that they didn't know was dead.

I'd been half hoping that they would scare him out, and half not. It had gotten easier to believe Ledsome had dissolved into the mists and disappeared than to think about him surviving out in the winter woods somewhere. How did you do that with no people, no friends, nothing?

His family had put a piece in the paper, asking him to turn himself in, and they'd done a TV interview as well. After that, they went silent. There was no way for them or anyone to link up the no-account kid with the monster who murdered Charisse. Of course, he hadn't actually murdered Charisse, like with a knife or something, but the law said that if someone died "in the commission of a crime," then it was murder. Blame was the easiest thing to spread around.

The posse came in for coffee and stood around dripping and silent until one of them made a little joke. That opened them up. It wasn't long until they were laughing and stomping around, full of life again. I couldn't take the levels of testosterone and went up to the picnic area for some quiet.

The horses were grazing, and the air was damp and still, like a blanket wrapped around the marina. All I could hear was the sound of big teeth ripping up grass. Fog was gathering. It reminded me of the time when Carl argued with the clergymen in Lapland who believed that the clouds were solid and when they hit the mountains were able to carry away trees and cattle. Carl got only scorn and scripture-quoting in response to his reasoned arguments that clouds and fog were water vapor.

A wild cry broke through the silence. *Killdeer, killdeer.* A plover was raising an alarm, up where we parked boat trailers during the busy season. *Killdeer, killdeer, killdeer!* It was living up to its scientific title—*vociferous.*

In early spring this was a hopeful sound, the circling of the birds looking for a place to nest. And then in summer with the peeps running around, the killdeer would alarm when someone came close to the nest. They would drag a wing and lure the predator away. When the danger was far enough from the babies, they would fly away again, *killdeer, killdeer.*

Now on this still, closed-in fall day, the cry was loud and terrifying, and who knows what had made the killdeer fly?

56

Tick tick tick.

I watched the time crawl through the afternoon. I was adding the sound effects—unlike the clocks at school, the one in the store moved soundlessly, the hand sweeping the minutes and hours away.

Clouds had been hanging low all day, the winds slowly clocking around the weak low as it passed. Beyond the no-wake buoys the lake ruffled and darkened with the shifts. In the backwater the protection of the hillsides kept the surface mostly still. The trees were bare, except for the oaks and the dark pine trees. It was like one of the Chinese paintings, the clouds rounded and gray, the trees black and gray, the water like jade.

This was the deadest season of all, between Thanksgiving and Christmas. After the holidays, the fishermen would begin moving, and sailors would go out on those unexpected warm days when it seemed like spring had come early. Right now, people were either shopping or hibernating.

I turned off the gas pumps. No sense using the electricity. I watched the loons as they floated in the area over the gas lines, then dove, to appear a long way away, sometimes with a fish. It was happy hunting grounds for them, since human fishermen weren't allowed to cast into the area around the gas lines.

Tick tick tick.

I raised the plywood Open sign on its hinges and turned the wing nuts to fasten it, simultaneously covering the big window facing the lake and showing boaters the "Closed" sign painted on the underside. Light from inside the store leaked around the edges, like the last of the sunset under the cloud edges. Everything just thin and dim and going out like the year, the days shrinking to a dark point. A few strings of Christmas lights showed on some of the houseboats and sailboats. All white here, cheery multi-colors there. A Cape Dory had green lights fore and aft, the stays outlining the triangular shape of a Christmas tree. There used to be a flotilla for Christmas but that fell off when the organizer moved away two years ago. I shut off the lights in the soda coolers and locked what needed to be locked. It was not yet five when I rang out the register, but Dad wouldn't know (or care) on a day like this. He was checking on the workmen doing winter maintenance, making sure they were finishing the repairs at the bathhouse and not sitting around a picnic table bullshitting. By the time he got back I'd be snuggled down in the houseboat with a book and a cup of cocoa.

As I pulled the blind shut on the small window, I glanced at the parking lot to see if he had come back yet. No truck. Just a couple of work vans and that red Miata that went with the second-to-largest Hunter.

I turned away, but movement caught my eye. A shadow.

A man emerged from behind one of the vans. He was wearing dark loose clothes and a ball cap, but as I ran through the list of contractors (plumbing, Carolina blue uniforms; electrical, tan) I couldn't place him. He had to be one of the workmen, so it was just me being paranoid.

But as he began to head down the walkway to the store, I knew.

He limped, almost dragging one leg. It was him. Ledsome.

My heart went banging around and I had to make sure I was breathing. I ducked behind the counter and went down on my hands and knees. The lights were on so he knew the store was open. He knew I was here. No place to hide, just four flimsy tin walls and a door that would pop open with one good shove. Nothing I could block the door with that was solid enough to make a difference.

I stared out through the display case and wondered if a collapsible gaff would be weapon enough. No, it wouldn't.

But he wouldn't be able to see the door from the walkway. The building itself blocked his view. I crawled fast, avoiding the ringer under the mat, pushed the door open, scooted out and pushed it closed behind me. Thank God I'd put up that Closed sign. He'd not be able to see me slipping away as lightly as my big feet would allow (don't set the halyards clanging) down the dock.

I crept past a couple of open boats, *Bellatrix*, a pontoon— there, the *Iolar*, buttoned down snugly under its boom tent. I was gently over the side and under the canvas in a flash. I looked back, peering through a space at the unsnapped corner of the tent edge.

The door was swinging gently, half open. *Idiot, idiot!* I hadn't closed it hard enough to catch. Rotten old cheap-ass lock.

I couldn't see him now. He was inside the store, hunting for me, looking under the counter and around the display racks. He knew my movements, my schedule. What did Vann say? I had been the target, *always* been the target. Not Charisse, beautiful Charisse. Why me? I couldn't figure it all out now, but I knew Vann was right. Knew it from that drawing, knew it from the bowers, knew it in my bones.

I waited, and waited. Maybe he'd go back up to the parking lot. Maybe someone else would pull in and scare him off. Maybe Dad was coming back. Maybe if I'd pulled my phone off the charger. Maybe, maybe.

And then a shadow crossed the gas dock, thrown by the light from the door. I heard the *bing-bong* sound, cheery as ever, as his feet crossed the mat. Ledsome was out of the store. He looked around and then headed up A dock.

I froze. Dad's *gotta* be on his way. Just wait like a rabbit in the thicket, a fawn in the woods, wait, wait. I made my breathing as shallow and silent as I could, until it seemed I would explode with lack of air. Footsteps went past. He walked heavy, stiff-legged, and dragged his foot along the dock. Fat Donna had done a number on his knee. The halyards clanged down the dock, growing fainter as he went toward the end.

In the movies he'd be shouting or threatening, taunting and teasing. Not a word. The silence was terrible, punctuated by dock sounds, groaning boards and squeaking lines and the tiny slap, slap of waves as the light chop made its way off the open lake and into the backwater.

I wanted to yell and run, wanted Vann to be there, wanted the cavalry or the Navy Seals, but it wasn't like that. It was just me.

I found the combination lock on the companionway and turned the tumblers gently. The numbers were white and big—old Mr. Showalter's bad eyes—and I could see them by the thin spray of light around the edges.

The clanging died out. End of the dock. End of the line.

I was on my knees. I gently lifted out the top door section and laid it on the seat. One, two. A little clunk as the board touched the other. Where was he? *Clang, clang,* far down but coming back. I lifted the third board from the slots and laid it silently on the others. Then I stepped, crouching, stepped light as breath down the steps into the cabin.

Now I really felt like an animal in hiding. Denned. Closed in, my back protected but no way to escape. I had thought briefly about going into the water, swimming to the far shore, but it was so cold—how long until help got there? No way now, because *Iolar* was a traditional boat and she carried a high, closed-in stern. I'd have to climb up and over, exposed as a bug on a wall.

I heard him dragging himself back up the dock. Thank God and all the little angels for sloppy sailors who didn't secure their halyards, letting them flop and bang every time the boats moved.

The dock lights shone through the portholes and gleamed on polished brass fittings. I heard Ledsome go past, step and drag, step and drag, and almost moaned when his shadow made the cabin go briefly dark.

Wait, wait.

The light flowed back and I could see the handheld radio hanging to the port side of the companionway. I knew where everything was on *Iolar*, everything in its proper place. I heard his steps retreat and I turned it on—it was charged, as I hoped it would be, *knew* it would be.

57

"M ayday," I whispered, loud as I dared. "Mayday, mayday. Filliyaw Pointe. Ledsome on A dock."
I heard the door to the store creaking.
"Mayday mayday mayday. Filliyaw Pointe."
I turned the radio off. Couldn't risk the squawk of a callback. Did anyone hear?

Please, let someone hear me on this dead night in the deadest time of year.

Oh, damn. Oh, idiot.

When I'd crept out, I left the radio on in the store. Someone had heard my distress call, that's for sure. Ledsome.

Those footsteps came back up the dock. "Where's my girl?"

His voice was light but gravelly, like someone who lived outdoors, under a bridge. Or a rock.

"I know you're here."

Think, Maggie.

I eased open the compartment under the steps. The flare pistol. I felt the slight weight of it as I lifted it with two fingers, making sure I didn't bump anything. It was nothing like a gun. A red plastic West Marine special, with extra cartridges riding piggyback. It was a signaling device, not solid and capable like a real gun.

I wished Dad had listened. Now there was no one to help me, just me, with nothing but this toy.

"You know how many times I've watched you? Out there in the woods, looking for me, even that time getting naked for me?" His voice was nearby, raspy and low. I didn't realize he was that close. He was sneaking now, sneaking up on me. I checked, loaded. I tightened my grip and put my finger on the trigger.

"Maggie, I waited and waited," he said. "You know I love you."

Oh, Jesus. I felt the shudders run up and down my back.

Silence. He was waiting as I was waiting. Listening for me to move. The fox patient for the rabbit.

He began moving again, and now he was walking and stopping. Looking at boats, maybe. Estimating which ones had hiding places.

Me, I'd start with the Party Hut, I thought, visualizing the line of boats bare or covered, with cabins or not. Then the orange O'Day with the big tarp tied over it. The houseboat—our houseboat—why hadn't he gone there? Because it was dark and he knew I was in the store, that's why. And the Boston Whaler with its cover. And, oh yeah, the *Iolar*.

I heard him step onto a boat. Must be the Party Hut. He walked heavily across the pontoon platform. The door rattled hard. Then I heard the creak of lines as he stepped back to the finger, and onto the dock.

"Girl," he rasped, "you know I've been watching you so long. You wanted me to see you, I know you did. You want me the same. I've stayed around, been cold and hungry and hurt, because you love me."

I heard the hollow sound of a foot striking against a hull, and the *clang, clang* of halyards. He was on the O'Day, just two spaces up and over. The tarp rattled. Something popped, a bungee or clip, and more rattling as the tarp was shoved around.

Mayday mayday mayday. My heart thudded in time. *Help me, help me, help me.*

I pulled my arms into my sides and leveled the flare pistol at the dark hole of the door opening. *Help yourself, Maggie.*

I visualized holding a real gun, one of those Smith and Wessons. If it were a real gun, I'd hold the pistol cocked and ready, and tell Ledsome to put his hands up. He'd be standing there as the blue police lights strobed across the water and the spotlights picked him out.

But this was no time for making up things or wishing they were some other way. There was nothing left but making the world work as it is.

"Ohhh, sweet Maggie, how could you keep teasing me?"

I heard him step off the O'Day and stand there. Waiting and listening.

When the flare went off, it would be incredibly bright. I'd have to close my eyes or be blinded.

I tried to slow down my heartbeat.

Heavy footsteps came down the finger beside the *Iolar*. I heard him pull at the loose edge of the boom tent. Snaps popped, one, two. As soon as he looked underneath, he'd see the companionway door open. I waited for the canvas to be yanked back, the dim dock lights to show my face, and he'd come at me and I would pull the trigger.

Maybe Drexel Vann. The headlights coming from the road, probing the dark, swinging across the water and stopping, and he would be leaping out of the car and running. *Hands up! Step away from the boat!*

But that was fictionalizing. Someone to rescue me, someone to be the hero.

But there was just me.

Another snap popped. Then another. I held the silly plastic toy gun like the real thing.

His shadow blocked the light.

Rip riiip rip-rip. He peeled the boom tent back and I could see his face. His eyes gleamed deep in his head and he was shaggy and bearded, worn out and in pain. I stayed crouched in the dark cabin, holding the pistol.

"You found a place for us." Then he grinned like he was seeing an old friend, and his teeth were white and normal instead of all snaggledy, which was even creepier.

He lifted his bad leg over the side to board the boat.

I stood up, closed my eyes against the flash, and pulled the trigger.

The flare pistol fired easily but it sounded like the real thing, *bang*. Then Ledsome began to howl like a wounded animal.

I looked and he was on fire. His *face* was on fire. He staggered backward, the flare burning with a hellish red fiery light that seemed to come from inside him, showed him a demon. He fell, pulled himself up, howling, went hand over hand along the rail until the boat ran out and he pitched sideways into the water.

I was out of my hidey-hole and onto the dock and running. When I hit the gas dock I looked back and could not see Ledsome. The flare must have already gone out. Not even a minute, that was all there was. A light in the dark and then gone. Maybe he was dead. I saw a head break the water. He began flailing. And howling. Howling. No sound an earthly creature should be able to make, rising and falling. And another sound. Big engines, rounding the point. This time I wasn't imagining. Sea-Tow always monitored the channel. He was coming in fast, and I started to wave him off before he ran over Ledsome.

Big Paul cut the engine and circled, shining his spotlight on me. I pointed to the water and he turned the light around until he saw the dripping head and white hands beating the black water.

Big Paul flung the yellow horseshoe of the Lifeline. I guess Ledsome wanted to live, because when it hit him in the back, he clutched at it. I was repulsed by him, enough that I wanted him to survive and pay for his crimes.

Now the lights in the parking lot were real. It was the truck, and Dad running.

"Maggie, my girl, I'm here!"

58

The lights and the sirens and the police filled the parking lot, just how I'd imagined it happening, and the detective loped down the walkway to take charge of Ledsome, who was slumped in a folding chair in the middle of the store, his hands and feet bound with cable ties. He was past howling, fallen into unconsciousness.

Drexel Vann walked in and took one look at his suspect, and though he tried to hide it, I saw the skin crinkle around his eyes. It was that bad.

I heard him turn to the deputy behind him and ask if the ambulance was on the way. Then he asked my dad what had happened, but he pointed to me. "I didn't have a thing to do with it. Ask Maggie."

A deputy handed Drexel some printed forms, and he asked Dad if we could use the houseboat while the deputies interviewed him and Paul in the store. I was happy enough not to have to spend any more time smelling that awful combination of seared flesh and burned plastic.

We sat at our "kitchen table" and Drexel pulled out a cheap pen and began to fill in the blanks. I guess we were beyond the little red notebook now. The table wobbled as he wrote. I saw him glance once around the kitchen. Not a bottle in sight.

After he had the basics filled in, place and time and such, he asked me for a statement. "Just tell what happened." This time, I could look him straight in the eye, and didn't have to fictionalize a single thing. When I told him about the radio, and the flare pistol, I saw his mouth move a little. I think he wanted to say "Good work" or something like that, but it wouldn't be professional.

"That mayday call wasn't a totally good idea," I had to admit. "Ledsome could hear it on the store radio. But I guess it worked out since I did get help."

I saw the ambulance roll in, back up to the top of the walkway, the spotlights shining down toward the store. They were about blinding. The crew took out a gurney and raised it on its wheels, then moved it down the paved part and across the metal ramp. When they took Ledsome out, he was strapped tight like a boat to its trailer with wide webbing, a deputy walking front and back.

He pushed the pages over for me to read and sign. "You know I worried for you."

"Not at first."

"Yes, even at first."

"So you didn't really suspect me?"

"I'm not saying that." He looked at me straight, and he didn't have to fabricate anything either. "Your public threats, and your secrets, made you a plausible suspect—more than anyone else for a while. Knowing you as I have come to do, I'm not surprised that you took care of yourself when the time came. You are a surprising young woman, Maggie. I knew that the day I met you."

I concentrated on my signature because I wanted to smile, but that wouldn't have been professional. "Lenore Marguerite Warshauer" filled the whole space.

The winter went on. Ledsome was hurt bad, blinded by the magnesium flare, but he didn't die. He confessed to thieving food and living in the boat and attacking Donna. His story was jumbled with stalker stuff about me and a woman up in Virginia, but he never would admit to Charisse's death. It turned out that when they searched him, he had a roll of duct tape in his pocket and a folding fisherman's utility tool in his sock. He had been planning ahead. He'd been planning for me.

The trial will be a short one. Unlike in Carl's day, he won't be hanged from a gibbet or have his head cut off or his body quartered and left to rot in the sun.

Spring has come around again, neither early nor late. Daffodils popped up around the old houses in the woods, redbud bloomed and then dogwood, and the leaves came out red before they unfurled into green. The air became softer, just this week, enough that I could crack open the vent windows at the bathhouse for the first time in months—the windows open but the door locked. Even with Ledsome in jail, I'd never again feel the same about being naked and alone.

I finished drying off and stood in front of the wavy metal mirror. No fiction here. Just me, Maggie, with a sturdy body pale from the winter, not yet sunburned or briar-scratched. I will be going off to college in the fall and wonder how I will stack up. As least I am solid and healthy, biceps and calves well developed, my muscles firm from walking and sports and sailing.

Carl got used to seeing people naked in Lapland, where they all slept together under reindeer skins and got up to put their clothes on without any shame or civilized modesty. *I could not but admire the fairness of the bodies of these dark-faced people, which rivaled that of any lady whatever,* he wrote. Later he married a woman named Sara and settled down and became a fat professor. Probably with a brood of kids. But he kept this little bit of a smile in those paintings made when he was old and prosperous, in a curly wig and a coat with big gold buttons. I'll bet he was remembering those days, living out in the mountains, chewing on wild plants and investigating everything from minerals to reindeer poop.

I looked at my body in the mirror, brown hair and crotch triangle like field marks. The same body plan, sure, as any woman, but nothing like the perfect woman. I thought about how Charisse was designed, and my once-upon-a-time mother. So much variation within the species. Humans were like dogs. We're variable in so many ways, but human all the same despite skin color and hair color and size. I was a mutt, an average, but that was okay because mutts have hybrid vigor and cunning. They can endure a lot longer than some pure-blood valued for its long legs or fancy coat.

My mother's body, seen in the dim glow of candles or the yellowish hue of the dusk-to-dawn light outside our beach shack, had been as soft as an arrangement of silk flowers. Pink and gold. Charisse was the same. If you couldn't have such beauty, you either longed for it or rejected it. For some time I thought of myself as a boy, a tomboy. Then I sort of morphed into being a geek, because it was better than admitting I'd never look like that.

I realize now that it was not really a sexual thing, when I responded to Charisse's lips against mine. It was a reflex, the automatic body response to stimuli. I never *wanted* Charisse. I had wanted *to be* Charisse, much as I hated to admit it. And, I guess, my mother as well. To have some of that kind of power. Beautiful women can cause all sorts of havoc, their attractiveness strong as riptides. But then I became an object of desire. It was still horrible to think about that. Ledsome had watched me, spied on me when I thought I was most alone, and he had desired me, even if it was in a twisted way. Me. Plain Maggie.

I wondered if a regular man would ever find me interesting for something other than my brains. I didn't want some perfect man that I cooked up from memories and wishes and bits of books and television shows. I thought maybe I could want some average, flawed person like me.

The air was chilly. I saw my nipples pucker and the fine hairs stand up on my damp skin. I spread out my arms and lifted them up, opened my hands, and then let my arms slowly down. My hair was longer now, collar length and cut evenly, so that it swung when I twisted my head. My hair was the color of a horse chestnut, dark and glossy.

Attractive.

Maybe. Maybe yes.

59

Well, at the end it was Drexel Vann again.

The semester was nearly over and I was coasting, counting down the days, sailing as much as the wind allowed, even enjoying time in the store. I was sitting at the dock, doing nothing, when I saw that white Chevy pull in.

The detective came right past the store and down the dock, plunking himself onto the deck box opposite where I lounged on *Bellatrix*.

"You'll get your pants dirty," I observed.

He brushed the palm of his hand across the top and looked at the grime. "Too late, it appears."

"What brings you out to the backwater?"

"I thought you'd like to know that the grand jury indicted Alan Ledsome."

"That should ease your mind."

"And yours, I expect."

"Sure."

"Maybe more than it should."

I gave him a look. "I'm happy we caught the creep and that he'll be going to prison."

"We did catch him." He caught my look. "*You* did. A feather in your cap, and a closed case for the London County Sheriff's Department. But there were times when I didn't think this case was solvable. Too many variables."

"Solve for X."

"Right." He took off his glasses and looked through them, but didn't polish them if they were dirty. He put them back on and looked at me.

"I like you, Maggie. You're smart and strong and capable. If the apocalypse comes, you'll be one of the survivors. But I keep thinking about the night Charisse died."

I waited, having learned that from him.

"You didn't like Charisse much," he said.

"We didn't have anything in common."

"Hated her, in fact. With good reason. She let you down, pushed you around, ridiculed you. And she reminded you too much of your mother."

I felt the flush of anger, or shame, or both. I wasn't going there. "She gave me her ring, remember?"

"I seriously doubt that a girl like Charisse gave things away, especially expensive, pretty things."

"She gave Nat her Tiffany bracelet."

"Not sure I buy that either."

"Well, you can ask him again. He's in Greensboro."

"We know. We keep track."

I looked at Drexel Vann and made a final categorization. He wasn't a johnboat or bass boat or clean-lined sloop. Not a Great Dane or a puppy. I had him pinned down at last. Half dog and half wolf, a hybrid. Dangerous, because he can pass among humans who will think he's just an average dog, but the eyes are always watching. Dangerous because he's smart in a world of not very smart people. I like him and admire him, maybe even love him a little, and sometimes I think he feels the same about me.

"You seem to have emerged pretty much unscathed from this, Maggie."

"I'm not raped or dead."

"Nor do you seem to be emotionally scarred."

"I rely on my brains, not my emotions. I'm a scientist."

"No, you're not." He didn't raise his voice or anything, but I could feel the edge. "You're a teenage girl who lives too much in her head, who imagines a world to fit what she needs."

"That's not very nice."

"But quite true. Now, this Ledsome character. Was he sexually obsessed with you? Yes. Did he want to harm you? Apparently. But there are a few things that still don't add up. Ultimately, you remain the last one to see your cousin that night."

"I saw her in the woods, at the plantation house."

"Not at the marina? Or maybe even after that, maybe even on the docks?"

I kept my silence.

I saw her fall. I looked back and I saw her trip on her ruined dress and sprawl in the mud where the path forked toward the storage dock, and I laughed.

"There are sins of commission, Maggie, and sins of omission. Things done and things left undone."

That sounded like church. I didn't think Drexel was a church kind of person.

"Omission, what you don't do?" I said. "Is it as bad as commission?"

He nodded. "It depends."

I didn't say anything more.

"Anyway, we have our man." He opened his hands out, as if he was accepting something. "Ledsome needs to be in prison for a lot of reasons, and he will be prosecuted and convicted based on the evidence that I present to the D.A."

"So that should make you happy."

"Not entirely. I'm a kind of categorizer too. I like to line up the evidence and make sure all the pieces fit. No loose ends. I nail down the motive, means, opportunity. How did things come together that night? Charisse and you both made it to the marina, but she ended up on that boat. Why? It's like the belt in Orion—if one star was missing, it wouldn't make a belt anymore, would it?"

"But the case is closed."

"Yes, but my mind isn't." He stood and brushed off the seat of his khakis. "Maggie, if you think I still believe that you murdered her, I don't. She didn't mean enough to you for you to do that. But I know you have secrets you'll never let go of. I'll just say that keeping them will do you harm."

The waves slapped against the underside of the dock and made that *tink-tink* sound against the hull of my boat. The swallows circled and cheeped.

"Then you're off to college," he said at last.

"Yep. I'm smart, right?"

"Where?"

"UNC-Wilmington."

"Just like you planned." He put out his hand, and I shook it. "I wish you the best, Maggie. But I'll be keeping an eye out."

"On me?"

"Let's just say for you."

60

I never did return to Filliyaw Pointe.
Dad finally made the break, left that job, and went back to Oriental, though he's still working for Mr. Malouf. I went to college to become a marine biologist, but things changed for me too. The science classes didn't attract me nearly as much as they once had, and after a year I changed to creative writing.

One of my professors said, "Stories tell themselves; it's getting them on paper that's the hard part." They're inside you like secrets that must be told, are burning to be told, but somehow, cannot be. At least directly.

Like that night. Prom night.

Charisse had fallen and I laughed at her, splayed out in the mud, and she reached up to me, crying and begging, *Help me, please, help me.*

I wanted to turn away and go home to my own bed. To be warm and safe myself, and not for once responsible for other people. But I couldn't. I helped her up and she leaned on me, dragging her dress in the muck, sobbing, barely able to stay on her feet. A mess.

We couldn't go home—not with Dad in the state he was in, and Charisse in the state she was in.

So I took her to the storage dock and the houseboat where I hid out occasionally. I always left the padlock looking like it was fastened but not quite clicked shut. Like the woods or the island, it was a private space—and now it was a place to ride out the storm.

We could have just gone to sleep. Easy enough. Nap until the rain was over. But the storm seemed to have roused Charisse from whatever pills she'd taken.

"It's all ruined," she moaned. "Everything's ruined."

The stink of vomit mixed with mud and booze and perfume

made me sick. "Don't worry, you'll get another overpriced dress."

"Nooooooo." The raw light of the dusk-to-dawn shone into the windows and fell across her, sparkling in the sequins, showing her perfect skin and perfect body. She rolled on the crushed velvet, shaking with cold, leaving dark water stains. "You don't know. Ruined. He didn't stop. He didn't stop. He put his fingers inside me."

That made me laugh. "Really? You suck dicks and worry about that?"

"What can I do? I'm not pure anymore. How can I tell Daddy?"

I shook with anger at her stupidity and helplessness. "Shut the fuck up, Charisse."

Instead, she began to moan, louder. "I'm hot."

I tried to pull the wet dress off her, but perversely, she clung to it.

"Help me get this off you." She seemed to understand, but instead of helping me pull off the dress, she reached down, slipped off her panties and delicately laid them on the bed.

"I can't go home," she sobbed. "I don't have any home anymore."

What did she know about home, or parents, or anything that meant anything? Crying and snotting and howling over nothing. I couldn't take one more minute. I picked up the nearest thing, the panties, and stuffed them in her mouth to stop the stupid moaning. Charisse went limp, not even trying to remove them, just whimpering. I threw the comforter across her and went to the other cabin to take care of my own wet, cold, miserable self.

I woke with the first bird (indigo bunting) and the smell of urine. That got me mad all over again—another mess I'd have to clean up.

"Damn it, Charisse." I threw back the comforter and she was just as I'd left her, on her back, panties wadded in her mouth. Her eyes were open. There wasn't any waking her up.

I guess most people would have panicked then. But dead is

dead. Whatever killed her, I wasn't taking the blame for it.

A mystery wasn't hard to fabricate. I pulled the utility bucket from under the sink, rubber gloves and shop rags. I took off the corsage, tied her cold wrists, and finished ripping apart that dress. If they thought she had been abducted and raped, so be it—at least they wouldn't be looking at me. I wiped things down and swabbed the filthy floor. The padlock I left hanging loose in the hasp, figuring someone would see it, just like Guillermo did.

It was dawn when I crept home. Dad was still passed out. I changed into my nightclothes and lay down for a while. By the time I woke it was full day and things had begun to change. Memories are strange things. They can burn deep into you like acid, or they can shimmer and evaporate, no stronger than a patch of dew when the sun hits.

Like my memory of that night.

Lately I've been finding my way back. Details of that night, ones I couldn't admit even to myself, have been rising like contours of the drowned land from the lake. I didn't kill her, but her death is mine. Like the death of Ledsome, who was killed in a prison fight. I had a hand in both. Alternative realities have real consequences.

I had learned from Linnaeus to look closely at the world—to count the veins on the wings of tiny flies that torment you. But it's another thing to look closely into people's minds, or into your own mind.

It seemed that all my energies had gone into protecting people—Dad, Nat, even Charisse—so how did that protectiveness turn into violence?

I still don't understand.

So I write. I write the story over and over, turning it around, with new faces, new names, new beginnings, new endings. Draft after draft, each revision coming clearer, closer to the bone.

Writers, we steal lives to shape a world, one we are able to live in for a while. Here at college I am learning to fictionalize for a living as I once fictionalized to protect my life.

That's how I remembered it.

Acknowledgements

I don't know about muses, but I've been fortunate to have people give me a nudge in the right direction—sometimes, a pretty firm shove. Fred Chappell's story "Linnaeus Forgets" rekindled my long-quiescent interest in the Father of Botany, and he went on to offer essential comments on the manuscript. Kevin Rippin pushed me to rewrite the ending, repeatedly, until it made that final necessary leap. Al Sirois, Grace Marcus, David Halperin, Marjorie Hudson, Catherine Luttinger, John Cochran, Shymala Dason, Susan Woodring, and Susan Schmidt offered cogent comments with honesty and grace, then encouraged me through many revisions.

I'm so grateful for Jaynie Royal and all the folks at Regal House for believing in this book. Pam Van Dyk's thoughtful editing helped bring the book into its final form.

This book took many years to come into being. Along the way, I gained both inspiration and information from the following:

Botanical librarian Jeffery Beam and the folks at the Couch Biology Library-Botany Section at UNC Chapel Hill (now Kenan Science Library), where I read the Lapland Journal in an edition of the period.

Lake Townsend Yacht Club.

Cape Fear Sailing Academy and Capt. Kevin Hennessey.

Steele Creek Marina and the communities around Lake Kerr.

With thanks to the Allen Boat Co. for specifications on the Blue Jay, used with permission.

Parts of the manuscript were written during residencies at The Weymouth Center for Arts and Humanities, a gift of time and space that was greatly appreciated. North Carolina Writers Network has been for many years an incredible resource and support for my writing. The Queens University of Charlotte

MFA Alumni Development Weekends provided opportunities to discuss *In the Lonely Backwater* with fellow alums and faculty. Thanks to John C. Campbell Folk School, where I've taught for many years, and where Maggie came into focus through a photo exchange exercise in my class on character development. That exercise became Chapter 13.

Many thanks to the North Carolina Arts Council for a much-needed fellowship during an early round of revisions, and the partnering arts councils of the Central Piedmont Regional Artists Hub Program and ArtsGreensboro for their support.

Sue Farlow and Marjorie Hudson were there when I most needed them, stalwart friends in a bad time. A tip of the hat to Marjorie's *The Search for Virginia Dare* for the legend of the White Doe.

Most of all, love and sweet memories of Mom and Dad, who provided safe harbor in Southport, NC, where the first draft was completed.

The opening pages of *In the Lonely Backwater* won the Seven Hills Literary Competition Prize for Young Adult Novel Excerpt and were published in *Seven Hills Review* in 2017. An early version of the book was a semifinalist in the 2016 William Faulkner–William Wisdom Creative Writing Competition.